Utterly Charming

KRISTINE GRAYSON

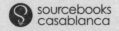

sourcebooks
casablanca

Published by Sourcebooks Casablanca, an imprint of Sourcebooks, Inc.
P.O. Box 4410, Naperville, Illinois 60567-4410
(630) 961-3900
FAX: (630) 961-2168
www.sourcebooks.com

Originally published in 2000 by Zebra Books, a division of Kensington Publishing Corp.

Printed and bound in Canada
WC 10 9 8 7 6 5 4 3 2 1

For my husband,
the secret romantic,
with love

Ten Years Ago

Chapter 1

HER FATHER USED TO TELL HER, *NEVER LOSE YOUR sense of humor, Nora. Sometimes it's all you need.*

And sometimes, it was all you had left. She hadn't lost everything, not yet, but she would if she didn't get another client, if she didn't find a way to earn some real money fast, if she didn't find a way to turn everything around.

Served her right for listening to her mother. *A girl needs to follow her dreams, honey.* Nora was following them. All the way to bankruptcy.

Still, she had to laugh as she left her office on the third floor of one of Portland's most exclusive buildings. The lower floors rented cheap because the offices hadn't been converted and the remodeling was shoddy. The carpet caught and bunched in places, and the ceiling tiles looked as if they might fall down at any moment. But that wasn't what made her smile.

It was the fact that the travel agency two doors down had picked that very morning—the morning she had received four *final, final, final!* bills, the morning her landlord had called and threatened her with eviction if she didn't pay the last two months rent, the morning her most promising client's retainer check bounced—to decorate the hallway with beautiful twelve-by-twenty travel posters of exotic places that Nora would never see. As she stepped out of her office, she found herself facing a bright blue ocean, a pristine beach, and a clearly exclusive resort in the distance. *Searching for Romance?* the poster read. *Try Hawaii.*

Nora smiled. Romance. She didn't have time for romance. Even if she could afford to go to Hawaii.

She clutched her battered briefcase to her side and hurried toward the elevator. The upper floors of the building had an express elevator, done tastefully in polished wood and brass. The elevator that served the first five floors was an ancient Otis with a cracked mirror that covered the walls. Every time she stepped inside, she was startled at the girl who looked back at her.

She wasn't a girl. She was a twenty-five-year-old woman who had graduated with honors from the University of Oregon Law School. She was the twenty-five-year-old crazy woman who had decided to open her own practice despite all the offers she had received from prestigious law firms around the state. She was the twenty-five-year-old crazy and unrealistic woman who believed she could make a living in Portland, Oregon's largest city, a city so full of *experienced* lawyers that no one with any sense would go to an inexperienced one, let alone one who had only recently received her JD.

And who happened to look like the head of the high school cheerleading squad. It wasn't her fault that she was only five two, petite, and blond. It wasn't her fault that her nose turned up ("like a little ski jump" her father used to say) or that her eyes were wide and blue, making her seem at first glance like an innocent adrift in the large, complicated world. The only asset she had was her voice, strong and strident and able to silence a room with a single word.

Her favorite law professor had told her that she had to learn to use her appearance to her advantage.

Obviously, she hadn't yet, not if the way she looked still surprised herself.

She got into the elevator, let the creaky doors close, and leaned against the mirror's crack. The only reason she was going to see this client—a doctor who had more malpractice suits filed against him than any other doctor in the state, a doctor who had gone through lawyer after lawyer—was because she needed the money. She knew it, and he knew it, which was why he could command her to come to his office instead of having him come to hers.

So much for her vaunted ethics. So much for not handling cases she didn't believe in.

Did all lawyers throw out morality in exchange for food? She didn't know. She suspected they did, though, which was why so many elderly senior partners were fat.

To give herself credit, though, she wasn't completely sure she was going to see him. She was going to treat herself to a cheap lunch at the nearby all-natural low-fat Mexican food place (which was as tasty as treating herself to a sugarless ice-cream cone) and she was going to decide on a full stomach. She couldn't make the decision in her office, not with the phone ringing and bills piled up on her desk.

The elevator clanked its way down to the bowels of the building, which hadn't been remodeled at all. She never told her clients—what few of them there were—to use the parking garage because she was afraid it would scare them. It used to scare her, until she badgered the landlord into putting in an extra bank of fluorescent lights.

She had been cantankerous about it too ("Women alone don't like dark places, Stan," she had snapped at him one afternoon), which was probably why he was pressing her so hard for the rent. The fluorescent lights did banish the darkness, but they also revealed spiders the size of mice and a crumbling concrete foundation completely at odds with the BMWs and Porsches parked beside the columns.

BMWs, Porsches, and of course, her mighty steed, an ancient Rabbit that belched blue smoke every time she put it into reverse. She parked it toward the back corner of the garage after one of the lawyers from the huge firm upstairs (the one that had tried to hire her out of law school and who had continued to belittle her dream of independence ever since) requested that she "Do Something about her *car* so that people knew this was a Reputable Building." She couldn't Do Something about the car, but she could hide it so that the snobbish people who worked in this Reputable Building didn't have to see the rust, dented fenders, and blue smoke.

Inside the garage, the cars were lined up like little soldiers, the most expensive closest to the express elevator and the rest scattered throughout the remaining spots. Despite the new lights, the place had an air of perpetual grayness, like an overcast day that kept promising, but never delivering, rain. It also echoed like crazy, and she was glad she had taken off her high heels and stuffed them into her briefcase before coming down. Her tennis shoes handled the concrete and the oil slicks much better, and they didn't make it sound as if she were an army of women on a mission.

But there were already people in the garage, and their voices were echoing.

"…still don't see why you've dragged me here," said the first voice. It was low and musical and sexy. She had always loved voices like that. The kind that had a faint English accent, the kind that made her think that a man could seduce her without her ever seeing him, just by listening to his warm mellifluous voice speaking softly in a dark room.

"You won't find out unless you go upstairs." The second voice was nasal and harsh. It was the complete opposite of the voice she had first heard.

"I really don't want to. I have a lot of other things to do, things that have nothing to do with Eals—"

"Really?" asked the second voice. "Is that why you were in Beaverton?"

"I'd heard she was there."

"She is there, but I don't know the exact address. There's all those little houses, you know, that go on like rabbit's warrens—"

The other voice interrupted, still speaking too low for Nora to hear. She rounded a corner, and as she did, her foot hit a loose piece of metal. It clanged, and the sound resounded off the thick concrete walls.

A man appeared on the back of a blue 1974 Lincoln—at least, it seemed as if he had appeared. One minute the car had been there—alone and slightly out of place—and one minute later, he was standing beside it. She would have sworn to that in a court of law.

Well, maybe not. After all, people didn't just appear. She could almost hear herself cross-examining herself. Perhaps she hadn't noticed him in her haste to get to her car. Perhaps—

But the hadn't-noticed thought stopped her. How

could she not have noticed this man? He was tall and slim with broad shoulders and narrow hips, and legs that went on forever. He had black hair in need of a cut, gray—or were they silver?—eyes, and smooth skin the color of toffee. His features were an odd mix of harsh angles and soft lines—an angular nose, high cheek-bones, and sensitive lips—none of which should have gone together, but which did in a way that made her heart beat faster. She couldn't tell how old he was; his face was unblemished, but his eyes held a wisdom most young men did not have. He wore a shimmery gray silk suit that accented his broad shoulders, and on his feet, he wore cowboy boots trimmed in real silver.

He was the most gorgeous man she had ever seen. He literally made her stop breathing, although her heart kept beating—so hard he could probably hear it. Color rushed to her cheeks, and she almost put her hands to them, until she realized it would draw attention. He would think her an actual cheerleader, blushing and stammering and completely out of her league.

The man turned, saw her, and his eyes met hers, hold-ing her. She had never felt such intensity in a man's gaze before. He tilted his head slightly, as if in recognition, and she nodded back.

It took her a moment to notice the snake he held in his left hand. In fact, she probably wouldn't have noticed if the creature hadn't turned toward her and hissed.

"Who's that?" the nasal voice asked. She couldn't see where it came from.

The man smiled at her, a small apologetic smile, as if to say that he had more manners than his nasal-voiced friend. "Probably someone on the way to her car."

He was the one with the beautiful voice. It suited him, so rich and warm, deep and smooth. She had been right. It was a musician's voice.

"Oops," the nasal voice responded, and suddenly a tiny man stood on the Lincoln's bumper. Nora would have used the word "appeared" to describe him too, but she didn't want to. That meant that he had been invisible one moment and visible the next. People didn't simply pop in. And people who saw people pop in, well, they were considered crazy.

The little guy grinned at her. He was perfectly proportioned, square with a pugnacious face, a chin that curved outward, and a nose that obviously had been broken several times. He wore dark blue jeans and a T-shirt with a pack of cigarettes rolled up in the sleeves.

He raised his eyebrows, making him look like the inspiration for Puck from *A Midsummer's Night Dream*. "It'd be nice to have a woman," he said, ruining the image.

She shook herself. What had she expected? Him to leap on the back of the car and intone, *What fools these mortals be?*

His companion rolled his eyes, almost as if he'd heard Nora's thoughts. Then she realized he was responding to the little man. "Things are different now," he said. "You can't just have any woman."

His gaze remained on Nora's, his silver eyes sparkling as if he knew that she understood the joke.

She didn't.

"Excuse me," she said, and shifted her briefcase again. The thing weighed more than a small child. She walked toward the Lincoln, not really sure if she wanted

the attention of these two men. The tall one was spectacular, but his friend was unnerving. Still, she had to go
by them to get to her car.

The snake wrapped itself around the tall man's wrist.

The little man watched. So did the tall one. In fact, he
didn't seem willing to take his gaze off her. She wasn't
really willing to take her gaze off him, but she did, just
to prove to herself that she could do it. Besides, that
blush had moved from her cheeks into her neck and
down her fake silk blouse. She probably looked like a
little blond tomato.

She was just past the car when the little man scurried
in front of her. She stopped. He moved quickly. If she
tried to go around, he would get in front of her again.
She didn't like this game (although she might have if his
friend had been playing it).

"Who are you?" the little man asked.

She had had enough. She rose to her full five feet two
inches and said, "My name is Nora Barr. I'm a lawyer."

She added that last so that they wouldn't mess
with her.

The tall man raised his eyebrows and looked at
the little man. The little man shrugged. "Told you we
needed a woman," he said. Then he grinned. It looked
like a triumphant grin. "And I had a hunch we'd find
one here."

―⁓―

It wasn't that hard for them to talk her out of lunch. They
needed an attorney, they claimed, and they had money to
burn. Actually, the little guy said that and the gorgeous
guy shushed him, but the little guy said that Nora needed

to know that, which she did. It allowed her to forget the malpractice doctor and to hang onto her ethics for at least one more day.

Besides, she wasn't really going to sell out for a single retainer, was she?

She didn't want to think about that question.

Instead, she found herself daydreaming about the gorgeous man as they rode the elevator to her floor. He was even better looking up close, and he smelled wonderful, a mixture of leather and something intoxicating, something exotic. She took several deep breaths and would have continued until she saw the little guy staring at her with that knowing grin on his face.

"Feeling faint?" he asked.

"Just practicing my calming techniques," she said. "I have a hunch I'll need them."

The tall man laughed, a deep, pleasant sound. "She's got you pegged," he said to his companion.

"It wasn't hard," she said, as the elevator doors creaked open.

The travel agency had added some potted palm trees to the foyer, such as it was, and so cramped the space that Nora and her would-be clients had to file out of the elevator one at a time. She had to admit that the travel posters gave the corridor a professional appearance which dissipated, of course, the moment she opened her office door.

Ruthie, her secretary, was sitting at the old metal desk, the telephone plastered to her ear. Several law books sat on the edge of the wall-to-wall bookshelves, waiting to be re-filed. Four separate files were open before her, and behind her, the cursor on the old PC screen blinked orange. When she saw Nora, she murmured an excuse into the phone and hung up.

"When does Bryan go back to work?" Nora asked, knowing the others hadn't quite gotten to the door yet. She wanted Ruthie to be as professional as Ruthie could be when they arrived, and usually Nora had to knock Ruthie off-balance to make that happen.

Ruthie swallowed. "He—ah—doesn't. He wants to be a househusband."

"I thought you don't have children."

"We don't, not yet. But he says with my salary, and his planning, we could do real well."

If Ruthie continued to get her salary. She was the only one who got paid regularly around here, and that probably wouldn't be happening for much longer.

The men had appeared in the doorway behind her. Nora could tell from Ruthie's gape-mouthed stare. She was looking up of course, and behind Nora the tall man chuckled softly.

For some reason, that small chuckle annoyed Nora almost as much as Ruthie's stare did. "Clients," Nora said and marched through the door into her office.

It was the larger of the two rooms, and it actually had a window, even though the view was of the roof of the building next door. Her desk was hand-carved oak, a gift from her father when she graduated from law school, given to her a few weeks before he died. She kept it highly polished and spotless. Everything had its place, from the phone to the blotter to her current cases (all three of them). Two mismatched chairs sat in front of the desk, and to the side, next to the small file room, was a ratty blue couch.

Certainly not the office of a prosperous attorney. But they probably knew that from the parking garage. She was willing to bet that the little man had her in mind from the very start. He had said something about going upstairs in the parking garage, before he had known she was there.

So they wanted an inexperienced attorney. That almost made them suspect. In fact, it would have made all of her clients suspect if it weren't for the fact that her last name began with *B* and was listed as the fifth attorney in the Yellow Pages. (And she was the first whose ad claimed reasonable rates.)

She slid around the desk and into the plush brown chair she had found at an estate sale. The men had followed her inside. The tall one was looking at her degrees, prominently displayed on the walls. The short one was staring up at the chairs with something like dismay.

"Have a seat," she said, somewhat perversely. She knew the little man would have trouble getting into the chair, and she didn't really care, not after his introductory remarks. The little man put his hands on the seat and boosted himself up. Then he settled in, looking for all the world like a particularly ugly child. His stubby legs extended over the seat and didn't pretend to try for the ground. Like a little boy, he put his hands on the armrests as if he were trying to hold himself in place.

The other man left her degrees, and slid into the remaining chair as if it had been built for him. He pushed the chair back so that he could extend his long legs. His booted feet hit the edge of her desk, rattling it. The snake had disappeared, probably hiding in his suit. The jacket was open, revealing a white shirt of the same material. He folded his elegant, ringless hands over his flat stomach and watched her with those sharp silver eyes.

That fluttery feeling was back. Was it ethical to have a client who attracted her like this, just from the way he looked?

Probably not. Although it was more ethical than working for the malpractice doctor. Of that she was convinced.

"All right," she said, leaning forward and folding her own hands into what she hoped was a businesslike position. "What can I do for you?"

To her surprise, the little man answered. "Can you have someone tested for a witch?"

"That never worked," the other man said.

"Exactly," the little man said.

Nora leaned back. Whatever she had expected, it hadn't been this.

"If she can't be tested for a witch," the little man said, "perhaps tarred and feathered—?"

"Wrong century."

"Hung from a tree until she's dead?"

"Wrong century."

"Boiled in oil?"

"You know no one did that."

Nora sighed. "Gentlemen, please. You only get one free hour before I must begin to charge you, so unless there's a realistic way I can help you—"

"I'm sorry." The tall man smiled faintly again. She wondered how powerful his smile would be at full wattage. On low, it was pretty strong stuff. She fought the urge to smile back. "I get so preoccupied that I forget the rest of the world doesn't work the way I do."

He stood just enough so that he could extend his hand. "I'm Blackstone."

She looked at the hand with its long fingers and did not take it. She was afraid that if she did, she wouldn't let it go. Instead, she said with just a trace of sarcasm in her voice, "*The* Blackstone?"

"Well, actually, yes, but not the one you're thinking of. He, in fact, was the impostor, but that's a long story that ended rather nastily for all concerned. He—"

"Blackstone." She shook her head. She should have known better than to take clients from the parking garage. "Is that a first or last name?"

"It's a surname," he said, easing his hand back to his side as if he didn't want anyone else to notice her obvious snub. "My given name is Aethelstan."

"Aethelstan?" She'd never heard a name like that.

He shrugged prettily. "It was in style once."

"A long, *long* time ago," the little man added.

"And you are?" she asked.

"Let's just call me Panza," the little man said.

"Let's not," she said. "Try again."

The little man crossed his arms. The cigarette pack slid under his sleeve until it hung beneath his right bicep. "My name is Sancho Panza."

She shot an exasperated look at Blackstone. His eyes were twinkling again. He looked even better when he was amused, not that it helped any. She would have to deal with the little guy on her own. "If you want me to do something for you in a court of law, I'll need your legal name."

The little guy leaned back in his chair. "It's not me you're helping," he said. "It's Blackstone."

She crossed her arms. She had the odd feeling they

were playing a game, and she didn't know why. Did they have some sort of scheme? If so, why all the subterfuge?

"All right, Mr. Blackstone," she said in her most haughty voice, "what can I help you with?"

For a moment, the mask dropped, and she saw something in his eyes, a vulnerability, almost a fear mixed with sadness. Then he seemed to notice her watching him, and the expression disappeared. He cleared his throat, glanced at his companion who was watching both of them, and said, "You charge what?"

The question was clearly meant to be rude, obviously because she had seen behind his facade. And the question was rude, at least the way he asked it. As he spoke, the snake stuck its head out of his shirt and looked at her as if it too expected an answer.

"One hundred dollars an hour, plus a"—she almost quoted her regular rate, then decided to double it because these two were proving to be so much trouble (not to mention the fact that she needed the money)—"plus a thousand dollar retainer."

"A thousand dollar retainer?" The little man strangled on the last word. "In my day, you could run a country on a thousand dollars."

"In your day, there was no such thing as dollars," Blackstone muttered. He hadn't taken his gaze off her. "What do you prefer? A check or cash?"

"Or gold," the little man added. She would be damned if she would think of him as Sancho Panza.

"A check is fine," she said. No sense in taking currency. With these two, it could just as easily be forged, and then where would she be? The worst thing a check could do was bounce.

Blackstone put a hand inside his shimmery jacket and brought out a checkbook. A pen appeared in his other hand—just as Blackstone had appeared initially. Just as the little man had appeared. Out of thin air.

She felt the muscles in her shoulders tighten. More games.

He poised the pen over his checkbook. "Do I write this check to you or to the law firm?"

"I am the law firm," she said. "Either is fine."

She was telling him that so that he could pull out. But he didn't quiz her about her background, or the types of cases she handled, or her past successes, of which there were quite a few, given the scant months she'd been in business. Not that those wins had brought more clients. It took time to build a business. But time was what she didn't have.

She watched him write the check.

He signed it with a flourish and then handed it to her. She glanced at it, noting his name in bold and only a post office box for an address. Her hand shook. She needed the money so badly. But she couldn't let that get in the way of her judgment. It was time to get serious.

With her left hand, she pulled open a drawer and removed a legal pad. Then she took her pen out of its holder. "Let's get your street address and phone, starting with you, Mr. Blackstone, and then going onto your friend here."

"You don't need me," the little man said. "I already told you."

She stared at him for a moment. He had just given her the opportunity she had been waiting for.

"Then I'll have to ask you to leave," she said.

"I don't mind him staying." Blackstone leaned back in his chair. The pen was gone. So was the checkbook. She hadn't seen him put either away.

The snake had disappeared as well.

"I mind," she said.

Blackstone raised an eyebrow. The little man scowled. "You got books in the waiting area?"

"Law books," Nora said.

"Good enough," the little man said and scooted off the chair. Blackstone held the back so that the chair didn't tip. As the little man's feet hit the floor, he brushed off his backside and adjusted his cigarettes. Then he let himself out the door.

The room felt three times larger without him. Nora wasn't certain how a person that tiny could fill such a big space.

"Mr. Blackstone," she said, keeping the businesslike tone to her voice, "street address and phone number?"

He gave her an address in the west side suburbs, in a new development that was only partially finished. The address surprised her; she would have thought a man like him belonged in one of Portland's older homes, filled with history and charm. Instead, he chose a cookie-cutter neighborhood without any class at all.

She must have paused long enough to catch his notice. He raised an eyebrow again—an expression which, on most people, would seem like an affectation, but on him seemed completely natural.

"Something wrong with my address, Miss Barr?"

The "miss" also surprised her, but she let it go. Unlike her mother, she did not make a federal case out of the misuse of the female honorific. It simply told her what sort of man she was dealing with.

She already knew he was strange; that he was also old-fashioned in some ways didn't surprise her much.

"No," she said. "I simply hadn't spoken to anyone who lives in Lakewood Development. It's fairly new."

His eyes narrowed a bit as if he knew she were lying but didn't know why.

"So," she said, before he could speak again, "how can I help you?"

He flushed. The faint redness ran from his high cheekbones, down his neck, and beneath the shimmering collar of his shirt. It was attractive and boyish and made her feel as if she'd found a kindred soul. She blushed more than she wanted, more than was seemly for a woman her age, and for a woman in her profession. His blush made him seem more approachable. It also made her wonder if he looked that way in bed. That thought made her uncomfortable, and she made herself look at the legal pad while she waited for his response.

He threaded his fingers together, glanced nervously at the door, and then said, "A—dear friend of mine—had, um, been in a, for lack of a better word, a coma—for, um, some time. Her, um, guardian won't—let me near her, and although I've fought for that right for, um, some time, I haven't made any progress."

For an articulate man, he suddenly had a great deal of trouble choosing his words. She didn't write anything down. Instead, she placed her pen across the page with his name and address on it.

"And you want me to—what? Contact the guardian?"

"Isn't there anything legal you can do?"

"Depends," she said. "What's your exact relationship to this woman?"

His flush grew deeper. She sighed inwardly. Girlfriend. Of course. A man who looked like that had to have a thousand of them.

"She's—ah—someone special to me."

Nora resisted the urge to pick up her pen and tap it against the desktop. "Special." She let her tone go dry. "As in fiancée? Lover?"

"No," he said. "But she will be."

Nora closed her eyes. *Will be.* He had hopes, but the girl probably didn't. Which meant he was some kind of stalker. Why were all the gorgeous ones also crazy? She opened her eyes. He was watching her, obviously puzzled.

She sighed again. So much money and it was now going to disappear. Apparently she had ethics after all.

"Look, Mr. Blackstone," she said. "I can't help you in any legal way unless the woman in question is in some way a relative. I'm sorry, but that's just the law. You'll have to accept the situation for what it is and move on."

She pushed his check back toward him.

"You can't help me?" he asked, sounding a bit astonished.

"Not me, not any lawyer," she said. "You have no rights with someone who is just a friend. I'm sorry. The guardian has legal control."

The snake poked its head out of Blackstone's sleeve and hissed softly. Its long forked tongue curled as it did so. He absently petted its flat head and then pushed it under his sleeve.

"This is becoming untenable," he said.

"I'm sorry," she said again. He had no idea how sorry

she was. Sorry that she wouldn't get to look at him any longer. Sorry that she wouldn't be able to use his money to save her law practice.

He took the check, stood, and held out his hand. "Sorry to take all of your time."

His mimicry of the pattern of her thoughts startled her. She wasn't sorry he had taken her time. He had shown her that she was thinking of walking the wrong path.

"I'm sorry that I couldn't have been of help to you," she said as she stood. This time, she took his hand. His skin was smooth and warmer than she expected. His touch sent a little shiver of pleasure through her, and it took all of her strength to keep from pulling away in surprise.

"Nonetheless," he said. "I appreciate your candor."

He bowed slightly, a courtly move that somehow seemed appropriate to him. Then he slipped out the door. She continued to stand for a moment, looking at the closed door, feeling vaguely unsettled. He seemed like a man who, despite his charming surface, was a bit lost.

Then she shook herself as if she were waking from a long, strange dream. It wasn't often she let good looks influence her that much. She sank into her chair and picked up her pen, pausing over his name and address.

After a moment, she reached for her phone and dialed the number of Abercrombie, Hazelton, Finch, and Goldberg. The receptionist answered, and Nora hung up. What had she been thinking, dialing up Max? Max had interesting cases and interesting clients, thanks to his accidental success shortly after he had joined Portland's largest firm. Max had been out of law school as long as she had, but already he had a buzz. Everyone was saying that Max would be the state's best defense attorney, and she had a hunch everyone was right.

Max wouldn't want to talk about this. Max would humor her, of course—he was nothing but polite—but he would think that she was even more marginalized than she already was.

Nora sighed and picked up her mini tape recorder. She would dictate a few notes about Blackstone and his little friend, just so that she had a completed file in case Blackstone did turn out to be a stalker and claimed he had done something on her advice.

Then she would close the file forever.

When she finished, she handed the entire mess to Ruthie and took off for her long overdue lunch. When she got into the elevator, which still smelled faintly of leather and something intoxicating, she let herself dream a little. It would be nice to have a man who looked like that be interested in her. A sane man.

But that would never happen, and she was smart enough to know it. Men always found her attractive at first—so little, so cute—and then she would open her mouth. So few men appreciated her blunt style, and even fewer of them appreciated her opinions. She didn't know how many men she had scared away. The ones who liked her mouth and her brains only saw her as a friend.

She sighed. She hated being practical. Her father used to say that it stole the magic from her life.

And he was probably right.

Of course, if she were really practical, she would have taken Blackstone's money. She had enough, if she were cautious, to pay one month's rent and hope her landlord would be satisfied. If she didn't have anything new on her desk in two weeks, she would have to apply at the law firms that had turned her down.

She would have to admit defeat.

And it was looking more and more like she would have no choice.

Chapter 2

TWO WEEKS LATER, NOTHING HAD CHANGED, EXCEPT that Nora had gotten a bit more desperate. She actually thought of calling her mother for a loan. But her mother would have given her a long lecture about responsibility, forgetting the admonition she had often given about following dreams, and then would write a check for three times the amount that Nora wanted to borrow. Nora hated going into debt. She hated it worse when it was accompanied by a lecture followed by kindness.

Fortunately, Ruthie had managed to get that client who bounced the retainer check to pay cash instead. Ruthie used to work for a collection agency, and for once her strange skills had proven useful. Privately, Nora believed Ruthie knew the end was near, and with her strange boyfriend Bryan to support, Ruthie would do anything to keep the office open.

Even with the lost retainer restored, Nora was still on the edge. She was sitting at her desk, checkbook beside her, a stack of bills on the other side, trying to see which ones she could skip and which ones she absolutely had to pay. No new clients had come in the door in over a week, and none had called. She was beginning to think she was going to have to chase ambulances to find work. At least then, she might have a chance of finding someone truly in need of her help, unlike the malpractice doctor who was the only person burning her phone lines these days.

As if on cue, Ruthie buzzed the intercom.

"Mr. Blackstone is on the line."

Nora felt her heart jump and then frowned at herself in annoyance. Blackstone had been a difficult man who would prove to be a more difficult client. She wasn't doing him or herself a favor by swooning over his looks.

Even if they were spectacular.

She thanked Ruthie and picked up the phone.

"'Bout time," said a nasal voice that clearly didn't belong to Blackstone.

Nora sighed. "Yes?" she said, pretending not to recognize the voice of the little man who called himself Sancho Panza just so she wouldn't have to use his name.

"Blackstone's in a lot of trouble. I think he needs an attorney."

"If he needs an attorney," Nora said, "why doesn't he call me himself?"

"He can't," the little man said. "The police are just arriving, and he's otherwise engaged."

"Police?" She felt a chill run through her. "I'm not a criminal attorney."

"Doesn't matter. You're the only attorney we know. Can you come?"

"You haven't told me where," she said, mentally kicking herself for the curiosity that made her ask the question.

He listed an address in Beaverton near the Washington Square Mall. She recognized the neighborhood; it was one of the older developments in what had once been a bedroom community for Portland, instead of an indistinguishable suburb.

"All right," she said. "I'll be there. But I may have to—"

She heard a click on the other line before she finished the sentence. She stared at the receiver for a moment.

"—find him a new attorney," she finished, softly, to herself.

Then she sighed and slipped on her trusty black shoes. She was glad she had worn a blazer, even though the shoulder pads made her look like a linebacker. Actually, they made her look like a cheerleader dressed in a linebacker's suit coat. She grabbed her cheap briefcase and her oversized purse and headed out the door.

"I don't know when I'll be back," she said to Ruthie. "Tell anyone who calls that I'm on an emergency and will talk to them later tonight or tomorrow."

Ruthie nodded, pretending, like Nora was, that someone would call, and Nora hurried out of the office, wishing she were busy enough to tell Ruthie to cancel her afternoon appointments.

When Nora reached the elevator, she wondered exactly what she was doing. She didn't have a criminal specialty. She should have called someone else. But she felt a need to see Blackstone, a need that she didn't want to analyze too closely. A need she suspected had nothing to do with her work.

Her drive from downtown to Beaverton took nearly twenty minutes in the hot afternoon sunshine. She spent most of the drive worrying about how she could get a retainer out of Blackstone and keep it while she found him a good defense attorney. It wasn't until she had reached

Highway 217 that she actually realized she had tried and convicted the man in her mind. Just because he was in trouble didn't mean that he didn't need a civil attorney. Just because the police were involved didn't mean she couldn't help. Just because he needed help didn't mean he was a criminal.

Gorgeous men shouldn't be criminals. In the world of her imagination, they couldn't be. Criminals looked like—well, criminals looked like Blackstone's little friend, Sancho Panza. Not that criminals were short (she thought most of them were tall) but in the world of her imagination, they all had improperly set noses and they all rolled cigarettes up in their sleeves.

Maybe the little guy had gotten Blackstone in trouble. Maybe that was why he was trying to get Blackstone off the hook.

As she took the Tigard exit off Interstate 5, she frowned at the cloud of inky black smoke that covered the horizon. It was field burning season—when the Willamette Valley's grass farmers burned their fields to prepare it for the next crop—but regulations required them to wait until the winds would take the smoke away from the city, not toward it. Besides, they would have to be burning fairly close to the west side suburbs for that much smoke, wouldn't they?

She frowned and rolled up her windows, wishing that she could afford to fix the air-conditioning in her ancient Rabbit. Immediately the air grew stuffy, but that was better than the smoke that she was driving into.

With a flick of her right hand, she turned on the radio. The local talk station had a single helicopter that was just going toward the site. The news stated what she already knew: something was happening ahead of her.

A prickly feeling grew along her back. She hoped that the smoke wasn't related to Blackstone, but that prickly feeling said it was.

Maybe she should stop at a pay phone and call another attorney now. But she was curious. She was broke. And she really, really wanted to see Blackstone again.

She rolled her eyes at her own thoughts. Maybe she deserved to look like a cheerleader. Only teenagers got crushes like this. Or, more accurately, only teenagers acted upon them.

She decided to take a back route to the address that the little man had given her. She took a side road, and then another, sweat running down the back of her cotton shirt beneath the blazer. The car was stuffy and smelled of smoke. The sky was so black here that she could barely see in front of her car, and what she did see was oily smoke and flaky ash.

There was no way one person could cause all of this. Maybe Blackstone wanted her to sue someone for burning his house down. Maybe. But then why had the little guy mentioned the police?

She bit her lower lip and turned into the neighborhood that the little man had told her about. Immediately she slammed on the brakes. Directly in front of her was a police barricade, and around that, fire hoses, emergency equipment, and more flashing red lights than she had ever seen in one place. She still couldn't tell what was causing the smoke, but she knew it was just ahead.

A cop rapped on her window. His beefy face was red and streaked with soot.

She shut off the radio and rolled down the window. "I'm Mr. Blackstone's attorney," she said, wondering if that would mean anything to the cop.

Apparently it did. He waved her forward. She had to drive slowly to avoid the hoses and the emergency personnel. Burning bits of wood littered the road, and she constantly had to swerve to avoid them. Several homes were on fire. The fire leaped out like a live thing, not responding to the water at all.

The smoke had gotten into Nora's throat, making it feel swollen. She had forgotten to roll up the window, and the stench was overpowering. She didn't see Blackstone anywhere.

She kept driving, cautiously. The address the little man had given her was right in the middle of the devastation. Police cars blocked the entire road. She couldn't drive any farther. She really didn't want to get out, but she felt she had no choice.

She grabbed her purse but left her briefcase, thinking that she didn't want to be too encumbered but she needed her identification. She opened the car door and slid out, gingerly putting her feet between fire hoses and charred debris.

It was worse outside. The stench permeated everything. Bits of charred wood and flame floated down with the ash. The sky was so dark, it seemed as if a severe storm were about to break overhead. Her eyes watered. Police band radios were crackling voices and static, and firemen were yelling directions at each other. Strangely enough, she didn't see any residents. Maybe they had been evacuated. But she would have expected at least one, screaming and shouting and defending his house. Instead there was no one. Other than emergency vehicles, there weren't even cars parked along the street.

For some reason that unnerved her more than anything. She walked around a parked police car, its flashing red lights a dramatic counterpoint to the artificial darkness.

There was a brown and orange Volkswagen microbus parked at the curb in front of the house that the little man had told her about. She walked around it, and then she saw Blackstone.

He was on a green lawn untouched by flames, its flowers a reminder of what the neighborhood had been just a short time before. He had not a speck of dirt on him. He wore the cowboy boots, and a tight pair of jeans, and a T-shirt so white, so clean, that it flared like a neon sign.

His hair was slightly mussed, but he seemed calm. And he was even more gorgeous than she remembered.

Five policemen stood around him—not protecting him so much as guarding him. Another group was on the driveway, including a man who was taking pictures. From her position on the street, Nora looked at what he was shooting, and the sensation that she was out of her league grew from a feeling to a certainty.

There was a woman on the concrete. She was sprawled, face down. With all the commotion around, Nora could only assume that the woman was dead.

Nora swallowed, then smoothed her skirt in a nervous gesture. Just as she had suspected, Blackstone needed a criminal attorney. But all he had at the moment was her. She would do what she could to get him out of here and call Max to defend him as soon as she was able.

Beside her the microbus rocked slightly. She looked up. Sancho Panza or whoever he was moved by the window. She was about to call up to him when he disappeared into the bus's interior.

She swallowed against the smoke-ravaged dryness of her throat. She had to stay focused. She had to get through these next few moments and then get out of here.

She stepped onto the lawn, and her movement caught Blackstone's attention. His face softened when he saw her. It had been all hard lines and angles before. Now it was gentle, rounded, as if someone had changed the lighting or he had become a different person somehow.

He looked at her as if she were a lifeline. She went to him like the schoolgirl whose crush she had appropriated. Only when she was halfway across the yard did she remember she was supposed to be his attorney.

She squared her shoulders and prepared to sound tough. Heaven knew, she couldn't look it.

She stopped beside one of the police officers, a middle-aged man whose soft stomach edged over his belt. His face was soot-streaked, and his eyes were red from the smoke.

"I'm Mr. Blackstone's attorney," Nora said in her best don't-screw-with-me voice. "What's going on here?"

"Honey," the officer said, "you don't belong here."

She raised her chin as if it would give her more height. She hated being called "honey," and she hated even more being called "honey" in that tone of voice.

"I have every right to be here," she said, louder and even more stridently than before. "I am Mr. Blackstone's attorney. I demand that you tell me what's going on."

"Nora," Blackstone said, and on his lips, the use of her name sounded like a poem. "What are you doing here? I don't need you. It's not safe."

"What's going on?" she asked again, this time to both Blackstone and the cop.

The cop stared at her as if she were a cat who had suddenly spoken. Then he looked around as if what she saw explained everything. "Your client destroyed this neighborhood."

She raised her brows, skeptical. "This doesn't look like the work of one person."

"Believe me, lady," the cop said. "It is."

"Nora," Blackstone said again.

She held up a finger, a silent command ordering him to wait. "I don't believe you," she said to the cop.

"We have witnesses," he said.

"Nora—"

"Just a moment," she snapped. Blackstone closed his mouth, obviously stunned at her curtness.

"And," the cop said, "those witnesses put that woman alive not fifteen minutes ago."

After the little man had called her. So he had called her while this—whatever it was—was going on.

She straightened. She had to take charge of this situation. "Are you charging my client with anything?"

It was the cop's turn to raise his eyebrows, as if he couldn't believe the stupidity of her question. "What aren't we charging him with? Carrying incendiary devices. Arson. Murder, and attempted murder. And that's just for starters."

Blackstone rolled his eyes and then shook his head, as if he couldn't believe what was going on. Nora's hands were trembling. She clasped them together to maintain her illusion of calm.

"Nora," Blackstone said. "Since you're here, find Sancho. Make sure he has secured the case."

"I can't believe you're speaking," she said, turning on him. "You're being charged with damn near every felony in the criminal code. Don't say another word."

"Nora—"

"I mean it."

He closed his mouth as if she had pushed it closed. The cop watched them. He hadn't called her honey since she got strident. And now he was looking at her as if she were someone to be reckoned with. The other officers who had been crowding around watched as well. One of them finally took out handcuffs.

"Are those necessary?" Nora asked in the same tone she had used with Blackstone.

The cop visibly flinched but nodded. He snapped them on Blackstone's wrists.

"Where are you taking him?" she asked.

"Downtown," the first cop said.

"Not the Beaverton station?"

"We're better equipped for this kind of criminal downtown, ma'am," the cop said.

This kind of criminal. She shook her head. "My client is not a criminal."

"All right," the cop said. "We're better equipped to handle this kind of *alleged* criminal downtown."

Now she remembered why she had avoided criminal work. It was so that she wouldn't have to deal with cops. "I'm coming with you."

"No!" Blackstone said.

"I told you to be quiet," she said.

"And I need you to find Sancho. We need—"

"One more word," she said, "and I'll gag you myself. You will not speak unless told to by an attorney."

"I promise," he said, "I won't say another word, if you promise you'll find Sancho."

"I'm going with you to the station," she said.

He shook his head. "You're my attorney, aren't you?" he asked. "You have to do what I ask."

Technically that was correct, but it was also her job to save her clients from themselves. The cops were watching the entire interaction with great interest.

"I promise to say nothing at all until you tell me when I can speak again, if you find Sancho and secure the case."

She didn't know what he meant by "secure the case" but she was sure she would find out. "All right," she said, wishing she had another choice. She probably did, but damned if she knew what it was. If he chose to speak without an attorney present, that wouldn't be her problem. She didn't do defense work. "But I won't meet you at the station. I'll be sending one of my colleagues."

No sense in using Max's name since she hadn't yet spoken to him. Blackstone smiled, full wattage. It hit her like a beam of light in the darkness. That smile was as powerful as she had fantasized it would be. She almost had to take a step backward.

"Thank you," he said, then he let the cops lead him away.

She watched. He was taller than the cops, but not by much. He only seemed taller because he stood so straight, even handcuffed when most people would have been humiliated.

Amazing how she could find him attractive, even now.

She brushed a strand of hair out of her face. The smoke was making her woozy. She adjusted her purse strap, and walked across the green lawn. Amazingly, none of the ash and burning debris had fallen here. The cops were still bent over the corpse, and as Nora passed, she paused to look.

The corpse was of a slender older woman with jet-black hair and a streak of white off the right temple. Her face, which might have been beautiful in life, was frozen in an expression of such malevolence that it took Nora's breath away. The woman's hands were splayed at her side, her legs bent, and her expensive dress torn. She didn't look like the kind of woman who normally frequented the suburbs.

She also didn't look dead. She looked more like she had—stopped—freeze frame, the way someone would pause a movie.

One of the cops moved in front of Nora, blocking her view. And she let him, feeling a bit odd lingering here. The fires were not spreading anymore, but it would take a long time for them to burn out—at least that was what one of the firefighters said as he passed behind her.

She walked across the sidewalk and down the curb. As she passed the microbus, the passenger window rolled down a crack. A tiny face pressed against it. Sancho.

"I'm going to your office," he whispered.

She suppressed a sigh and didn't even nod as she passed him. The last thing she wanted was for the cops to investigate the microbus. Who knew what they would find inside? She couldn't believe they hadn't cordoned it off as part of the crime scene. It was as if no one seemed to notice it. No one but her.

She climbed over hoses and returned to her own car. It was covered in a film of ash. As she settled into the driver's side, she turned on the wipers. The ash smeared all over the glass.

The cops said Blackstone had destroyed a neighborhood and maybe killed a woman. She didn't believe it. Was that because she had spent the last two weeks fantasizing about him? Or was it because she had some innate belief in the goodness of people? Or was it because this feeling that she had—that she had had from the beginning—that this was a decent man was growing stronger instead of weaker?

She started the car and executed a series of small Y-turns in the tiny space, careful not to run over any hoses. Why didn't she see this destruction as something awful? It looked as make-believe as the dead woman, the one who looked as if she had been a video stopped midframe.

Whew. Nora had never thought she was one who practiced denial. At least, she hadn't thought it—until now.

———✦———

Before Nora drove to the office, she stopped at a pay phone just off 217 and called Ruthie. Ruthie asked if Nora had heard about the disaster in the west side suburbs, and Nora said, yep, she'd heard. No sense telling Ruthie that she'd been in the middle of it. Ruthie would panic, and Nora would spend the next few minutes calming her instead of getting business done.

And she suddenly had a lot of business, although she doubted she'd be paid for it.

Not that it mattered. Some part of her really thought Blackstone was being framed. By whom and for what, she didn't know, but she was convinced of it.

She had Ruthie set up a conference call with Max, and while she waited on hold, she brushed ash off her blazer. There was a lot of ash, and as she brushed, she changed the color from a faded blue to a dusty gray.

When Max came on, she told him about Blackstone ("You're kidding about the name, right?") and asked him to go to the police station. Max sniffed money immediately and all the fame and publicity a good local defense attorney wanted. He agreed to go the police station before Nora had told him about the dead woman. She was left holding the receiver, Ruthie on the other end, asking her if she was all right.

Nora lied and said she was.

She was shaking as she drove back to her office, shaking and slightly woozy from the smoke. Her nylons were ripped, and she didn't know how she had done that. She smelled like charred wood, and she doubted the smell would ever come off.

The traffic was horrible—backed up for miles as people gawked at the smoke and pulled aside for the emergency vehicles. Nora ran a hand through her hair, and her fingers came away covered with dirt. She was filthy, but she couldn't go home. This might be her only chance to meet Sancho.

She was a bit amazed she hadn't told Max about him. The police would be looking for Sancho, particularly after Blackstone's three requests that she find him.

The little man would prove important to all of this, she knew that somehow. But she didn't know exactly how. And she didn't relish meeting with the man without Blackstone around.

Still, she couldn't stay away either. She was too involved. If Sancho told her something pertinent, she would send him to Max. It was the least she could do.

So after this meeting, the problems would no longer be hers. She would bill for these few hours—any attorney would, right?—and then she would get on with her life and not think about the case at all, except maybe a few phone calls to Max, and those would be an excuse to talk to him, not necessarily to find out about Blackstone. She would act as if nothing unusual happened. Not that she would succeed, of course. She knew, deep down, that this afternoon had changed her life.

But in the spirit of pretense, she flicked on the radio to focus her mind on something else.

Instantly a shrill female voice, filtered through a phone line, grated on her nerves. She was about to flip away when a professional radio voice broke in and clearly hung up on the caller.

"Crackpots," the announcer said. "We have a situation, and all we get are crank calls."

"Several dozen of them, though, Dave," said a professional female voice. "Don't you think we should pay attention to them?"

"No," Dave said. "To recap, there's been an incident…"

He started to describe the neighborhood she had just left, adding nothing to what she already knew. Fortunately he didn't have Blackstone's name and he didn't seem to know about the dead woman. At that moment, the radio was reporting that no one had died. In fact, it said that no one had even been injured and that all of the residents had seen the trouble brewing and had been able to leave as the fires started.

"...another caller from the neighborhood," the female announcer was saying. "And this one we both happen to know. It's Rick Ayers, our morning news announcer. Rick?"

Traffic had slowed to a crawl. Nora had turned on Highway 99, but it seemed as if all of Tigard was at a standstill. In the westbound lanes, traffic had completely stopped as the police tried to prevent anyone from heading to Beaverton. She didn't know what was causing the tie-ups in her eastbound lanes. She just wished it would end. She wanted to get out of here.

"Stephanie." Rick-the-Morning-News-Announcer's voice crackled over the phone lines and through Nora's radio. "Even though Dave thinks the other callers are cranks, they aren't."

Nora felt a shiver run down her back. It was a warning shiver. She turned up the volume.

"Come on, Rick," Dave said. "Two people fighting with fire that gets out of control? A big wild fireball battle like something out of Tolkien? We're supposed to believe that?"

Now they really had her attention. Nora glanced at the radio as if she could gauge its truthfulness just by looking at it.

"'Fraid so," Rick said. "I was across the street. I got the kids out and down the block as fast as possible. There were two people involved—a man and a woman. The man had been coming out of the woman's garage. He had a glass case shaped like a coffin in front of him, and there was something inside it. That's what caught my attention. He wasn't carrying the case. It was floating in front of him."

Glass case. Nora gripped the wheel tightly. Blackstone wanted her to talk to Sancho about the case. Not his court case. A glass case.

"And what were you drinking this afternoon?" Dave asked. It didn't sound like banter.

"I wasn't drinking anything," Rick said.

Behind Nora, a horn honked. She glanced in her rearview mirror and saw a red pickup and its driver waving his fist. Then she looked forward and realized the traffic had started to move again. She drove, the muscles in her shoulders so tight that it actually hurt to move the wheel.

"The guy put this case in an orange and brown Volkswagen bus," Rick was saying. Nora resisted the urge to close her eyes. "And then this woman comes out of her house and lobs a ball of fire at him."

"A ball of fire, Rick?" Dave asked.

"The size of a basketball," Rick said, unperturbed. "The guy deflects it, and it lands on a neighbor's house. That's when I got the kids and sent them down the block, knocking on doors."

"You sent your kids into that mess?" the woman, Stephanie, asked.

"It was smarter than staying inside," Rick said. "Believe me. The entire neighborhood fanned out. I think we got the place evacuated by the time the fire-fight started in earnest."

"According to the police, you did," Stephanie said.

"What does 'started in earnest' mean?" Dave asked. The man was a bulldog. Nothing could sidetrack him. Maybe he saw the morning news anchor slot opening up. He had to be thinking: *If I can discredit old Rick here, I'll be getting drive time.*

Nora was finally at full speed, heading toward downtown. She drove like a madwoman, not sure if she wanted to see Sancho now or not.

"They were throwing fire at each other like kids throw water balloons," Rick said, "and the fire was landing everywhere but on them. It was ugly and scary and—"

"I hope you were hiding somewhere," Stephanie said.

"There was nowhere to hide," Rick said. "Most of us had moved to the far side of the block, but the way that fire was flying, we were no safer than we had been up close."

Nora took her usual exit. It was dark, even here. The smoke had settled over the valley.

"So, what?" Dave said. "Someone was passing hallucinogens through your neighborhood this afternoon, and everyone had the same bad trip?"

"No—"

"It sounds more like David Copperfield came to visit," Stephanie said and laughed.

"Really," Rick said. "It happened. I'm not lying to you. My neighbor Alex, he took out one of those camcorders and…"

Nora pulled into the underground parking garage near her building and lost the radio signal, just like usual. Another thing she didn't like about the garage.

The fluorescents glowed as brightly as they did at night. It felt like night here, with the overcast caused by the smoke. She drove past the usual decrepit cars to her parking space. There she shut off the car and leaned her head against the steering wheel.

The thing was, she believed this Rick, this voice on the radio who claimed he had seen two people hurling fireballs at each other. She believed him, and she knew, without a doubt, that one of those people had been Blackstone, and that somehow, Blackstone had killed his opponent after he had stolen a glass case from her, a glass case that he wanted Nora, somehow, to help Sancho with.

What she didn't know was whether believing all of that made her as crazy as she was afraid it did.

She sighed and sat back up. Her eyes were swollen, her throat scratchy, and the entire car smelled of smoke. Those were the facts. That was all she could know. From there on, she would have to see what happened. No supposing, no guessing, no relying on disembodied radio voices for her information.

Her father used to call her ability to set aside her beliefs as great a magic trick as the ones he used to perform. She still missed him, more than she wanted to admit. The Great Maestro, Portland's best birthday entertainer, who had always wanted to be something more, who had always wanted, in his heart of hearts, for the magic to be real. That was why her mother left him; not for the lack of money or the hand-to-mouth existence, but her father's stubborn belief that, beneath the tricks and the sleight of hand, real magic did exist.

He also believed that he had the ability to do real magic, if only someone would teach him how.

She still couldn't believe how much she missed him.

He'd only been dead a year, and sometimes she still felt him beside her, laughing and pointing out the beauty in the world. He was the one who taught her to look at sunsets. He used to drive toward the end of rainbows, searching for gold. All his life, he never lost that belief, that childlike belief, that there was more to the world than most people could see.

Oh, how she needed him now. He would have listened to her stories about this afternoon. He would have had suggestions.

But she was on her own, with only his memory for company. Somehow that had to be enough.

Nora opened the car door and heard a clang. She frowned, wondering if she had hit the car next to her. She looked over and saw that it wasn't a car. It was a brown and orange VW microbus.

Sancho, or whatever his name was, crawled from under her door. "Man, am I going to have a headache," he said, one hand cradling the side of his face.

"What's going on?" she asked, wishing he hadn't come, wishing he had taken that damn vehicle somewhere else.

"You don't want to know," he said, then murmured something in a language she didn't understand, rubbed his temple, and added, "Better."

The bruise that had been forming on the side of his face had completely disappeared.

"I'm supposed to know," she said, gathering her purse and her briefcase and pretending she hadn't seen anything unusual. "Blackstone said I'm supposed to help you."

"Let's go to your office," Sancho said.

She wriggled out of her car, nearly beaned Sancho again with her briefcase, and then used a hand to wave him forward. He wasn't covered with anything. His T-shirt, the cigarettes missing, was as white as Blackstone's had been, and his tiny jeans looked new. Only his shoes seemed out of place. When she really looked at them, she realized he was wearing cracked leather shoes that buttoned instead of tied.

He walked through the garage, his arms swinging fiercely like he was punching imaginary (short) opponents. She kicked her door closed with one foot and followed him, feeling dirty and short of breath.

When they got into the elevator, she concentrated on the door instead of looking at her reflection in the mirror. Even then, she saw, through the corner of her eye, that her blond hair had gone streaky brown, her normally clear skin looked like it had been finger-painted by five-year-olds, and her clothing was coated with gray ash. She tried to brush some of it off, raising a dust cloud. Sancho began coughing and only just managed to croak out an offended "Hey!" before she stopped.

The ash was still billowing when the elevator door opened and, for the first time since she had taken the office, there were people in the corridor. They stared at her as she led Sancho down the hall, most of them shrinking back as if getting close to her would contaminate them as well—which, if she were being fair, it probably would.

She opened her office door, and Ruthie shrieked.

"Ms. Barr! Ms. Barr! Are you all right? When you said you knew about that mess on the west side, I didn't know you meant you *really* were there. I mean, *actually*. You know, I—"

"You mean literally," Sancho said. "That's what you mean."

Ruthie looked at him as if she was seeing him for the first time. "All right," she said, her voice as cool as his. "I mean literally, whatever that means."

"It means—"

"Ruthie," Nora said, not wanting to hear any more of this discussion. "Can you get me a Coke? Would you like anything, Mr.—?"

"Pan-za," he said slowly, as if he were speaking to a particularly dumb child. He waited. She didn't repeat the name. "And no, I'm not thirsty."

Nora rolled her very dry eyes and walked into her office. It looked as it did when she had left it, cluttered but clean. She turned. She was tracking gray dust behind her. Sancho was avoiding it as he followed her.

She went to her desk and sat down, knowing she would have to clean the chair afterward. She didn't touch the desk's surface or anything else. Sancho climbed into the chair he had used before.

"I won't do anything for you," she said, "until I know your real name."

He stared at her for a moment, his eyes an icy blue. Then he rolled to one side and pulled a swath of paper from his back jeans pocket. Until that moment, she had thought the pocket empty.

He placed a birth certificate, a Social Security card, a passport, and a driver's license on her blotter. She leaned forward, careful not to brush the desk, and stared at the papers. They all showed his name to be Sancho Panza, and the driver's license and passport photos confirmed that the name belonged to him.

She put her index finger against the edge of the blotter and shoved it toward him. "I don't deal in fake IDs," she said.

"Neither do I," he said, shoving the blotter back toward her.

She looked at the papers again. She couldn't tell if the birth certificate and Social Security card were real, but the driver's license had been done on the special paper that the DMV used to discourage forgers. She picked up the passport, getting gray fingerprints all over the blue leather. It was four years old, with several stamps inside, as well as the raised stamp specially done by the State Department. If his identification was good enough for several governments, including this one, it was good enough for her.

"I still don't believe it," she said, because she didn't.

"You don't have to." He settled in his chair. "Just help us."

"I already got a defense attorney for Blackstone."

"Fine," Sancho said as if he didn't care. "The most important thing is the glass case."

"Yes." Nora was amazed at how calm she sounded. So Rick the Morning News Anchor had been right. There had been a glass case. "I understand it levitated out of someone's garage."

"How he got it isn't your concern," Panza said. "Helping him with it is."

"I don't deal in stolen property," Nora said.

"It's not stolen," Panza said and stopped as someone knocked on the door.

"Come in," Nora said.

Ruthie entered, carrying two cans of Coke. She too avoided Nora's gray footprints. "Want a glass?" she asked.

Nora shook her head.

"I suppose you want me to call the cleaning service."

Nora smiled. At last, Ruthie was thinking on her own. "Please."

"Good," Ruthie said, "because I sure as hell don't want to clean up this mess." And with that, she let herself out.

"Nice secretary you got," Panza said.

"You get what you pay for." Nora grabbed a can and pulled the ringtop. "Sure you don't want one?"

He wrinkled his nose. "Ever since they removed the cocaine, it hasn't been the same."

She gave him a flat-level look. "I don't appreciate drug jokes in my office."

"You don't appreciate much, do you?" Panza said. "I thought you had more sense than that. Maybe I misjudged you."

"Maybe," Nora said. She crossed her arms. "Your choice."

He stared at her a moment. "You're not that ruffled by the events of this afternoon."

"I'm a good actress."

"Not that good." He nodded. "We can proceed."

She wasn't sure she wanted to. "I don't mind if you find another attorney."

He grinned. The expression made him seem like a ferocious twelve-year-old. "Naw. You're perfect."

"Have you checked my credentials?"

"Enough," he said.

She took a long, long drink from the can of Coke.

The sweetness helped bring up her blood sugar, and the liquid felt cool against her dry throat. She would eventually need water—she was probably dehydrated—but this would do for now.

The movement gave her a chance to plan and take control of this interview.

"Why did Blackstone destroy that neighborhood?" she asked.

"He didn't."

"Someone did."

"Don't worry about it," Panza said.

"I have to worry about it." She ran a hand over her face, felt the soot flake off. "People make jokes about lawyers having no ethics, but that's not true. I can't help him and stay true to myself if I know he destroyed a neighborhood."

"It was a diversion."

"Really?"

Panza nodded.

"Blackstone would destroy people's homes and kill a woman just to divert attention from—what?"

"He didn't kill her," Panza said.

"She looked dead to me."

His eyes narrowed. "Well, she wasn't. He just knocked her out."

"The EMTs thought she was dead."

Panza shrugged. "It's amazing how susceptible some people are to the power of suggestion."

"I'm not," Nora said. "And I am not sure I want to represent someone who performs wholesale destruction as a means to an end."

Panza clenched a fist, hit the arm of the chair softly,

and then shook his head. "What if I told you everything would be fixed?"

She laughed and felt its bitterness. "That can't be fixed. Not in the way I would want."

"And that is?"

"To make it seem as if today never happened. But people don't forget. Even if everything were made better, people would remember and—"

"Say no more." Panza stood in the chair. She was constantly amazed at how small he was. "We can do that."

"Sure," she said. "And pigs fly."

"Not without help," he said, and he seemed perfectly serious. "Now. Assist us."

He wouldn't go away. And no matter how ethical she got, the images wouldn't go away. She might as well see what Panza wanted. "Tell me what you need."

"I need you to store the microbus," he said.

"You can do that."

He shook his head. "We can't know where it is. Only you can know. You'll store it for us, and then when we come and get it, everything will be safe."

"It doesn't sound legal."

"It is. All you have to do is find a garage, rent it, and keep the microbus there. We might not come for it for years."

"Years?" Nora asked.

"Years." Sancho reached inside the breast pocket of his T-shirt (she hadn't realized there was a breast pocket until he did that. Didn't most T-shirts come *without* breast pockets?) and removed an envelope. The envelope was four times the size of the pocket. "This should cover rent for the next fifteen years, plus your fees and time, based on the estimate you gave Blackstone when we first met. There is also a periodic cost of living adjustment factored into the amount. I've included a worksheet so that you can see how I came to the enclosed figure."

She took the envelope. It was too thin to be holding cash.

"Of course," he said, "if it takes us longer to come for the van, we will send more money."

"Of course," she murmured as she used one short fingernail to slit the envelope open. Inside she found a very ornate check made out for a huge amount of money. More money, in fact, than she had ever seen in one place in her entire life. If she thought about that, she would start trembling again and lose any advantage she might have in this interview.

Sancho was watching her, a bemused expression on his face.

"I'll have to verify funds," she said, using the primmest tone she could muster.

"Of course," he said, echoing her earlier words.

She took the check and walked to the front office. After the door closed behind her, she let out a deep shaky breath. *Please let the check be genuine*, she prayed to any god that would listen. *Please*.

Ruthie was watching her as if she had grown a new head. She probably did look strange, still covered in soot and ash, carrying a check and shaking as if she had won the lottery. Which, if this check were valid, she had.

She made herself swallow and focus on the piece of paper in front of her. The check was issued by Quixotic Inc. and signed by Sancho Panza. His signature was as ornate as the check.

"Ms. Barr?" Ruthie asked.

Nora shoved the check toward her. "Verify this," she said.

Ruthie took the check, and her eyes grew wide. "Holy shmoly," she said. "What does he want you to do?"

"Not much," she said and sat down because she was shaking so badly.

"This is a lot of cash for not much," Ruthie said. "What'd you do? Quote him the rate for billionaires?"

"No, actually," Nora said. "Just the standard fees." Then she grinned. "The standard fees for troublemakers."

Ruthie held up a well manicured hand. "All right. I don't want to know." She shoved the phone between her ear and her shoulder and dialed with a pen. Nora took several calming breaths while Ruthie verified that the check was valid. Then, for good measure, she asked about another check, making up the number, for an equal amount of money.

When she was finished, she hung up and whistled. "These guys are *loaded*," she said.

"You didn't have to do the second," Nora said.

"Actually," Ruthie said. "I used to work for a debt collection agency—"

"I know," Nora said.

"—and they always made you do that," Ruthie continued, "so that the check you had wouldn't bounce if someone took $5 out of the account. It also gives you a sense of how much a person is worth, you know, by how much he keeps in his checking."

For the first time, Nora didn't regret hiring Ruthie. "Thanks," she said as she took the check.

"Does this mean I get a bonus?" Ruthie asked.

"The money goes in escrow," Nora said. "This isn't a debt collection agency."

"Obviously," Ruthie muttered.

Nora ignored her and went back into the office, tapping the check against her hand. The little man was still standing on the chair. He was watching her. She closed the door and leaned on it, thinking only a second too late of the smudge she was making against the presswood's veneer.

"Here's what I'm willing to do," she said. "I'll take your money and put it in a special account. I will have the rental for the garage removed from that account, as well as my monthly fee. I will keep the keys here, and I will not inspect the microbus. I will not touch the microbus after I take it to the garage, and I will not relinquish the keys to anyone but you. *Ever*. Is that clear?"

He nodded. Then he tilted his head. "Will the account bear interest?"

"Yes," she said.

"And who gets the interest?"

"Probably the person who owns the garage, when you don't show up in fifteen years," she said.

The little man smiled. "I like you," he said. "If Blackstone's heart weren't imprisoned, I bet he would too."

Chapter 3

AFTER SANCHO LEFT, NORA USED HER MINI VOICE recorder to dictate the necessary instructions to Ruthie. Then she put the check in the tiny safe that one of her instructors recommended she get (and which she so far had had no occasion to use), so that she could put the check in the bank in the morning. Nora was leery about waiting; she had a horrible feeling the check would vanish in a puff of blue smoke overnight. But she had to trust Sancho, much as she hated to. He was the one who wanted her to guard his case. And if his check did a disappearing act on her, well, she'd tell him where the case was.

Sounded like such a meaningless threat. But she didn't have anything else. And she couldn't cash the check today. The bank was only open for a few more minutes, and she didn't have time to go home and change first. She simply wasn't dressed to open an escrow account this afternoon. She could imagine the looks she would get, coming in all dusty and tattered and trying to cash a check this large when she had never done so before in her entire banking life. It wouldn't be pretty.

After she'd finished tending to the details, she went home. She lived in a loft not far from her office, in a building she one day hoped to buy. She had a hunch that downtown buildings would soon be premium housing, although right now, they were considered the next step above shoddy. The loft had a lot of space, and she had divided most of it herself: living room, spacious kitchen with a view of the Willamette River, study/guest bedroom, and a half bath on the first floor. Up a flight of spiral stairs was her bedroom and a large bathroom.

Her black cat, Darnell, who had been sleeping exactly where he wasn't supposed to be, on the white linen duvet her mother had given her as a housewarming gift, opened one eye as she passed, then rubbed his nose with his front paw, as if in disgust.

"The same to you, pal," she said as she took off her clothes and stuffed them in a garbage bag.

He sneezed, as if the smoke smell trailing after her was an affront, which, she supposed, it was.

Her other cat, Squidgy, who was also black, watched the entire procedure from the bedroom window. She didn't get down to greet Nora either.

"Some companions you are," she said. "I expect a little sympathy."

Squidgy turned back toward the window, as if sympathy were the farthest thing from her mind. Nora grinned. Cats were cats, and their opinions were always quite clear. These two didn't like what they were smelling, and they made sure she knew it.

"Guess that's better than you liking this smell," she said as she walked, naked, to her bathroom. She took a long hot shower and then spent fifteen minutes applying every lotion she had in the house to protect her skin. She wrapped a towel around herself, drank a gallon of water, and finally changed into jeans and a Powell's Books T-shirt. Her eyes were still red, and her throat still ached, but she figured she would suffer like that for the next few days.

Using the downstairs phone, she called several garages before she found one with enough space for a VW microbus. Then she went back to her office and got the microbus. It drove like an old Bug that was about to explode. Something weighed the back down and made corners difficult. But she didn't look. She didn't want to.

When she got to the garage, she parked outside the makeshift office and went in to call a cab and to fill out paperwork. She signed a year's lease with an option for renewal, and in return, got a padlock and a number. She drove down the narrow stalls until she found a metal garage door with that number painted on it in white.

It took some effort to pull the door open, and when she did, it squealed. She put her hands on her hips, squinted at the cobweb-covered interior, and hoped it was long enough for the microbus. If not, she'd have to go back to the office. Who did they make these short garages for anyway? People who drove Le Cars?

She got back into the microbus and pulled it into the garage. Then she took the keys and her purse and exited. As she had promised, she didn't scan the interior, didn't know much more about Sancho than she had before, except that he liked Hershey's Kisses, and kept most of the wrappers on the floor.

It took two tugs to pull the garage door down and a bit of work to get the padlock in the place. Then she was done. The cab was waiting for her at the mouth of the driveway, and she took it back to her office.

For a while, she closed her eyes and rested. Then,

when she felt the swerves that meant the cab had gotten on the bridges over the river, she opened her eyes, expecting to see a darker twilight because of the smoke. Instead the sky to the west was a brilliant pink with no hint of smoke at all. For a moment she stared at it, wondering how all that smoke cleared out of the air. It must have been windier than she realized. That, and the authorities must have gotten the fires under control quicker than they thought they would.

The cab driver let her off in front of the building, and she climbed the three flights to her office. The corridor was dark; everyone had gone home. As she unlocked her office door, she heard the phone ringing. Without thinking, she sprinted across the floor and answered. As she picked up the receiver, she realized she should have let the service get the call.

"Nora?"

It took her a moment to recognize the voice. "Max? How did it go with Blackstone?"

"Buy me a drink," Max said. "No. Buy me fifteen drinks and pour me into a cab. I really don't want to go home."

That bad. It had been that bad. It had to have been, if Max was worried about it. She swallowed. "All right. Where?"

"Grady's."

Grady's. It had been a favorite Portland escape when she and Max were attending the University of Oregon Law School. They would drive north with a dozen other cars filled with law school students from Eugene and spend the weekend drinking and studying and studying and drinking.

Sometimes she missed those days. Especially after days like today.

She grabbed her purse and drove to the bar, which was in a section of Portland she usually didn't go to alone.

Fortunately there was a parking spot in Grady's lot. She went inside. The bar hadn't changed at all. It was just as seedy as it had been a few years ago, with its name painted over the previous bar's name in a metallic gold. The windows were filthy, and the air inside was so blue with smoke—of the legal and illegal varieties—that for a moment, she thought she was back in Beaverton. The bar was full, and for the first time, she felt old. Everyone inside had to be at least twenty-one, but they all seemed carefree. She could barely remember feeling like that.

It wasn't hard to spot Max. He sat alone in what had been Law Student Row, still wearing his three-piece pinstripe. He looked as trim as ever, almost dapper, with a red breast pocket handkerchief that matched his red silk tie. His blond hair had an expensive angle cut. Since she'd last saw him, he had grown a thin mustache, probably in an attempt to look older, but which really made him look like he belonged in a bad World War II movie.

She pulled up a chair, and he grinned at her. His smile didn't have the power that Blackstone's did, but it did make her realize how much she had missed Max. He was good-looking in a mild mannered sort of way, which she actually had trouble seeing after looking at the stunner who was Blackstone.

More than that, though, Max had a charisma that made him good at what he did. Everyone wanted to be his friend. Women hung on him. Yet Max had always had time for Nora, had, in fact, always *made* time for Nora. Sometimes she thought he flirted with her, and then she decided he wasn't. Men who were interested in her always asked her out, and they had never been men she had known from class. They had always been men she'd met at basketball games or in supermarkets. And those men had lost interest so fast, she sometimes wondered if she unintentionally insulted them.

Her father always teased her, telling her that was what she got for dating men whose IQs were lower than hers. Her mother had said that Nora was hiding while she waited for her one true love. Sometimes Nora wondered whether both interpretations were true.

Nora and Max had been the only two members of their class who had come to Portland, and they had promised to keep in touch, which they had, but by phone, not in person. She had often fantasized about him, not just during law school, but after, fantasizing that he would call, not on business, but to ask her out. Max was the only man—until Blackstone—who Nora had ever fantasized about. Ruthie had told her she thought that Max was shy, but who had ever heard of a shy defense attorney? Ruthie had said that some people weren't shy on the job, but they were shy in person.

Nora wished, just once, that Ruthie was right.

A waitress wearing too much lipstick and not enough blush found her way to the table. Nora ordered a beer, and Max did the same, then insisted on paying for everything. When she protested, he shook his head. "You got me the case."

"You asked me to buy on the phone," she said.

"I've just made more money for doing nothing than I've ever made for doing something," he said. "I'll buy."

He had to shout slightly to be heard over the din.

"Let's move to a booth," Nora said. The booths had high wooden walls and their own lights, which meant that she could see Max better and hear him without worrying about what anyone else would hear.

He nodded. They took the only open booth and had to signal the waitress when she came looking for them at their table. After she left, Nora said, "What do you mean, you did nothing?"

He held up a slim hand. "I'm as confused as you," he said. "Maybe more confused." He grabbed his beer like it was a lifeline. "I cashed one very large check on the way back from the jail this afternoon, and I verified funds before I did. It's good. I'm supposed to give some to you. Finder's fee."

She had her own very large check waiting to be cashed. She was about to protest when he slid another check across the table. She gasped at the amount. The check Sancho had given her would pay her monthly expenses for fifteen years. This one was big enough for her to invest and live off the interest. "Max—"

"No," he said. "Don't argue. After what I saw today, don't argue."

She rubbed her eyes, not wanting to ask the next question, but knowing that she would have to. "What did you see?"

"You know where the coroner's office is?"

"In the basement of the main police station. Why? Did you see something?"

He shook his head. Then he stopped, nodded, and shook his head again.

"Max," she said. "What did you see?"

He drank the entire beer in one long gulp. Then he slammed the stein on the table, and signaled for another round. She hadn't broken the head on hers yet.

"Max?"

"I saw," he said slowly, staring at his empty stein as if he were wishing it was full, "the police forget a crime had been committed. I saw a dead body get up and walk. Your friend Blackstone promises me I'll remember all of this, but he said no one else will. No one else—except you."

"Tell me," she said.

And so he did.

<center>~~~</center>

When Max arrived at the police station, he pulled into the parking garage behind an ambulance traveling with its lights off. The ambulance parked in front of the double glass doors that led into the coroner's office. Max found a parking space nearby and kept his gaze on the ambulance. From what he'd heard on his police band radio, he guessed that the ambulance carried the body of a woman found on the driveway of the house where they arrested Blackstone.

Max wanted to catch a glimpse of the body before taking the case. He had made a pact with himself when he became a defense attorney: if the case sickened him, he wouldn't take it because he wouldn't be able to provide a good defense. So far in his young career he'd had no problems, but this whole burning of a neighborhood thing had him spooked, more than he wanted to admit.

So he got out of his car and walked toward the ambulance. He was coming up behind it as the attendants pulled the doors open. One of the men stepped inside while the other waited below. Max heard the sound of metal bumping against metal as they took the gurney out.

The body on the gurney was a woman's, just as he had suspected, and he was surprised to see that she wasn't in a body bag. Her long black hair flowed freely down the sides. She wasn't strapped in either, which he thought odd.

The attendants set the gurney down, and one of them bent over to reach for the strap that was dangling close to the pavement.

The body moaned, and the attendant who was still standing sighed. The other attendant stood. "A little soon for that, isn't it?" one of them asked.

"Soon for what?" Max asked. He stopped beside them as if viewing bodies was a normal part of his day.

The attendant closest to him—a beefy man with a bit of a sunburn and an embroidered name tag that read "Lane"—one of those names which was impossible to tell if it was a first or a last—said, "Dead bodies fill with gas, and the gas moves, and sometimes the bodies make this awful moan as the gas leaves."

"You're kidding," Max said.

"Nope," said the other attendant, a slender reedy man whose pasty-white skin made him look like a native Oregonian—the kind that never saw the sun. His name badge read "Bill," answering the mystery question of first or last once and for all. "Sometimes bodies'll even—"

The body on the gurney moaned again. Hair rose on the back of Max's neck. Then the body sat up.

"—sit up," Bill finished weakly.

The body looked right at Max. It—she—it—had stunning gray eyes that he could have sworn were filled with laughter. Then she threw the blanket off her legs and got off the gurney.

"Sit up?" Max asked. "You mean like that?"

"N-N-No," Lane said.

The woman grinned. She had dark red lips and a silver streak that ran along one side of her dark black hair. She got off the gurney. She was six feet tall and at least forty, maybe older, and stunningly gorgeous in a buxom but expensive Cruella de Vil sort of way. Then she tilted her head, held her hands out as if in apology, and started for the bank of elevators near the double glass doors.

Max watched her go, thinking she was the most beautiful woman he had ever seen and, out of the corner of his eye, he saw the attendants staring after her as if they felt the same way. She pushed the elevator call button with one long red fingernail and then Max remembered that he hated women with long red fingernails—it meant, to him at least, that they were incredibly self-absorbed— and the spell—if that's what it was—was broken.

He had just seen a dead body up and walk. His mouth went dry, and he stepped on the curb, not sure what he was going to do. His movement seemed to stun the attendants out of their stupor. Lane gasped as if the sound had been bottled up inside him, and Bill ran for the bank of elevators but wasn't even halfway there when the woman got on her elevator, turned around, and smiled as the doors closed.

It wasn't a nice smile. In fact, the smile made Max shudder.

He took a deep breath and tried to pull himself together, using all the tricks he had learned in law school and his brief career as an attorney—which then reminded him that he *was* an attorney, which then made him think about his potential client, under arrest for a murder that he couldn't possibly have committed.

At least, not if the body was up and walking around. Dead bodies didn't grin. Murdered people didn't get on elevators.

Max hurried to the elevator banks. An elevator opened in front of him, and he was grateful that it wasn't the one the woman had just used. As the doors closed around him, he saw Lane and Bill bounding up the stairs.

Max used the few minutes in the elevator to calm himself. Obviously, Lane and Bill or the cops who had called them hadn't checked the woman's pulse. She may have had the whitest skin Max had ever seen, and those red lips made it seem even whiter, and that black hair gave her an undead look, but that still didn't excuse their mistake. They should have checked her vitals before assuming she was a murder victim.

Oh, he'd have a field day with this one.

By the time the elevator door opened, he had worked himself into a proper defense attorney lather. He was almost rubbing his hands with glee. Which disappeared as the elevator beside his opened and the not-dead woman got off. He had a creepy feeling that somehow she had held the elevator to wait for his.

He ignored her and headed for the desk sergeant. The sergeant spent most of his day behind a large counter with an open window. He was a muscular balding man who looked like he could take on all comers. Max had gone there a dozen times before and had a casual relationship with the sarge. When Max reached the counter, he leaned on it, thinking it was built to make short attorneys feel even shorter.

Max introduced himself and asked where he could find his client.

Before the sarge could answer, though, the ambulance attendants reached the top of the staircase.

They were screaming something about death and gas and dead women and dead bodies walking, and the entire squad grew silent. Police officers turned in unison to see the two attendants, still in uniform, shouting and screaming and pointing at the not-dead woman as if she had committed a horrible crime.

She, on the other hand, had come up beside Max. Only she seemed unperturbed by the screaming behind her. She was wearing a strong musky perfume—the kind that always overwhelmed him when he walked through the cosmetic section of a department store on his way to the menswear—and she had elaborate jeweled rings on every finger. She was taller than Max by a good four inches. She leaned on the sarge's desk, her thin gold watch clinking against the wood, and asked in a very cultured, very reasonable voice, "Is there someone I can talk to?"

The sarge looked at Max, then glanced over Max's shoulder at the shouting ambulance attendants who, for some reason, weren't getting much closer. Apparently the police academy hadn't prepared people for moments like this, because the sarge decided to use the same tack Max had.

The sarge ignored her.

"Let me take you back," he said to Max, then came around the desk, grabbed Max's arm, and pulled him through the door that led to holding.

Blackstone was in one of the interview rooms, the first one just off the corridor. Max braced himself as the sarge opened the door. Most clients Max saw in places like this were upset or angry or in tears, and Max always had to deal with the rush of emotion first and the problem later.

But Blackstone wasn't upset at all. He was leaning against the peeling green wall paint, his arms crossed, looking as if he were waiting for a cab. He was one of the most striking men Max had ever seen—and Max never usually noticed whether other guys were good-looking—a man who looked like he should be on television, not standing in a grungy interview room near a fake Formica table with a tape recorder built into it.

"You must be the attorney Nora Barr sent." Blackstone's voice was deep and had a faint English accent that somehow seemed just right. "I'm sorry to have wasted your time."

Max suppressed a sigh as he stepped into the room. Any time clients said they were wasting Max's time, they were clients who really needed to go to jail. But Blackstone was attempting to dismiss Max as if Max were a bellboy waiting for a tip.

"You aren't wasting my time," Max said, and then he turned to the sarge. "May I have a moment with my client?"

The sarge shrugged, and that was when Max noticed that no one seemed to care that Blackstone's arms were crossed. Blackstone's hands should have been hand-cuffed, but no one seemed to have thought of that.

Max frowned. He had never encountered anything like this before. What kind of situation had Nora gotten him into?

"Are they letting you go?" he asked Blackstone.

Blackstone smiled, and Max had to take a step backward. It was as if someone had lit up the room. For the first time ever, Max felt jealous of another man. Blackstone probably had to beat women off with a stick.

"You'll see," Blackstone said.

And then, as if on cue, the not-dead woman shoved her way into the interview room, trailed by five cops and the two ambulance attendants. She pushed Max aside, and he fell against the table, his feet tangling in the connections to the tape recorder. But she didn't seem to notice. She headed toward Blackstone. She was as tall as he was, and she seemed to sizzle with energy.

They looked matched somehow, not like they were related, but like they had been painted with the same brush, a brush filled with glitter that only Max could see.

He untangled himself as she raised her arms in a classic sorcerer pose. It looked as if she were grabbing air and holding it. Then she said in that elegant voice, "Where is she?"

The voice made Max shudder. If she had been asking him, he probably would have told her everything, including his underwear size. But Blackstone didn't seem upset at all. He got a self-satisfied cat-that-just-ate-the-canary grin and shrugged.

Max's heart stopped. Somehow he knew that little smile would piss the not-dead woman off. Max headed for the nearest wall and saw that the sarge, the cops, and the attendants were doing the same thing.

"I know you know," the woman said as she got closer to Blackstone.

"Actually, I don't." Blackstone let his arms fall to his sides. Max glanced at the cops, thinking they should have been doing something—anything—about this, but they were mesmerized. It seemed like they had forgotten where they were and that they were supposed to be in charge.

"Tell me where she is," she said.

Blackstone rolled his eyes and said, "You know, Ealhswith, you'd think this would grow old after a thousand years."

She took a step closer to him. Max pressed himself against the wall and pretended to be invisible. He'd represented arsonists and murderers and generally scary people, and never in his life had he felt like this.

He felt like a child in the presence of giants.

"I will not let you have her," the woman said as if Blackstone hadn't spoken a word.

"That's been clear from the beginning," he said.

She took another step toward him. Max was starting to think she was moving slowly for dramatic effect. He wanted her to launch herself at Blackstone, do what she was going to do, and then leave. Immediately.

"This has gone on too long," she said, "and we're getting sloppy."

Max glanced at the cops. This was criminal talk. The cops should have noticed. And they did. But they looked as scared as Max felt.

Which didn't reassure him.

"*You're* getting sloppy," Blackstone said. "Who would have thought to have a battle in the middle of a suburb?"

"Fields are getting harder to find."

"Not really," he said and tilted his head against the wall. He seemed to be watching her and, despite his relaxed posture, he seemed ready to fight. "I knocked you out."

"You should have killed me," the woman said.

"And then what would have happened to all that we hold near and dear?" He said this last with so much sarcasm that Max got a sense the reference was important.

She took a final step and was within touching distance of Blackstone. She bent her arm slightly, as if she were restraining herself. "Tell me where she is," she said.

Blackstone grinned again, and everyone in the room—except the not-dead woman—cringed. "She's somewhere even I can't find her," he said, and then he closed his eyes like someone expected to be slapped.

The not-dead woman extended her hand, and Max slipped farther down the wall. She grabbed Blackstone's head and held it, her fingers bent like claws. Sparks flew everywhere. It was as if Blackstone's head had become a Fourth of July sparkler. His head even made the same hissing noise, complete with sulfur smell. Max had a sense that the woman was trying to pull every thought from Blackstone's brain.

Around Max, the cops and the attendants and the sarge ducked and covered their heads with their arms. Max did the same, but he kept his eyes open, watching the not-dead woman, determined if she came toward him he would run, hide, do anything except let her touch his skull.

Slowly the sparks faded. She cursed and shoved Blackstone away. He was still grinning, even though there were shadows under his eyes that hadn't been there before.

"You think this will work, but it won't," the not-dead woman said, her voice ringing with threat. "I'll find her."

"You have ten years, Ealhswith, and then she's on her own."

"She's too young."

"She's too beautiful. Women leave home well before they turn one thousand. You're just jealous."

A thousand? Max slowly rose to his feet. Surely he had misheard that.

"She's too young, Aethelstan," the not-dead woman said. "She hasn't lived those thousand years like we have."

"And whose fault is that?" It sounded like an accusation. How could it be an accusation? Was it normal for these people to live a thousand years?

"You have to tell me where she is." The not-dead woman's threats seemed to lack the teeth they'd had a moment before. Max had to give Blackstone points for attitude. His unflappability made it clear that the not-dead woman had no power over him, even if she could turn his head into a sparkler.

"You want me to tell you where she is?" Blackstone said, uncrossing his arms and rising to his full height. Max had been wrong. Blackstone was the taller one. "So that you can keep her on ice until your body gives out? I don't think so."

The woman drew in a sharp breath. Then her eyes narrowed and her red, red mouth became a thin line. She whipped her arm in a circle like a pitcher warming up on the mound—and she disappeared.

Max blinked three times and saw the outlines of sparklers against his eyelids. But no matter how many times he blinked, he couldn't make the woman return.

He swallowed, wondering when he was going to wake up.

Blackstone crossed the room and grabbed Max's arm. Max tried to yank away, but it didn't work. He'd had enough of arm-grabbing for one day.

"There's going to be chaos in a moment," Blackstone said. "Just follow my lead."

But there didn't seem to be any chaos. No one seemed upset. The cops, the attendants, and the sarge all stood, unwrapped their arms from their heads, and filed out of the interview room like actors who'd just been told "Cut!" The cops went back to the main area, the attendants walked toward the stairs, and the sarge headed for his desk.

Max glanced at Blackstone, who still had a grip on his arm. They walked out of holding. The sarge looked up from his desk and said, "Max! What're you doing here?"

Max flapped his mouth like an afternoon talk show host, but no sound came out. Blackstone smiled that smile of his—the warm one, the one that made everyone notice—and said, "He's been showing me around. I hope you don't mind."

If Max had been able to get a word out, he would have contradicted Blackstone just to maintain his own credibility. No one got a tour of the police station, and no one but no one, not even the reporters who did ridealongs, got a tour of the interview rooms. But the sarge smiled and said, "No problem," as if Max gave tours of the station every day.

Max's mouth was really fluttering then. Blackstone led him to the elevator. They got on, and as the door closed, Max found his voice.

"What just happened here?" he asked.

Blackstone's smile was gone. He looked tired, drained, as if he had been up for three days straight. All the glitter seemed to have faded from him. He almost looked like a normal person. "Let's get out of here before I answer that," he said.

So Max leaned against the elevator wall and waited for the slow car to bump its way to the parking garage. Finally the elevator stopped, and the doors opened. Max stepped out only to see Bill and Lane, the ambulance attendants, leaning against the side of their vehicle.

"You didn't call for an ambulance, did you?" Bill asked.

Max frowned at him. Bill knew better. Lane knew better. They'd just gone through a traumatic experience together, the three of them. What was this? Some sort of elaborate butt-saving?

"No," Max said, sounding as affronted as he could while Blackstone spoke over him, saying, "Have you checked upstairs?"

"Yeah, at least, I think so," Lane said. He looked at Bill and shrugged. "I just don't get it. How did we end up here?"

Bill looked even more confused.

Blackstone still had a grip on Max's arm. That, and the fact that Blackstone was taller, made Max feel like a child with an upset parent who was leading him somewhere he didn't want to go. Blackstone tugged and Max moved, even though he wanted to continue the conversation with the attendants.

Blackstone led Max to his car—and it was only later that Max wondered how Blackstone knew which car that was—and handed Max a check for his "time and services."

"Please," Blackstone said. "Split the money with Nora."

He spoke Nora's name with a softness he hadn't used at any other point, and Max looked sharply at him. What was between the two of them? Nora always picked losers. And while this guy was certainly dramatic, he didn't seem like a loser.

He actually seemed like a threat. Maybe Max should be paying more attention to Nora instead of letting this guy close to her. After all, Max didn't want to lose his chance with her. He'd been waiting until she got out of her loser phase.

Then Blackstone said, "I'm sorry you had to see this. You can't forget because you were of service to me at the time. And Nora needs to know, because if she doesn't, I'll be, as your generation so aptly puts it, screwed. But do tell her for me that we did as she asked and put everything back the way it was."

That speech was the topper. Max didn't get a word of it. He felt as if Blackstone were suddenly speaking Greek. Only warmly. And as if Nora had a part in all of it. Which, for some inexplicable reason, irked Max more than anything else had.

"What *is* going on here?" he asked.

"You don't want to know," Blackstone said.

Hmm. Hidden information. Max crossed his arms. "But I do," he said.

Blackstone sighed.

"All right," he said. "I'll tell you what I can. But it's not my fault if you fail to believe me."

———

Max paused long enough to make Nora wonder if he'd

lost his ability to hold his liquor since law school. She'd lost count of the number of beers he'd had—she still had barely touched her first—but he was beginning to look bleary-eyed. He flagged down the waitress and asked for another beer. The waitress looked at Nora as if Nora were the one who had to approve the order, and when Nora nodded, left.

"Max," Nora said. "What did Blackstone tell you?"

Max rolled the empty beer stein between his hands. He didn't look at Nora. "You know, when I drove here, there wasn't any smoke. And no one said a word about it on the radio."

"Max," Nora said, feeling more impatient than she probably had a right to. "You were going to tell me about Blackstone."

"So I drove by the neighborhood, just to see all this destruction for myself. And you know what? It looks fine. No burned houses. No ashes. Just flowers and porches and electric lights."

"Max," she said, worrying that he might lose complete control before he got to the point. "What did he tell you?"

The waitress set down Max's beer, and Nora paid for it, just to get her out of the way before Max forgot the question. He looked at Nora, waved a hand in thanks, and said, "What did Blackstone say?"

"Yes," Nora said, clenching her fists in her lap. If she didn't, she would shake Max, and that wouldn't be good.

"He said that fairy tales are true. Sort of."

"Great," Nora said, leaning back.

"And we got stuck in the middle of *Sleeping Beauty*, only there was a dwarf. At least the glass case is correct—"

"Max." A chill ran down Nora's back. It wasn't that she was afraid she didn't follow him. She was afraid she did. "From the beginning. Please."

He looked up, his eyes bleary and sad. So very sad. "I told you about the police station. Didn't I? I thought I did."

"You did. But you were going to tell me what Blackstone said when he took you to your car."

"Oh, yeah. From the beginning." Max ran a hand over his face, as if he were trying to hide. "Blackstone said— are you sure you want to hear this?"

"*Yes*." Maybe she would shake him. Maybe that was her only option.

"Blackstone said he was a wizard."

"A wizard?"

"Only he used the word mage."

"Mage?"

"You asked."

Nora bit back a sharp response. "Go on."

"Over a thousand years ago, he fell in love with a witch's daughter. Or was she a stepdaughter? I'm not clear on this point. It's the mention of fairy tales. You know, you hear them all your life, you don't pay attention, and suddenly it becomes relevant. Kind of hard to deal with, don't you know?"

"I know," Nora said. "The witch's daughter?"

"Or stepdaughter. Yeah." Max drained his beer stein. "Shouldn't do that," he muttered. "Will get drunk."

Nora took the stein away from him. "Will pass out before finishes story. I need to hear this."

"Right," Max said. "That's what Blackstone said."

Only now his *s*'s were sounding like *sh*'s.

"Anyway," Max continued, "this daughter, step-daughter, whatever, had a hell of a witchy mother who didn't want anyone near her stepdaughter or daughter or whatever, and so she hid the daughter with her assistant, a magical dwarf named—"

"Sancho Panza," Nora said, beginning to see the pieces.

Max looked at her strangely. "No," he said with great precision. "The magical dwarf was named Merlin. No one talked about Don Quixote de la Mancha. Besides, that was less than a thousand years ago, right?"

"Right," Nora said, sorry to have interrupted him.

"This Merlin dwarf had something to do with the great Merlin of old, only Blackstone said he wasn't that old then. And that it was in a different kingdom. There are lots of kingdoms, I guess, some magical, some not." Max waved a hand as if clearing the cobwebs from his own mind. "If I tell you all the tangents, I'll never get another beer."

"Just the main points," Nora said, wondering how long they had before Max anesthetized his memory into oblivion.

"Okay," Max said. "This dwarf, he was a good friend of Blackstone's, and he managed to get Blackstone and the girl together. What they didn't know was that the witch had put a curse on them so when they kissed, the girl passed out."

The waitress stopped to offer Max another beer, but Nora shook her head. Max looked after her longingly. "When you finish," Nora said.

Max sighed, then looked down at his empty hands. "Merlin knew this girl would die if she didn't get back to the witch to remove the spell, but Blackstone outsmarted the witch. He put the girl in a glass coffin. She would remain as she was, not alive, and not dead, until the spell was removed. Merlin knew the witch's spell would wear off in ten years if the witch didn't know where the girl was. But before they could hide the coffin, the witch stole it. Over the centuries, Blackstone has stolen it back, but he's never been able to hide it from the witch. She's got this weird form of telepathy—that was those sparks, I guess—and she's always been able to pull the information from him. Until now. As long as he doesn't know where the coffin is, the witch won't either."

"Oh, no," Nora said, taking a big slug of her own beer.

"You know, don't you?" Max asked.

"I have a hunch," Nora said.

Max held up his hand. "Well, don't tell me. I don't want to be any more involved than I already am." He got up and swayed once. "I told you what I know. Now I'm leaving."

"Max," she said, feeling suddenly alone. "Don't you think we should investigate?"

He shook his head then caught the table to hold himself upright. "It would raise too many questions. Like, if there is a woman in a glass coffin in your possession, is she dead? And if she is, are you an accessory after the fact? And if she isn't, are we supposed to believe she's been alive but asleep for a thousand years? Doesn't the prince get to wake her with a kiss? What's all this waiting ten years stuff? Or has the oral tradition really screwed up? Was it going to sleep with a kiss after all?"

He leaned closer to her. "And is there such a thing as a happily ever after?"

"Only in fairy tales, Max," she said.

"But Blackstone said this is a fairy tale." He leaned even closer and whispered in that stagy way that drunks had, "It all seems wrong to me."

"It's seemed wrong to me from the moment I met Blackstone," she said.

"Tell me no more," Max said, waving a hand and nearly toppled backwards. He caught himself again, and she found herself amazed at how well he could control his mind when he was drunk but not his body. She doubted she could have been as coherent as he just was when she was drunk.

He stood up straight, brushed his expensive suit with exaggerated movements, frowned as if he were trying to concentrate on each flick of his hand, and then announced, "I am going to call a cab. Then I am going to go home to pretend this was all a drunken fantasy."

"And the money?" Nora asked.

"I'll pretend I defended a mobster and it was so traumatic, I forgot all about it."

"A mobster? In Portland?"

Max frowned at her. It took her a second to realize he was trying to be serious. "Stranger things have happened," he said and wandered out, clutching the back of booths as he went for support.

"No kidding," she said when he was out of earshot. She only wished the stranger things weren't happening to her.

She shoved her beer aside. She no longer wanted it. It made her queasy stomach worse.

Max was right, and she didn't want to think about that. She had said she wouldn't investigate what was in that van. But now, it seemed, she had no choice.

Or did she?

She shook her head. Max was right; these were the things they didn't teach in school. Did magic alter the law? Or did it work the same way? And who would decide?

Then she heard her mother's voice as clear as if her mother were in the bar with her. *There is no such thing as magic, Nora. It's all tricks that someone does to make you do exactly what they want.*

"I know, Ma," Nora whispered. "That's precisely what I'm afraid of."

—⁓—

She had to go to her office first to get the key to the lock she had put on the garage. As she stepped out of the bar, she looked at the night sky. It was dark, just like it was supposed to be, but the city lights illuminated part of it.

And from here, at least, she couldn't see the smoke.

Maybe Max had had the wrong neighborhood. Maybe he was looking in the wrong place. Maybe he had been disoriented from his experience with Blackstone and merely wished that nothing had gone wrong.

Heaven knew, she did.

She got into her car and deliberately took the long route to her office, going out of her way to the west side suburbs to see if that neighborhood had been repaired as Blackstone claimed it had been.

The inside of Nora's car still smelled of smoke. She would probably have to get the thing professionally cleaned. She rolled down the windows and didn't get any fresh smoke scent from the air. In fact, the city smelled like it usually did this time of year; like car exhaust mixed with roses, lilies, and other flowers that seemed to grow everywhere here.

Streetlights were on the entire way, and the roads were clear of debris and emergency vehicles. She tried to tell herself this meant that the Portland authorities were just unusually efficient, but she found herself holding her breath, hoping that she was wrong. As she pulled off 217 onto the residential streets, she saw the silhouettes of houses trailing off into the distance. Some had lights on. Many, by this time, had their lights off. Vehicles were parked in the street as if they belonged there.

She pulled over to the curb, parking between the two houses where she thought, but wasn't certain, the van had been parked earlier. She got out and wandered the lawn, recognizing its greenery and flowers from the afternoon. This was the place. She would bet her practice—meager as it was—on it. And yet the neighborhood stood around it. Nothing was destroyed.

A porch light came on at the house behind her. She frowned. That house probably belonged to the radio personality. He had seemed like the nosy type. She slipped back into her car and drove away.

A feeling of disorientation that had nothing to do with the beer swept through her. Maybe when she got back to her office, she wouldn't even find a key. Maybe in the morning, Max would deny having had that conversation with her. Maybe none of this had happened.

Maybe.

But it felt as if it had.

She pulled into the parking garage beneath her building and got out of her car. As she walked to the elevators, she passed a blue 1974 Lincoln. A little man stood on its fender, and a tall man leaned against its hood. He was still the most stunning man she had ever seen. He wore a shimmery gray silk suit that accented his broad shoulders and long legs, and on his feet he wore cowboy boots trimmed in real silver. A snake peeked its head out of his sleeve.

"You know," he said in that rich voice of his, with the accent that made her warm all over, "if you get the key and go to the van, I'll simply have to follow you. And if I follow you, all of this will be for naught."

Nora stopped. She put her thumbs in the pockets of her jeans so that she could look casual even though she didn't feel that way. She wanted to hug him because he was safe. She wanted to yell at him for confusing her so. Instead she said, "Max tells me there's a woman in that glass case."

"And she's alive," Blackstone said. "She's been asleep for a thousand years. If you help us, she'll sleep for ten more."

"Why can't your friend get the information out of my brain?"

"Because it isn't there," Blackstone said. "Right now, all you have is supposition. She could probe, but her powers won't let her unearth supposition. They'll only unearth fact."

Nora dug her thumbs in harder. She could feel the hard seam against the thin webbing between her thumbs and forefingers. The pain let her know this wasn't a dream. "The fact is, I have your van. She'll know that."

"You have *my* van," the little man said. "Sancho Panza's van."

"And we all know that's not your name," Nora snapped.

"No," the little man said. "You *suspect* that's not my name. You *know* that I have all the legal documents to prove that it is."

She took a deep breath. "This afternoon, I saw a destroyed neighborhood and a dead woman. I saw the police lead you away in cuffs."

"Yes," said Blackstone.

"But you're here, and the neighborhood's back the way it was, and Max said the woman's not dead."

Blackstone's smile was small. "We live differently from you, Sancho and I."

"So you're saying what I saw was real."

"For that moment," he said. "But you asked us to fix it, to put it back the way it was. So we did. Just like we were supposed to."

"For the record," the little man said. "*She* was the one who destroyed everything, not us."

"What if she's the one who is in the right?" Nora asked.

Blackstone crossed his arms. He glared at her as if he couldn't believe anyone would ask that question. "You don't even know what the battle's about."

Nora tilted her head slightly. "You're right. I don't. Enlighten me."

"Love," said Blackstone. "The battle's about love."

She was mesmerized by the way he said the word. He said it as if love were everything there was to life, as if love were the entire focus of his existence.

And then she shook herself. That might be what he said, but that wasn't how he acted.

"Seems to me it's about possession," she said. "I mean, there's a woman who has been asleep for a thousand years because her family and her boyfriend are fighting over her. Seems to me, she has no say in the matter."

Sancho put his face in his hands. Blackstone frowned. The snake hissed at her.

"She loved me," Blackstone said.

"Then," Nora said. "But you've lived for a thousand years. She hasn't. That has to have some effect on a person."

"You don't understand," Blackstone said. Sancho was peeking through his fingers, watching her.

"Apparently not," Nora said. "I suppose you're going to paraphrase F. Scott Fitzgerald again? The magical are different from you and me?"

"You don't understand," Blackstone said.

"What I understand," Nora said, "is that people who resort to using the phrase 'you don't understand' in an argument already know they've lost."

The snake slid out of Blackstone's sleeve and headed toward her, mouth open, fangs revealed. Blackstone caught it with his other hand and shoved it into his jacket pocket. Sancho's fingers were splayed farther, and Nora got the distinct impression that behind them, he was laughing.

"Sometimes," Blackstone said, "people use the phrase 'you don't understand' because the concept they are trying to discuss with another person is well over that other person's head."

"The other person's stupid," Nora said.

"I didn't say that. But the other person has—shall we say—a different life experience?"

"Like a woman who went to sleep in the Dark Ages and wakes up in the computer age?" Nora asked.

The little man guffawed then choked and hit himself once on the chest, as if the sound were not laughter at all. Blackstone turned to him, glaring, the snake working its way out of his pocket.

"I suppose you agree with her?"

"I always thought this was more about you and Ealhswith than you and Emma," Sancho said.

"Emma?" Nora asked. "Sleeping Beauty is named Emma?"

"What did you expect, Osborg?" Blackstone snapped.

"No," Nora said. "Maybe Guinevere."

"You're mixing your legends."

"Sounds like you are too," she said. They stared at each other for a moment. There was something in his gaze, something bright, as if he enjoyed the sparring.

And then he looked away. "Her name is Emma," he said. "It's probably good for you to know that."

Nora took a deep breath. Her heart was pounding. She wasn't used to arguing with clients like that, not even strange and magical clients.

She ran a hand through her hair. "What happens if I raise the coffin lid before the decade is up? Will I wake her?"

Blackstone snapped his head around to look at her so fast, she felt as bad as if she had actually tried opening the lid. "Don't do that. You'll destroy my spell. She'll die."

"She'll die?"

"Ealhswith's death spell will not be broken," the little man said. "It'll continue just as if it had never been stalled."

"You're sure that was a death spell?" Nora asked. "I

mean, it seems weird that a mother would do that to her own child."

"Ealhswith is not her mother. She's Emma's mentor."

"The same comment applies," Nora said.

"Things were a bit different then," Blackstone said.

Nora frowned. "That comment is only one step up from 'you don't understand.'"

"It's just as true," Blackstone snapped.

"I'm sure it is."

"Children," Sancho said, his lips twitching as he clearly tried to suppress a grin. "Fighting gets you nowhere."

"That's right," Nora said. She started for the elevator, then stopped. "If all of this happens in ten years, why did you pay me for fifteen?"

Blackstone hadn't moved. The snake had crawled out of his pocket and back into his sleeve. Just its tail was sticking out. Sancho grinned and started to answer, but Blackstone spoke first.

"I didn't pay you," he said.

"I did," Sancho said. "I figure you have it right. Emma's been asleep for a thousand years. She'll need time to adjust. She'll need to make decisions, choices, and she can't do that if she doesn't understand the world she's in."

"What choices?" Blackstone asked.

At the same time Nora said, "You expect me to baby-sit?"

Sancho shrugged. "I expect nothing," he said, answering Nora and ignoring Blackstone. "Except that you find competent help for any problem that might arise while you're my lawyer. If that's too much to ask, let me know. I'll find someone else."

There was a lot more here than she had initially expected. She couldn't see herself training a medieval woman—check that, a woman from the Dark Ages—how to survive the modern era. But he did say competent help. She could always find help. Especially since he had paid her up front.

Nora pushed a strand of hair off her face. The hair still smelled faintly of smoke. She looked at Blackstone. "The battle between you and this woman, this so-called witch. Is it over?"

"It will be," he said, "when she can't find what she's looking for."

"And she won't find it, as long as I work for your sidekick here."

"Hey," Sancho said.

"You're the one who chose the name," Nora said.

"Yes," Blackstone said, seeming at first to confirm what Nora had just said. Then he added, in clarification, "She won't find it as long as things remain as they are now."

Nora frowned. "That's giving me a lot of control over something that's important to you."

"Yes." Blackstone stood. He seemed taller than he had before.

"Why?" she asked. "Why me?"

"Because," he said, "you're perfect."

She felt a flush build in her cheeks. She knew she'd be reliving that sentence for days. But she had to make a pretense at keeping her distance. "Thanks. But flattery won't work. Why me?"

"Because," Sancho said quickly as if he were covering for his friend. "You believe just enough to take a chance."

Believe? Believe what? In magic? In them? "I don't believe in anything," she said.

"If that were true, you wouldn't be standing here, now would you?" Blackstone asked.

She supposed not. She closed her eyes, shook her head, and bit back the retort that came to mind, a retort as ridiculous as his "you don't understand."

"What happens to you now?" she asked as she opened her eyes. The sentence sort of trailed off. Blackstone was gone. There was no Lincoln, no snake, and no annoying little man. She was the only person standing in this section of the garage.

She looked over her shoulder. No, she hadn't gotten turned around. She was alone.

"Damn," she said. "I've decided I hate it when people do that."

But there was no answering reappearance, no giggle from Sancho, no hiss from the snake. She was well and truly alone.

She didn't like the feeling.

She adjusted the purse strap on her shoulder and headed toward her office. Maybe they were invisible and watching her. Maybe she had imagined the whole thing.

But of course she hadn't. The smell of smoke trailed her like a homeless puppy. She got into the elevator and leaned on the cracked mirror, like she always did. She looked no different, except for her swollen and reddened eyes, but she felt different—angry, yes, at being left alone like that, but beneath the anger was an exhilaration. Her father would have given everything for a day like the one she had had. Her father would have seen it as proof that magic did exist.

She didn't know how she could doubt it. And then she stood up. Of course she did. It had been what she had been thinking of when she came back to the office. She would get the key, go to the garage, and look in the microbus. If there was a dead woman in the coffin, then she had a problem on her hands.

She let out a small sigh. But if Blackstone was to be believed, she would have a dead woman on her hands if she opened the coffin. If she left it closed, then she kept the woman alive.

Theoretically.

Well, in ten years, if that person in the coffin was really dead, at some point the decay would cause a smell that someone would notice.

Nora winced. The elevator door opened. The lights in the corridor were dim. Now there was no one here. Of course, when she finally looked presentable. She walked through the hall to her office, and as she opened the door, she noted that the cleaning service had already been there. The place had the faint odor of lemon. She thought about the added cost and then realized that with the check Max had given her, and the fees she would be taking from Sancho's escrow account every month, she would never have to worry about incidentals again.

Max. She hadn't even checked to see if the cab got him home safely. Before she thought about what she was doing, she leaned across Ruthie's desk and dialed Max's number. It startled her to realize that she had it memorized.

The phone rang six times. She was about to hang up when someone answered.

"Max?" she asked.

"You looked," he said.

And in that response, she felt a deep and profound relief. She hadn't imagined any of this.

"No," Nora said. "But I did realize that we'd skipped dinner. You want to go?"

"Now?" he asked. It was nearly midnight.

"Yes," she said.

"Is this… a date?"

There was enough hesitation in his voice to make her hesitate too. But dating Max was something she had wanted to do since she met him years ago. She had just never had the courage to take the initiative before. Maybe she had learned today that if she didn't do what she wanted, no one else would make her wishes come true.

"I guess it is," she said.

He laughed. "Who'd've thought—after a day like this—well, maybe dreams do come true."

"Max?"

"Sorry," he said. "Muttering. I'd love dinner. I think I'm a little more sober now than I was before."

"I'll pick you up," she said. "In ten minutes."

She hung up before he could change his mind. And then she did a small dance around the office. Maybe some good would come of this after all. She smiled. How strange. She had met a magic man, and he had indirectly granted her two wishes—a date with Max and enough money to keep her law firm open.

Be careful what you wish for. The voice belonged to her grandmother, her father's mother, a kind old woman who had been raised in a strict Germanic community in the Midwest. Nora stopped dancing. The voice had come from her memory, hadn't it?

Be careful what you wish for, Norrie. You might not like it when it comes.

Of course she would like it. How could anyone not like her dreams? She was simply being too cautious, unable to believe the strange luck that had visited her these last few days.

She decided to leave the garage key in its place, and she promised herself she would check on the microbus once a month, just to earn her fee. And then she walked out of the office, heading toward dinner, heading toward Max, heading toward her future, and leaving this weird incident behind her. Maybe she could convince herself she'd gotten the money from mobsters too. Maybe, but not likely. First, that meant she'd sold out her vaunted ethics. Second, it would really complicate things with the garage.

No. She would look on it as a strange side trip, a place where she had stepped into the twilight zone, where she had learned that her father's dreams had a basis in fact.

And that was enough for one life.

Wasn't it?

Now

Chapter 4

NORA HUNG UP HER CELL PHONE AND STEERED THE Lexus that Max had bought her for their last anniversary across the Banfield bridge. Maybe she should trade the Lexus in on a new Volkswagen Bug. She had always liked those, and she had never had one of her own. The Lexus just wasn't her, and it never had been. That was one of the many things Max had never understood.

Besides, she hadn't felt right driving the car since the divorce had turned so sour.

Portland was beautiful this morning: clear blue skies over the equally blue river, the mountains in the background, and the city sparkling in the amazingly pure light. No matter what happened, she loved it here. She loved it enough to continue sharing the city with Max, no matter how ugly things got.

She ran her hand over the phone's receiver and frowned. She hadn't been entirely honest with Ruthie. Ruthie, who had become her right hand, deserved to know why Nora was postponing her 9:00 a.m. with the head of the legal team for one of the largest athletic shoe manufacturers in the country, if not the world. The appointment had been on the books for weeks, and it had bothered Nora for weeks, even though she hadn't admitted it to herself.

And she would have gone to the meeting, too, if she hadn't had the dream again last night.

The dream was quite vivid and quite horrifying. She had been having it for ten years, ever since she had met that strangely beautiful man, Blackstone, and his even stranger companion, Sancho Panza or whatever his name was.

The dream would begin as Nora awoke in a glass box, in semidarkness, confused and alone, pressing her hands against the top and unable to get out. In the logic of dreams, there was a digital clock above her, giving the day and the time and the date. As she shoved on the glass top, trying to break the glass sides, trying to find a way to move within her narrow prison, the hours ticked by. Eventually she would gasp for air and wonder how long she had before she stopped breathing altogether.

At that point, she would always wake up, coughing as if she really hadn't gotten enough air and holding her pillow above her as if it had doubled for the glass coffin's lid.

In the early days of their relationship, Max hadn't laughed at the dream. He had confessed to similar dreams himself, and he had always held her and comforted her. In those days, he had believed in magic. Sometimes sharing moments with him as simple as a sunset made her think of her father and his beliefs.

But Max stopped talking about magic as time went on. As his fame grew, not just locally but statewide, and he began eyeing the careers of really famous defense attorneys like F. Lee Bailey and Johnnie Cochran, he seemed to lose any sympathy for the strange events that had brought them together.

Fantasy doesn't win cases, Nora, he would say. *Talent, hard work, and clear-eyed perspective does.*

She believed in talent, hard work, and a clear-eyed perspective. She really did. But ever since that strange day ten years ago, she also believed in magic. The story-book kind.

The head of legal for the shoe company would re-schedule. After all, it was her expertise he was coming to see her for; she had developed several specialties, and one of them was suddenly of use to the company. If they needed her badly, they could wait. She certainly didn't need them, not even with the divorce.

As the Banfield left the river, she took the first exit in the Hollywood District. She had had to find a new garage; the old one had burned years ago, all but her rental, which was left standing in the middle of completely flattened devastation. The police—who were investigating the fire as an arson tied to insurance fraud—said they had never seen anything like it. It was as if, they said, that particular garage was shielded from the flames. There wasn't even a charred stretch of paint.

She had moved the microbus to a new garage owned by a reputable national company and had left it there for the past three years. In the past ten, she hadn't seen or heard from Sancho or Blackstone. Max came home pale and shaken one afternoon about five years ago and said he had seen the not-dead woman in his courtroom, but when Nora asked him about that later, he denied it. He said he had only thought someone looked like the not-dead woman. Nora wasn't so sure.

Nora monitored her rear and side mirrors carefully as she went to the garage. She wasn't being followed—at least, she wasn't being followed by someone obvious.

She drove into the garage and storage unit place, parked in front of her rental, and took a deep breath.

Did she really believe dates and times she saw in dreams? Did she think that something was going to happen on this day at this time or was she here to destroy the last bit of belief she had? Max had done a good number on her. He was, in some ways, helping her reenact her parents' relationship: she was the believer in magic, and Max was the one who wanted to destroy that. At the very last party they'd attended, before the very last screaming fight they'd ever had, he had told a colleague that in his first years of practice, the largest payoff he'd ever had was for getting a mobster out of jail before the man had ever been charged.

The colleague had frowned as if he had known Max was lying and said, "A mobster? In Portland?" and then walked to the other side of the room. Nora had seen that as a small victory. But she still couldn't believe that Max had bothered to tell the story, even though he had once warned her that was how he chose to remember things.

Nora hadn't confronted Max in person, but she had on the way home. She had asked him about the magic, about the fires, about the ruined neighborhood, about the not-dead woman, for heaven's sake, and he had an explanation for all of them. There is no such thing as magic, he had said. There were no fires. I never saw the neighborhood you talk about, and the woman was merely riding in the ambulance.

Nora found she couldn't argue with such intense denial, and she finally admitted what she had been denying herself: the marriage didn't work. It hadn't really worked from the beginning. They had been too shy with each other. He had been too ambitious, for himself and for her. She didn't live up to his idea of what a good defense lawyer's wife should be. And so on and so on. She had suggested irreconcilable differences and thought the divorce would be easy.

Of course she was wrong. Two attorneys couldn't order a pizza without filing several briefs; they certainly couldn't let something like a divorce occur without some sort of legal warfare.

She glanced at her watch. It was 8:50 a.m. She had used the Internet that morning, checked Greenwich Mean Time, and done the math so that her watch was on Pacific Daylight Time to the second. Somehow she had felt that to be important.

As she got out of the Lexus, she looked around. The storage and garage units were simple structures with rippled metal doors and relatively thin walls, mostly built for holding things, but not for keeping them in any kind of good condition. There were no other cars parked on the asphalt near hers, and the office was far enough away that no one could see her. As far as she could tell, she was alone.

She took the key out of her pocket and unlocked the padlock holding the gate shut. She hung the lock in one of the holders and pulled the door open.

The garage looked just like she'd left it: the microbus parked haphazardly in the space. The tires were low, and the entire front end was covered in dust. She remembered the drive from several years ago; years in storage had left the interior with a thousand spiderwebs, and she had brushed them off as she had driven, wondering what weighed the thing down in back and

made it corner so poorly, and vowing, yet again, not
to find out.

She went inside. Her heart was pounding. She had
promised herself that she would never look in the back
of this thing, and she was breaking that promise this
morning. She was even dressed for it, in frayed denim
jeans and one of Max's ratty University of Oregon
sweatshirts. She pushed up the sleeves and grabbed the
rusted handle on the microbus's back end.

For a moment, she thought the handle wasn't
going to turn. Then it did, with a creak that sounded
like the squeal of bad brakes. The door popped open,
and surprisingly the dome light went on, faint, but
somehow comforting.

She glanced at her watch. It was 8:55 a.m.

The floor and walls and ceiling were carpeted in
brown and orange shag—a detail that hadn't been in her
dream—and in the very center of that was a glass coffin. It wasn't clear glass, like she had thought it would
be, but frosted glass, or glass that was so very old that
moisture had gotten into its layers.

On top of the coffin was an envelope with *Quixotic
Inc*. in the upper left-hand corner. She remembered the
ornate logo as if she had just seen it the day before. But
the envelope had been there a long time. The tape holding it in place was brown and brittle. In familiar flowing
script below the logo were the words, *Read Me*.

She felt as if she had stepped into Lewis Carroll's
Through the Looking Glass. Maybe if she pushed
hard enough she would find herself in another world,
with a bottle that said *Drink Me* and a talking cat that
dispensed advice.

It was 8:56. She was running out of time. If Nora's dreams were right—and who was to say they weren't—the girl in the coffin would wake at precisely 9:00 a.m.

Nora ripped the envelope off the top of the coffin. She slid an unpainted fingernail behind the flap and pulled out the paper inside.

Nora Barr: If you are reading this before 9:00 a.m. on July 15, ten years to the day from the moment we met, the paper read, *then things have gone according to plan. You must follow the enclosed instructions precisely. A life is at stake.*

It was signed, quite simply, *Sancho*.

She felt a small wave of disappointment at that. When she had seen the envelope, she had somehow thought it was from Blackstone.

She turned the page. On this second page, the handwriting was completely different, not ornate at all. It was full of angles and slashes and had an almost artistic look to it. The paper was yellowed, and after a moment, she realized that the instructions were written in India ink, faded, and almost illegible. The signature at the bottom of this page was as familiar as her own, even though she had only seen this signature once before:

Aethelstan Blackstone.

Nora glanced at her watch. It was 8:58 a.m. She scanned the instructions. They read like gibberish to her. But she would do as they said.

She had come this far.

She stuffed the paper into the back pocket of her jeans and climbed inside the bumper of the microbus. There she sat on the wheel well, staring at the glow-in-the-dark digital readout on her watch.

At 9:00 a.m. precisely, she took a deep breath and gripped the lid of the coffin. And yanked.

It didn't come up, of course. It had been closed for a thousand years. It didn't even budge. She felt her heart's pounding move into her throat. If she didn't get this open, then the girl might die, and then what? Then she really would have problems with a possible murder, although she had no idea how she would explain it to the police.

But Max would find a creative way to do it.

Max.

She shook her head. Max was a defense attorney. If things got that bad, she just might have to hire the bastard.

The thought made her try harder, and the lid moved. She felt an answering pressure from inside, thought she saw movement through the glass, and that gave her an adrenaline burst.

The lid groaned as it moved sideways. A small hand came through the opening, and inside a woman started yelling.

"I'm here to help you," Nora said, hoping that the yelling would stop. The last thing she needed was some Portlander stopping by his storage unit, hearing screams, and coming to investigate. How could she explain the ancient VW, the glass coffin, and the living woman inside?

The yelling didn't stop, but the hand turned and applied pressure to the lid. Then another hand popped out, followed by the most gorgeous head Nora had ever seen, and a pair of creamy white shoulders that she had once thought only existed in airbrushed magazine photos.

A dress of homespun material hung off the edges of two perfectly sized breasts, just barely hiding the nipples.

The woman—and she was quite a woman—braced her hands on the sides of the coffin and squeezed the rest of herself out. After she escaped, she collapsed on the edge of the shag carpet and took several large breaths.

Nora was shaking. The woman had black hair the color of night, lips so red that they looked as if they'd been painted, and eyes the color of an angry sea. She was the perfect complement to Blackstone, the yin to his yang as the cliché went, and suddenly Nora understood why he had spent a thousand years trying to protect her.

The woman had gotten control of her breathing. She looked up at the ceiling, then at the windows, and then she rolled, looking out the back end of the microbus.

Nora tried to imagine the view through the eyes of a woman who had just gone from the Dark Ages to the computer age in the space of a single night's sleep. Nothing would be familiar. There was asphalt on the ground, a Lexus (how would the pre-medieval mind translate that?), the storage units with their metal doors glinting in the morning sun. Even the air had to smell different. It probably, if Nora were honest with herself, smelled better.

The woman turned and in a voice so musical, it made Nora wince, asked—something completely indecipherable. It sounded like Danish, only Nora knew Danish, and it didn't have any words like the ones the woman was using.

"I'm—I'm sorry," Nora said. "Could you try again?"

The woman pushed herself onto her elbows, then

sat up. There was real fear in her eyes. She was under-
standing enough of this to know she was in a strange
place with someone who didn't speak her language. She
leaned forward, earnestly it seemed to Nora, and said
the same thing she had said before, only much, much
slower, as if she were speaking to a very elderly person
or a very dumb one.

The language still sounded like mutilated Danish.

Then Nora remembered the letter. "Wait," she said,
reaching into her back pocket. Step Two required her to
repeat some words, words that clearly weren't in English.

Nora wrapped her mouth around the letters, hoping
she was pronouncing things clearly. The woman frowned
at her. She started to speak again. The more panicked she
got, the more her language sounded like baby gibberish.
She reached for Nora just as Nora finished.

"...help me?" the woman said.

"Oh thank God," Nora said. "I was beginning to think
I needed to find someone who spoke Norse."

"I can understand you!" the woman said.

Nora nodded. "You're Emma?"

"Yes," the woman said. "How do you know me?"

"I'll tell you what I can in a moment," Nora said.
She ran through Steps Three through Five. They all
required her to speak unpronounceable words, except
for Step Five, which included an obscene gesture that
didn't seem to bother Emma. None of these other steps
seemed to have any discernible effect.

When she was done, she looked up from the paper to
find Emma staring at her.

"You do not have any magic powers, do you?"

Nora shook her head.

"Yet you have me."

"It's a long story," Nora said. "But first I think we should get you out of here. You want to take anything with you?"

She peered into the coffin to see if there was anything there. It had the imprint of Emma's body against the glass, as if all the time she had spent there left an indelible mark.

Emma shuddered. "No," she said. "I am very glad to leave that thing."

"You were unconscious the whole time, weren't you?" Nora asked, remembering her dream and not wishing that suffocating feeling on anyone.

"I guess so," Emma said. "Since the last thing I remember was Aethelstan—" And then she blushed. The blush went from her cheeks down to the tops of her breasts and looked as if someone had faintly touched her beautiful skin with a complimentary shade of rouge. Another blusher. Only this time, it didn't make Nora feel as if she'd found a kindred spirit. Instead she felt as if she'd found blushing perfection. When Nora blushed, her face looked blotchy for hours afterwards.

"He was kissing you, right?" Nora asked.

Emma looked at her. "How did you know?"

"It's all part of the story. Come on. This is no place to talk." Nora climbed off the wheel well and onto the pavement. She took Emma's hands and helped her down as well. Emma was shorter than Nora, which was unusual, and very delicate.

"How old are you?" Nora asked.

"Twenty," Emma said and blushed again. "I know it is old, but—"

"It's not old," Nora said, although by Dark Ages standards, it was probably elderly, especially for a woman to be unmarried. Nora felt positively ancient at thirty-five, and she wasn't the one who had been in a coma for a thousand years. "I'm going to take you to my carriage. It has magical properties. Just ride with me, and I'll explain what I can later."

"What is this place?" Emma asked.

"A long way from where you grew up," Nora said.

"And how did you find me?"

"I'll tell you when we get somewhere else," Nora said, opening the door to the Lexus. She extended a hand, as a butler would do, indicating that Emma should get inside.

After a moment's hesitation, she did, and Nora found herself admiring the girl's guts. If Nora woke up in a place as strange as this one clearly was, Emma, she would be completely freaked out and letting everyone know about it.

Emma sat down, ran her hand on the seat as if she couldn't believe the material, then frowned at the glass. Nora swallowed hard. Things had just become a lot more complicated.

She turned, closed the back of the microbus, and heard a small squeal behind her. Emma had her hand to her mouth, watching. The sound must have startled her. Nora nodded once, in reassurance, and then grabbed the door to the garage and pulled it closed. That noise really alarmed Emma, who cringed in her seat. Nora took the lock and replaced it, then she came to Emma's side of the car.

"This carriage is like nothing you've seen. It'll feel

strange to ride in it," she said, hoping that her words would be enough.

"There are no horses," Emma whispered.

"That's right," Nora said and closed the door gently. Emma put her hands on the dash, then removed them as if she had been burned. She was touching everything. It almost seemed like she was a blind woman trying to get her bearings. Nora felt incredible sorrow at this woman's confusion. How would she ever adjust?

Nora went to the driver's side and got in. "We call this a car," she said.

"The carriage?"

"Yes," Nora said as she put the keys in the ignition. She had the forethought to turn the radio off. "It makes a lot of noise, but it allows you to go fast."

Then she turned the key. The car rumbled to a start. Emma put her hands over her ears. Nora sighed and was about to put on her own seat belt when she realized that Emma wasn't wearing hers. Of course. Nora reached across, excused herself as she did so, and buckled Emma in. Emma's eyes widened, and she started to squirm, when Nora said, "I have to wear one too."

She leaned back and put hers on quickly, hoping that would calm Emma. Emma watched, her lower lip trembling. Then she touched the seat again, obviously feeling the vibration of the running motor.

"We are not moving," she said.

"I haven't started driving yet." Nora put the car in gear and eased out of the storage area. Emma put her hands on the dash as if she expected to be killed. If driving this slowly made her nervous, then going fifty-five miles an hour on the freeway would terrify her.

Emma gazed out the front window, like a deer caught in headlights, as Nora turned onto the road. The color had drained from Emma's face. Her fingers gripped the dash tighter and tighter, making Nora wonder if they would leave dents.

Nora executed a series of left turns until she reached the interstate, and then she merged, ignoring Emma's whimpers of fright. The girl sat, her back straight, her arms rigid, as if she expected to crash at any moment.

Nora couldn't watch her. At this time of day, Nora had to pay attention to the road. She toyed for a moment with taking Emma to her office, then decided that would be a bad idea. Even though Ruthie had seen Sancho and Blackstone all those years ago, seeing was different than actually experiencing those strange and magical events. Trying to explain Emma would be next to impossible. At the moment, Nora needed to do this on her own.

She took the exit that led to her loft. She hadn't sold it, as Max had wanted her to do when they got married. Maybe she had always known it wasn't going to work. After she'd given him the ultimatum, she had moved back into the loft and found she loved living there more than she had ever loved their big home on the hills overlooking the Columbia River. In the years since she left, the downtown loft had become chic, and she could sell it for five times what she had paid for it, a fact Max had reminded her of often. But she was glad that she hadn't.

Not that any of this mattered to Emma. All that mattered now was to get Emma off the road and someplace where she could calm down.

Nora turned on her street and parked curbside. She had the car off and her seat belt unlatched before Emma even moved.

"We did not fly," Emma said.

"No," Nora said.

"But we traveled forever."

"A long distance," Nora said. By horse and cart standards, anyway.

"Everything is so strange," Emma said, and there was sadness in her voice.

"I know," Nora said. "Stay put."

She got out, then went to the passenger side, helped Emma with the seat belt, and then had her get out of the car. Emma stood on the sidewalk, pressing her toes against the concrete as if she were amazed that the ground didn't move.

"What happened to dirt?" she asked.

"We still have it," Nora said, locking and closing the car door. "But we like to cover it up now."

She took Emma's arm and decided to forgo the elevator. They climbed the stairs until they reached Nora's loft.

Emma was shaking, even though she probably looked, to anyone who saw them, like a woman who hadn't given up her hippie past and was a bit uncomfortable being in the city. Only Nora could feel the bottled-up terror. Emma's muscles were rigid, her spine so straight that Nora felt like a false move would break her. Nora had to get Emma inside, in a protected space, and then figure out how to care for her.

Damn Sancho. Damn Blackstone. They had known this would happen.

I expect you to find competent help for any problem that might arise.

Competent help. Yeah, right. Who would know how to deal with a woman who had been in a coma for a thousand years?

They reached the top floor and the small corridor that was little more than a catwalk over the lower parts of the building. Emma was looking down at the mesh, watching her feet, her trembling growing worse.

Nora saw the man in her doorway first. Her heart, traitor that it was, leaped, and she had to suppress a smile of greeting. Intellectually, she was angry at this man. Emotionally, she wanted to throw herself in his arms.

Instead, she stopped, and Emma stopped obediently, still looking down.

Blackstone was leaning against the door, arms crossed. He wore a loose shirt and faded blue jeans, but his cowboy boots were the same and still trimmed with real silver. His face looked no different. The last ten years hadn't aged him at all. Still gorgeous. Still guarded.

When he saw Nora staring at him, he smiled slightly. "I see you found her," he said.

Emma looked up at the sound of his voice. She shook herself free of Nora's grip and ran toward him. "Aethelstan!" she cried as she launched herself into his arms, just as Nora had fantasized about doing a moment before.

Blackstone held Emma, but his gaze hadn't left Nora's. His look measured her, took in her reaction—although she tried to have none—and then, slowly, deliberately, he brought a hand up and cradled the back of

Emma's head, pulling her close. He didn't kiss her, but he ran his hands along her in an attempt to comfort her. Apparently he knew how terrified she was.

Nora looked away. It was a private moment for them, a moment she should have no part of. She did wish, however, that they'd move away from her door.

As if he heard her thought, Blackstone stood and eased Emma aside, still keeping a hand around her waist. He was looking at Nora again.

"Did you follow my instructions?" he asked.

"All of them," she said. "Even though after Step Two they seemed to have no effect."

His smile was small. "The others you couldn't see," he said. "Immunization spells, so that she wouldn't catch any modern diseases. Muscle strengthening spells, so that her long sleep didn't debilitate her. Adaptation spells that prevent the worst of culture shock—"

"Long sleep?" Emma asked, looking first at him and then at Nora.

His lips tightened. He frowned at Nora. "You didn't explain?"

"I got her out of there first, figuring she should at least be comfortable." Nora pushed past him. The brief touch of her shoulder against his chest burned her. God, why did he have to be so attractive? "Which I still think. Besides, I don't think it was part of my job description to explain what you did."

"Aethelstan?" Emma asked.

"Inside," he said, and Nora could have sworn that he was biting back anger.

Nora unlocked her door and held it open. Blackstone pushed Emma forward, one hand on her back, and then followed her inside. Emma stopped, staring at the room as if it too were as alien as everything else. Which it probably was.

Nora had remodeled the loft just before moving back in. She had had an architect simplify the design and add a shower in the half bath. The living room was sunken slightly and done in reds and silvers; the kitchen which could be seen from the door, was done in chrome. The staircase had been redone also in chrome and steel, and her bedroom, walled off with a stylish silver screen, was barely visible above. Sunlight poured in from the open windows, making the silver and chrome sparkle.

"I would have expected something else from you," Blackstone said.

"Warm and kitschy?" Nora asked as she walked to Emma.

"Yeah," he said, sounding not that certain. "I guess."

Nora put a hand on Emma's arm and led her farther inside. "I know it's not what you're used to—"

"Nothing is," Emma whispered.

"Come in anyway," Nora said. "And let me get you something. Water, maybe, or even some tea?"

"Tea," Emma said.

"Remember we didn't have caffeinated teas until the British East India Company," Blackstone said softly.

"I think I can find some chamomile," Nora said. She helped Emma to the couch. "Would you like anything to eat?"

"She won't need anything for a day or two. That's when the magic wears off."

Emma looked at her skirt, smoothing it as she sat.

Nora kept a hand on her arm. "Emma," she repeated. "Would you like anything to eat?"

Emma glanced at Blackstone, and then shook her head.

"You don't have to do what he says," Nora said. "You can do what you want. Are you hungry?"

"Not yet," Emma said and looked down.

This time, it was Nora's turn to glare at Blackstone. He shrugged and sat beside Emma on the couch. She had to put out a hand to brace herself, as the cushions bent beneath his weight. He put his arm on the back cushion, behind Emma, as if he were guarding her, and Nora suppressed a sigh. How many times had she imagined him in this loft, sitting just like that, his arm behind her? Too many. He hadn't left her mind, not for a single day, even during her marriage to Max.

Nora went into the kitchen. She took the kettle from the back burner and filled it, deciding to put some cookies out anyway. Emma had seemed interested in food but had been more interested in not displeasing Blackstone.

The swine.

They were talking softly in the living room. Nora caught only a few words.

"...long sleep?" Emma asked.

Nora peeked around her cabinets. Blackstone had his head bowed. "It was Ealhswith," he said. "Remember the day you snuck to my cottage?"

"And we kissed," Emma said, raising a hand to his lips.

The gesture made Nora look away. She went back into the kitchen and pulled open a cupboard, looking for cookies or crackers or something that might look familiar to Emma. Probably nothing would—except bread or fruit. And Nora wasn't even sure what kind of fruit was native to Emma's part of the world. England, Blackstone had led her to believe. Did they have apple orchards in England?

Nora shook her head at her own ignorance. Funny how she could go through life and not know how other pasts, other cultures worked. It had never been relevant before, and the man in the other room had failed to inform her that it would be relevant when Emma awoke.

"…to sleep?" Emma's voice rose over the rattle of the teakettle as the water warmed. "Why?"

"I didn't put you to sleep. Ealhswith did. Her spell would have killed you."

"But you did not reverse it."

"Hell, Emma, I was just a boy. I did what I could."

"But you are no longer a boy. Surely at some point you could have reversed the spell."

You go girl, Nora mouthed. She smiled to herself, and as she did, she found the tea bread she had bought on a whim a day ago. She began to cut it into small slices.

"I didn't always have you. Ealhswith—"

"But when you did?"

"It's more complicated than that. Ealhswith—"

"You should have woken me."

"It might have killed you."

"But I do not understand. A thousand years. Surely you could have settled things in a thousand years."

"I could have," Blackstone said. "But Ealhswith had other plans. She wasn't thinking of you. Just herself. And I was trying to protect you from her."

"You were?"

"Yes," Blackstone said. "I tried a hundred things. Only this last one worked. And it worked because of Nora."

"Nora?"

"Miss Barr. The woman who was with you when you woke."

The teakettle whistled, cutting out part of the conversation. Nora removed it from the burner. Apparently it had reminded the two in the other room to lower their voices. She could hear them talking, but she couldn't make out the words.

She opened her tea and coffee cupboard and dug until she found the chamomile. Then she put the requisite two tea bags into the pot, and poured steaming water over them. She continued cutting the bread, hoping they would raise their voices again.

They didn't.

After the tea had steeped, she removed the tea bags. She put everything on a tray—teapot, cups, sugar, and cream, as well as the bread, and carried it into the living room.

Blackstone was leaning toward Emma, his hands outstretched as if in supplication. Emma's cheeks were bright red, not with shame or embarrassment, but with anger. Nora suppressed a grin. Good for Emma. The girl had some fight in her then.

As Nora set the tray on the glass coffee table, Emma looked up at her. "Aethelstan says I have been asleep for a thousand years. Is that true?"

Nora shrugged. "I can't say for certain because I've only been involved in this mess for ten, but I'd say it's likely."

"A thousand years," Emma said. "I do not even comprehend a thousand years."

Blackstone reached toward her head. "I can give you the history, the memories, all of it—"

"No!" She slapped his hand away. "You will not

touch me again." She moved to the other end of the couch. Nora sat on the leather armchair and wondered if she should pour tea. Probably not yet. Not if she wanted her china to survive this fight.

"I don't know a lot about magic," Nora said. "But it might be a good idea to let him do that. I mean, time can't run backward, can it?"

She looked at Blackstone as she asked that.

"You mean, can I give her back that thousand years? Of course not. She has to go forward."

"Forward?" Emma's voice broke. "Forward? To where? Everything I know and love is gone."

Blackstone looked at her with such shock on his face that, for the first time, Nora felt sympathy for him. "I'm here, Emma."

"You? You are not Aethelstan! Aethelstan was a green boy whom I had just met, a boy whom I wanted to get to know. He was tall and awkward and silly. You are merely tall. And old. You are so very old." Emma looked around the room as if she wanted to flee but didn't know how or where to.

"I'm still Aethelstan," he said softly, taking her hands in his own.

She pulled her hands out of his grasp.

"Emma—"

Nora reached between them. "I think that's enough," she said to Blackstone. "She's made it clear she doesn't want your attentions."

"But I'm all she has," he said, looking at Nora. And in those silver eyes, she saw that vulnerability, that confusion, she had seen only once before.

"Really?" A haughty female voice boomed from the

doorway. Nora looked up, startled. The woman was tall, with hair so black that it didn't reflect light except for the white streak along one side. She wore a black-and-white dress that emphasized her hair and stiletto heels, which made her seem even taller.

"You have no right to be in here." Nora stood rapidly, wondering how the woman had gotten in.

"Oh, I have every right," the woman said. "You have my daughter here."

Nora glanced at Emma. Emma had pressed herself against the back of the sofa, making herself seem very small. Blackstone had moved so that his body was between Emma's and the woman's.

"She's not your daughter," Blackstone said.

"By rights of law, she is," the woman said. This had to be the famous Ealhswith that Max had once told Nora about and whom Blackstone had mentioned just this afternoon with a touch of awe and disgust in his voice.

"What law?" Nora asked. She had pulled herself to her full five two. It didn't make her any taller, but it made her feel taller.

"Our law," Ealhswith said, motioning with an elegant hand at herself and Blackstone.

"Not good enough," Nora said. "You happen to be in my apartment which happens to be in the United States, and as long as you are here, you are governed by my country's laws."

"Horseshit," Ealhswith said delicately. "With a simple flick of my finger, I could turn you into a toad."

"Perhaps," Nora said. "But that still doesn't change the fact that here, in the United States, a person who is twenty years old or one thousand and thirty, depending on how you want to count it, has reached her majority and belongs to no one if she so chooses."

"Is that true?" Emma whispered to Blackstone.

He didn't look at her. He was staring at Ealhswith. Nora couldn't help thinking at that moment that long ago this battle had ceased to be about Emma and had become something personal between Ealhswith and Blackstone. Something personal and something ugly.

Nora put a hand on Emma's shoulder in reassurance. Emma jumped. "It's true," Nora said.

"And irrelevant," Ealhswith said. "You cannot stand in my way."

"Sure I can," Nora said. She didn't know how, but she knew she would try. "I will do anything I can to protect my client."

"Emma's not your client," Blackstone said.

"That's right," Nora said. "But she is under my protection at the behest of my client. I answer to him, not to either of you."

Blackstone turned to her with a stunned expression on his face. "Surely you don't mean that."

Nora raised her eyebrows. "You were the one who first reminded me of it ten years ago," she said.

"You know that was a ruse to protect Emma from Ealhswith."

"I don't know anything, remember?" Nora snapped. "It was better that way. And because I don't, I follow the letter of the law in which I was trained. And that letter instructs me to act in my client's best interest."

"Who is this 'client'?" Ealhswith asked.

"Sancho Panza," Nora said, feeling, even now, slightly ridiculous when she said the name.

"Sancho—?" Ealhswith frowned. "She doesn't mean that disgusting little man who once pretended to be my assistant?"

"Merlin?" Emma whispered.

"He's in the South of France," Blackstone said. "At least, I think he's in the South of France. He promised to stay away while Emma and I became reacquainted."

"He didn't tell me that," Nora said, "so I can only act on his ten-year-old instructions, and those were to take care of the things within my protection and to make sure, if I couldn't handle it personally, to find someone who could help me."

"Enough of this," Ealhswith said, extending a hand. "I think a toad is too good for you. I would rather summon a bolt of lightning—"

"I wouldn't," Nora said. Her heart was pounding, but she wasn't going to back down.

"You are being a bit clichéd," Blackstone said to Ealhswith.

"You shut up too."

Blackstone shrugged. "I'd love to see how you're going to get yourself out of this one."

Emma wrapped a hand around Nora's wrist. "Don't," she whispered. "Not for me."

"Listen, Emma," Nora said. "They've been fighting over you for a thousand years, and no one has defended you. Well, now someone is."

"You don't know what she can do."

"I have a pretty good idea," Nora said, remembering that neighborhood.

Ealhswith's magnificent eyes narrowed. "Then you shouldn't argue with me."

Nora put her hands on her hips. "I think too many people have been intimidated by those threats over the years and have given you what you want. I suspect that's why you've been so angry at Blackstone for so long, because he was one of the few who dared stand up to you. Well, you don't scare me, lady. I don't know what you get out of keeping your thumb on Emma, and I don't really care. All I know is that you have to go through me to get to her."

"Don't worry," Ealhswith said, splaying her hand against the air. "I will."

"But you should know," Nora said, "that my ex-husband, schmuck that he is, can remember what you did to that neighborhood ten years ago, and if I'm found dead any time soon, especially if the circumstances are strange, both you and Blackstone fall under suspicion."

"As if that matters," Ealhswith said.

"It might," Nora said, "if your magical presences here are discovered. Then you might have to be subject to our laws after all. And the penalty for murder here is life imprisonment."

"No prison can hold me," Ealhswith said.

"Or death," Nora added. "Can death hold you?"

"Sometimes," Blackstone said, and this time there was no amusement in his voice. He tilted his head toward Ealhswith. "Neither you nor I know where the glass coffin is. If the husband knows where it is, and he finds Nora dead, today of all days, then that much at least will back up his story."

"I'll make him forget his story," Ealhswith said.

"You cannot." This came from Emma. She leaned

into Nora as if she needed Nora's strength. "Not if the information came from a source with which you are unfamiliar."

"When did you learn the intricacies of magic?" Ealhswith asked, inadvertently confirming what Emma said.

"When I first moved in with you," Emma said. "I had to learn how to protect myself."

"I was going to teach her more," Blackstone said.

"She couldn't have used it for another thirty years," Ealhswith said.

"And then you would have had to watch out, wouldn't you, Ealhswith? Especially if she had been taught by someone like me?" Blackstone stood. He moved between Nora and Ealhswith. "Nora has done us all a great favor. She has brought Emma back to us. You will not repay her by venting your petty rage on her."

"She is an inconvenience."

"She is Emma's protector, as she said. You might be tempting more than her silly ex—?" he turned to Nora to confirm. Nora nodded once. He half smiled and shook his head. "Her silly ex-husband's desire to reveal our presence." Something in Blackstone's tone made Nora believe that he didn't believe that Max would do anything of the sort. "You might be tempting the Fates."

"The Fates?" Ealhswith crossed her arms. Obviously the mention made her forget that she was going to destroy Nora with a bolt of lightning. "That group of legalistic crones. They—"

"They've been trying to pin something on you and me for years. Killing a civilian has been illegal since the sixteenth century, or have you forgotten that, Ealhswith?"

Ealhswith actually shuddered. "How could I?" she asked. "If they hadn't made that ruling and held it up with the absolute death decree, I wouldn't have been hanged in Salem in the 1690s. I still am due some revenge on that, I think."

"But the hanging didn't last," Blackstone said. "It would have if you'd had real revenge."

Ealhswith touched her neck. "The mental scars remain."

This time it was Blackstone's turn to snort. He glanced at Nora in something like amusement, but she didn't smile in return. This was not funny. It was her life they were discussing so casually.

"I could still turn her into a frog," Ealhswith said.

"But you'd have to turn her back."

"Eventually." Ealhswith's smile was slow and cruel.

"And she'd have to forget the entire incident. You know the rules," Blackstone said.

"Rather defeats the point, doesn't it?" Nora asked.

"No one spoke to you," Ealhswith snapped.

"Only about me. And I really don't like to be discussed in the third person."

"You're still the powerless one here," Ealhswith said.

"Actually, sounds like I have more power than I'd thought." Nora smiled. "And since we're discussing rules, entering a person's home without her permission is also against the law. Should I call the local authorities?"

Ealhswith's eyes narrowed. "You wouldn't."

"I would." Nora reached for her phone.

"Looks like you've been kicked out," Blackstone said. "The uninvited. So sad."

Ealhswith turned the glare on him. "I'll give you one warning, Aethelstan. Don't kiss the girl. Don't even consider it."

Nora put her hand on the receiver of the phone. She was watching this interchange with great interest.

"Couldn't think of a new spell, could you?" Blackstone asked.

"I didn't have to," Ealhswith said. "The old one hasn't worn off yet, at least, not entirely. So act accordingly. You wouldn't want to lose your one true love now that you've found her again?"

Emma made a small whimpering noise. Nora picked up the receiver and started to dial 911.

"I'm a lot more sophisticated than I used to be," Blackstone said. "I'm sure I can handle one kiss-and-tell spell."

"Are you?" Ealhswith asked. "Are you sure it's that simple?"

And then, with a twirl of her arm, she disappeared.

Nora hung up the phone before it even rang. She stared at the place where Ealhswith had been. "Somehow I expected to see a puff of black smoke after she'd done that."

"A bit of fire and brimstone," Blackstone said, arms crossed.

"I did not realize she was here," Emma said, her voice so soft that it almost sounded as if she had whimpered.

Blackstone and Nora turned around at the same time. Emma was cringing against the couch, clutching the leather fabric in one hand. "You did not tell me she had come here too."

"I was getting to that," Blackstone said. "It's hard

to cover centuries in the space of a few minutes. I wish you'd let me do the spell. It would—"

"Actually," Nora said, "on this one, it's not that hard. They've been fighting over you for the past thousand years. She put the kiss-and-tell"—Nora looked at Blackstone for confirmation. He rolled his eyes but nodded—"spell on you, and it nearly killed you. He stopped it by putting you in a coma, but no one could wait the requisite time to get you out. They kept stealing your damn coffin, back and forth and back and forth—"

"For a thousand years?" Emma whispered. "A thousand years?"

Blackstone swallowed so hard that Nora saw his Adam's apple bob. "It was more complicated than that."

"Why could you not set aside your differences for even ten years?" Emma asked him. "God's blood, that is barely a heartbeat in the amount of time you let go by."

"Emma, if you would give me a chance—"

"Why?" she asked. "You gave me none." Then she bowed her head and hid her face against the cushions. She apparently felt that she had nowhere else to go.

And she didn't. Not really.

"I think it's time you should leave," Nora said.

Blackstone smiled at her, the full-watt, how-can-you-refuse-me? smile. She had forgotten how very gorgeous it was. It sent shivers all the way through her and reminded her how long it had been since anyone had touched her.

"I'll take Emma with me, then, and get out of your way," he said.

"Sorry," Nora said. "You can't have her. Not unless she wants to go with you."

"Emma," Blackstone said, putting his hand on her shoulder. She jumped so violently he had to pull his hand back. "Would you come with me?"

"You can stay here," Nora said as Emma raised her head. "I'll do my best to protect you. I think you'd be safest here."

Her thin bloodred lips narrowed. "I do not want to go with you," she said to Blackstone. "I am not even sure I want to see you again, Aethelstan."

"Now, Emma—"

"You heard her," Nora said. "I think it's time you leave."

"Nora, you know better—"

"No," she said. "I don't. I told you, ten years ago, that I'm an attorney with ethics and one who likes to play by the book. I expected you to honor that then, and I expect it now. She has no tie to you, not as far as I'm concerned, and you are in my house. I am telling you to leave. If you do not, I will call the police."

"You know I can manipulate them."

"I know," Nora said. "But I can keep calling them until one of us tires of this game."

"I've been known to have a stubborn streak," Blackstone said.

"A thousand-year-long one," Nora said. "That still doesn't change my mind. Get out."

"Emma—"

"It's better for her to have you leave."

"I want to hear her say that."

"You have become obtuse in your old age, Aethelstan," Emma said, turning her back on him and crossing her arms. "You have been asked to leave."

Again, that vulnerable, wounded look filled his silver

eyes before he had a chance to mask it. He reached for Emma, then curled his fingers into a fist. Then he turned to Nora. "You're making a mistake."

"Threats don't bother me," Nora said.

"It's not a threat," he said. "It's a fact. You don't know what Ealhswith can do."

"No, I don't," Nora said, "and at the moment, that's not my concern." She inclined her head toward the door. "Are you planning to leave now?"

He raised his hands in a gesture of mock surrender. "I'm going," he said. "But call me if you need me."

"What, am I suppose to call out your name in rhyme?" she asked, thinking of Dr. Bombay in the old *Bewitched* television show. "Or am I supposed to use the phone?"

"Don't be sarcastic, Nora," he said.

"It was an honest question."

"I have a cell." He took a business card from his pocket and threw it on the table. "I expect to hear from you."

"I don't expect to hear from you." Nora put her hand on his back, intending to lead him out of the apartment. It was the first time she had touched him deliberately in ten years. Through the fabric of his linen shirt, his back was smooth, tense. A jolt of energy ran through her, and he turned as if he had felt it too. His eyes softened as they gazed at her. She shoved him forward.

He frowned, as if he weren't quite sure what happened, took two steps, and nearly stumbled up the stairs leading to the door. She followed him. They both avoided the spot where Ealhswith had stood.

"Please," he said softly, as he glanced over Nora's shoulder at Emma, "call me if she needs anything."

"I'm still not sure if you're the good guy or the bad guy in all of this, Blackstone," Nora said.

"You don't know how to take care of her," he said.

"It sounds like you don't either."

"I at least have some abilities at my disposal."

"I'll be fine," Nora said. "Good-bye, Blackstone."

With one last look at Emma, he went through the door. "I'll be in touch, Nora."

She closed the door after him, thinking it strange that he didn't even try to say good-bye to Emma. She didn't know if that was him being sensitive, since Emma so clearly wanted nothing to do with him, or if it was something else altogether, something Nora hadn't yet figured out. She opted for the something else. Blackstone hadn't exactly shown himself to be sensitive where Emma was concerned.

Nora turned the dead bolt and put on the chain lock, even though she knew that would do no good against a determined Ealhswith. She wasn't even sure it would do any good against Blackstone.

She came back down the stairs and crossed to the couch. Emma had her face buried in her hands. Nora sat down in the armchair and poured them both some tea. The liquid still steamed. She held a cup in one hand and with the other, tapped Emma on the arm.

"Here," she said as Emma looked up. "This might help calm you."

Emma took the tea, holding the saucer as if she had never seen anything like it before. Nora picked hers up, then offered Emma some cream and sugar as well. Emma looked surprised at the milk in a little pitcher, the sugar in blocks, but said nothing. She shook her head slightly, refusing, and then took a loud, slurping sip of the tea.

"Ah," she said, "it feels as if it is cleaning cobwebs out of my mouth."

Nora didn't want to think about it, but she couldn't stop herself. How would a mouth feel after not tasting anything for a thousand years?

Emma drank the entire cup and then looked at Nora. "Is it all right if I have some more?"

Nora grinned. "That's why I made it." Simple things, that was what her father had once taught her. Simple things were the most important after a traumatic experience. They showed that the business of life continued. "Some bread too, if you like."

Emma picked up a piece and took an experimental bite. Then she smiled. "It is good."

"Yes," Nora said. "It is."

They sat in silence for some time. When they were finished with the bread, Nora said, "I expect you might want some rest."

Emma shook her head. "I have been resting for a long time. Right now I need to remain awake, at least for a while."

"If you don't mind my asking," Nora said, "what happened with you and Blackstone?"

She was more interested than she wanted to say. His reactions were so different from Emma's. Nora had expected Emma's hug when she saw him, but from that moment on, everything seemed different.

Emma smiled for just a moment, and then the smile faded. "He was so different then," she said. "Young. He was just a boy early in his magic."

"Why don't you have any magic?"

"Girls get theirs later, but it is more powerful when it comes. When I am fifty, I will gain my magic."

"And when do boys get theirs?"

"When they reach twenty-one summers," Emma said. "I met Aethelstan just after his twenty-first summer."

"And Ealhswith? She didn't like him?"

Emma cringed at the name. "Ealhswith wanted him for her own."

"She's not your mother?"

"No."

"But she is your guardian?"

"My mentor," Emma said. "My parents gave me to her when it became clear that I would have the power."

Nora poured herself another cup of tea. "But what's the point of mentoring if you haven't come into your magic yet?"

"The magic arrives full strength," Emma said. "You must know how to use it when it arrives or it could kill you."

"I don't get it. How can you practice?"

"You cannot. You must simply imagine it. Knowledge comes first, then the power, then control."

It all sounded very strange to Nora. "How did you meet Blackstone?"

"I met him when I arrived in the village to see Ealhswith. He was the one who helped me find her. We saw each other every day after that."

"So you were with her a very short time."

Emma bowed her head. "Less than a month."

"Yet you learned several things about her magic."

"Not enough," Emma whispered. "I had been warned

that she would be jealous. I did not listen. I thought Aethelstan could be mine."

"Did you love him?" Nora found herself holding her breath after she asked the question.

Emma sighed. "Perhaps. I certainly wanted to kiss him." She raised her eyes. "That boy. Not this man."

Nora couldn't imagine this. To Emma, only a day had passed. "How can you see the difference?"

"He speaks in a way Aethelstan would not."

"It's the language."

Emma shook her head. "It is the tone. And he moves like a man filled with anger. And there are lines on his face that were not there before."

"I thought magic could prevent that."

"Magic may slow it down," Emma said. "But age happens to all of us." She set her cup down. "I do not want to talk about this anymore. I need to learn where I am, and what I can do. And is this Sancho you work for really Ealhswith's dwarf?"

Nora took a deep breath. "That's something we need to talk about," she said. "I worked for Sancho— and I don't know if he's Ealhswith's dwarf, but I had heard he was—but only to guard the microbus you were in. I've been thinking, since we had that altercation with all of your old friends, that you might want to hire me."

"Hire you? What do you do?"

"I'm a lawyer."

Emma frowned. "You do not look like a lawyer."

Nora took a sip of tea, mostly to prevent Emma from seeing the bemused expression on her face. "What's a lawyer supposed to look like?"

"A fussy dry little man with squinty eyes, who is more concerned with rules than with people."

Nora almost said she was surprised that there were lawyers in Emma's time, but then she remembered the mention of law and its keepers in the Bible. Hers was an old profession. "There are still men like that," Nora said, "but there are people like me too."

"I do not need a lawyer," Emma said.

"What will you do then?" Nora set her cup down.

Emma opened her mouth, as if she were going to answer, and then closed it again. A flush covered her skin.

Nora put a hand on hers. "Lawyers have many purposes now. If you hire me, I can help you. I can protect you while you learn about this new world. I can keep Blackstone and Ealhswith away from you if that's what you want, and I can do it all in a way that they have to follow."

"They follow their own rules."

Nora smiled. Not after that little discussion she had had with them earlier. "Perhaps," Nora said. "But they also need to follow mine. You can teach me their rules, and I'll teach you ours, and together we'll be quite a team."

Emma ran a hand over her face. "Everything is so different," she murmured.

"Yes," Nora said, "it is."

Emma stood. She walked around the couch and headed to the windows, staring through the large plates of glass at the brick and concrete below. The bridges were visible over the river. The sky was bright blue, and the river reflected it. Portland looked beautiful, for a modern city. Did it look like a fairy-tale city to

Emma? Something out of fanciful stories? Or did it look like a nightmare? Something only a demon could have imagined?

Emma leaned her head against the glass. "I assume payment is still required in the hiring of a lawyer."

"Yes," Nora said.

"Then I cannot hire you. I have no coin, and no way of getting any."

Nora stood and walked to the window. She looked down, just as Emma was doing. Below them, people walked, men in suits and women in dresses. A couple in jeans had their arms around each other and their hands in each other's back pockets.

"We can defer payment," Nora said. "In my capacity as a lawyer, I can help you find work."

Emma laughed. The sound was glorious, like the ringing of chimes. "You cannot find me work. I am unschooled in this world, unable to understand this place you live in and the carriages you use, let alone how to earn my keep." She reached out and touched the sleeve on Nora's shirt. "I do not even know how this fabric is made. I see no fireplace here, and do not know how you make your evening meal or even how you heated the water for the tea. I cannot do simple things. I do not know how I would work."

Nora smiled. "I have some ideas, if you'd let me work for you."

Emma leaned her shoulder against the glass. The blue skyline was visible behind her. It seemed, from Nora's perspective, as if Emma were leaning against the sky.

"Will I make you rich, then?" Emma asked.

"I doubt it," Nora said.

"I do not understand, then, why you would like me to hire you."

Nora put her hand on Emma's shoulder. It was rigid. The stress that she wasn't showing was evident in her body.

"You're going to need help," Nora said. "Whether it's me or Sancho or Blackstone, someone is going to have to take care of you while you learn about the world you're in. First of all, hiring me makes the choice yours. You are taking your first action on your own, as an adult in this century, not the century into which you were born. Secondly, by hiring me, you give me the ability to defend you in ways that I don't have as your friend or the person you're staying with or as someone you know. I'm a defender, a knight, for lack of a better term. I will be able to handle the intricacies of this century while you're learning them."

"But you cannot protect me from Ealhswith."

"Yes, I can," Nora said.

"You have no magic."

"There are other ways to protect you from Ealhswith. We just have to find them. I'm sure, if we need magical protection, that Blackstone will help."

Emma turned away from Nora. "I am not sure if I want his help. He is part of what happened to me. He let me sleep for a thousand years."

"I know," Nora said. "But he says he loves you." Although he never did say that, at least, not in so many words.

Emma shook her head. "And you, you know him. How can I trust you?"

"I haven't seen him for ten years," Nora said. "I know him because his friend hired me. That's all."

Emma looked out the window. She seemed forlorn.

"If you don't like my work," Nora said, "you can fire me."

Emma put a hand against the glass. She did not say anything.

"If you want," Nora said, "I can find you another lawyer, someone else who will help you. It'll take time. In my world, people do not believe in magic or curses or spells that last a thousand years."

Emma turned her head. Her eyes were sharp, flashing with anger. "Then why do you?"

"Because I saw it in action. I tend not to deny the things I see."

"But others do."

Nora nodded.

"Someone of your acquaintance saw the same thing and has denied it."

"Yes," Nora said. "We would have to find someone else with a more open mind than that."

Emma closed her eyes. Her face was drawn, pale, paler than it had been when Nora found her. The girl needed care, not decision making. She needed help, whether she realized it or not.

Something crashed in the living room. Nora turned to see Squidgy bolt across the room, Darnell behind. Darnell turned, ran toward the window, and tried to stop when he saw Emma. His little black cat legs pinwheeled, and then he managed to regain his feet only to find himself sliding into the wall.

Emma knelt and caught him. Darnell looked at her

with his large yellow eyes. Nora knew the look. It was Darnell sizing her up. Then he leaned his big black head on Emma's shoulder and started to purr.

Nora had never seen the cat go from panic to purr that fast. She looked at the coffee table. Her tea set was all over the floor. She wondered how much of it was broken. Halfway across the living room was a half-eaten piece of bread, the prize apparently that Squidgy had been going for. That cat liked anything made from dough.

"You did not tell me that cats lived with you," Emma said, running a hand along Darnell's side.

"Actually," Nora said, sighing, "I think I live with them."

Emma smiled. "You protect them. This one is very soft."

"They're not allowed outside. It's too dangerous for them here."

"Cats are—were not considered pets in my world. To keep them was to be considered a witch." Emma studied her over Darnell's back. "Perhaps you do not know of your powers."

"I'm not fifty yet," Nora said.

"No," Emma said. "Cats like you. Perhaps they know."

Nora shook her head. "If that were true, then over half the pet-owning families in America have witches."

"You sound as if that were unusual. It is not."

"You don't know how many people there are in America." Nora smiled and petted Darnell. He purred louder.

Emma raised her chin slightly. "I will hire you, Nora Barr. But you will keep me apprised of the debt I am accruing. If I do not like what you are doing, then I will ask you to find me another defender. Is that agreeable to you?"

"Yes," Nora said.

"Good," Emma said. She hoisted Darnell on her shoulder. The cat was like a limp rag. "Now let us see what kind of damage the cats have done to your dishes."

She walked toward the living room, Darnell bouncing along as if he belonged cradled against her. Nora watched her go. This girl was not a girl, but a strong woman in a difficult situation. Nora wasn't quite sure what she had gotten herself into, but she had a hunch it was like nothing she had ever done before.

Chapter 5

BLACKSTONE STEPPED OUT OF THE APARTMENT BUILDING into the full force of Portland's July heat. His fists were clenched and his muscles were tight.

Something had gone very wrong inside that building. He still wasn't sure exactly what it was, but he knew that because of the events of the morning, his entire life had changed.

He had expected—he had hoped—to see Emma, and when she and Nora left the stairs, everything had happened just as he'd planned. Well, almost. Emma had run into his arms, and she had felt so warm, so soft, and he had realized how much he missed her.

But he hadn't expected the look of hurt surprise on Nora's face.

Nora. He shook his head. She had messed everything up. Nora had kicked him out of the loft, and Emma had let her. He was officially uninvited, just like Ealhswith, and that wasn't good. Neither Emma nor Nora had magic, and even if they did, they wouldn't know how to combat all those years of experience—nasty experience—that Ealhswith had.

He shook his shoulders and made himself relax his fists. He took a deep breath. A woman passed him, clutching her purse to her side. She smiled at him. He didn't smile back.

Maybe he should go back up to the loft and get Emma

out of there. He'd take her to his place and give her the information spell whether she wanted it or not.

But that wouldn't do any good. He had forgotten how stubborn Emma could be. He had forgotten many things about her, including her temper, which he'd seen flash in her eyes just a few moments ago.

And she had every right to be mad at him. He was just beginning to realize what it meant to be in her shoes. He had thought he would give her that last magic spell, and life would go on as it had before. He hadn't really thought what the loss of all those years would mean to her.

Nor had he realized, until she turned those angry eyes on him, what he had done. In protecting Emma from Ealhswith, he had harmed Emma, and he hadn't meant to.

Blackstone sighed and crossed the sidewalk toward his car. The 1974 Lincoln was in storage—it was too distinct a car for a man in his position. Instead he drove a glimmering black Porsche that made him feel as if he had to fold himself into thirds every time he got inside of it.

He wasn't sure what Emma would think of this. He wasn't sure about Emma at all. He kept looking to Nora for guidance—she had such wisdom for someone who'd only been on the earth thirty some years—but she was angry at him too. And justifiably.

He ran a hand through his hair. He wasn't sure how to make this right, and he had to make things right. The Fates had told him Emma was his soul mate. And when he first saw her, with her lovely black hair and beautiful skin, he had believed them. He had believed them even though Emma had been living with Ealhswith. He had thought that he would rescue Emma, that he would teach her magic, and that together they would spend eternity in perfect harmony.

Over the centuries he had forgotten so much about her. Everything, it seemed, except that she had been fun to kiss—until she had passed out and nearly died.

He reached the door of the Porsche and pulled it open. Hot air streamed out, and he sighed again. He walked back to the sidewalk and opened the passenger side. What had he been thinking when he bought this thing? A black car always absorbed the heat. He would wait a few minutes before folding himself inside and then trying to find the switch for the air-conditioning.

While he waited, he gazed back up at the windows of Nora's loft. If anyone without magical powers could defend Emma against Ealhswith, Nora could. She had shown such fire, such spark. And that intelligence of hers intrigued him more than he wanted to admit. He even liked the sharpness of her tongue. It was a wonderful contrast to that petite beauty, which made her look so vulnerable at first glance.

She was anything but vulnerable. She was tough and smart and confident. In his very long life, he had never met a woman like her.

In fact, the feeling he got when he looked at her— well, he would have thought that was what it felt like to gaze on your soul mate. Of course he was wrong. The Fates had told him a millennium ago that Emma was his soul mate. Apparently feeling had nothing to do with it. Having a soul mate was an assignment like everything else.

Magic was not as simple as mortals believed.

He crumpled himself into the driver's side of the Porsche, leaned across the stick, and pulled the passenger's door closed. Then he started the car, pressed the clutch, put the car in first, and pulled out, letting the engine roar. Nora had to hear that. She had to know that he wasn't happy. And he wasn't. He had expected to take Emma home with him. He had imagined laughing in Ealhswith's face. He had imagined a happily ever after.

Instead his soul mate was staying with a woman he couldn't get out of his mind, and they were both being threatened by a creature who made the Wicked Witch of the West look like she needed wickedness lessons.

Nora had made it clear that he was uninvited, but he couldn't accept that. He had to get her to change her mind somehow. Surely after a few hours with Emma it would become clear to Nora that she was in over her head. After a few hours, she would be ready to let Blackstone take Emma off her hands.

He would see Nora at the office. By then, she would have changed her mind.

By then, he would know how to fix all that he had done wrong.

"The cover story is this," Nora said after she and Emma had cleaned up the spilled tea, found the other cat, and had a rather lengthy and too technically accurate discussion of how the sink worked. They had also discovered that Emma wore the same size clothing as Nora and managed to squeeze her into some jeans and a loose blouse. It did make her look a bit more modern.

Thank heavens.

"Cover story?" Emma asked. She was standing beside the sink, one hand on the metal basin, the other toying with the faucet. She would turn it on, put her fingers beneath the water, and then turn it off. Nora didn't want to think about how Emma would react when Nora showed her the shower.

Nora had just finished using the phone. Emma had clearly thought that odd but hadn't said anything. Which was good. Nora was getting tired of explaining things. The argument they had had over the toilet made her lose some of her enthusiasm for the job.

"Cover story," Nora said. "We have to have some kind of tale to tell other people about you."

"Would it not be simpler to tell the truth?" Emma asked.

"No," Nora said.

"I do not understand why. Truth is always best," Emma said.

"You haven't met my mother," Nora muttered.

"I do not see why I have to," Emma said. She turned the faucet to hot, and before Nora could stop her, stuck her fingers in it. Emma screeched, then pulled her fingers back and shoved them in her mouth. The water pouring into the sink was steaming.

"Now do you see why you can't be alone? I've already explained the sink, and you've burned yourself anyway." Nora took Emma's hand out of her mouth and examined the reddened fingers. "No blistering, but let's ice it just in case."

She opened the refrigerator and pulled some ice cubes from the ice maker. Frost spilled out around her.

"It is winter in there."

"Yes," Nora said. She wrapped the ice in a washcloth and then wrapped the cloth around Emma's fingers. "This should take some of the pain away."

Emma stood there like an obedient child. "You do not seem to like your mother. Why would you leave me with her?"

"She's the only person I know who doesn't work during the day." Nora closed the refrigerator door and shut off the faucet. "Besides, she's the only person I know who would probably scare Ealhswith."

"Then I do not want to be alone with her."

"Relax," Nora said. "Mother genuinely likes people, and most people like her. It's magic she's not fond of."

"This is why we need a 'cover' story?"

"Partly," Nora said. "But we also need it for others as well."

"What would this 'cover' story be?"

Nora had been thinking about that since she decided to call her mother. "We'll tell them that you've lost your memory. All of it. Down to the simplest things, like how to work a sink."

"She will believe this?"

"Yes," Nora said.

"More than the truth?" Emma asked.

"Absolutely," Nora said. "People will believe that you've lost your memory a lot easier than they will believe that you were in a magically induced coma for a thousand years."

"But—"

"Don't argue, please," Nora said. "Just go with it." She was feeling impatient. She needed to get to her office to establish Emma as a client and start forging

Emma's identity. She wasn't sure how she would do that one without breaking a few laws herself; after all, Emma had been born more than a thousand years before. Birth records would be rather difficult to obtain.

Nora glanced at the kitchen clock. Her mother had said she would be right over. But her mother was never quick about anything. And Nora had made the mistake of telling her to pick up some lunch on the way. It could take even longer.

"Since you don't want to sleep," Nora said, "I suspect it's time to educate you on the one thing that might help you learn more about this century. Kind of." She started toward the television, then stopped. How do you explain television to a person who had never experienced radio, or movies, or probably books?

Emma followed her, and as she did, Nora realized that one thing was missing, the very thing she would need to forge Emma's new identity. Nora shook her head. Her mind was jumping everywhere, a sure sign that she was overwhelmed.

"Emma, do you have a last name?"

"Is it necessary to know to learn this thing?" Emma asked as she came closer.

"No," Nora said. "I need it for my work."

"A last name?" she asked.

"You know, like Aethelstan Blackstone."

"He did not have the second name when I knew him."

"What was his name then?"

"Aethelstan, son of Elwin."

Nora put a hand on the top of the television. "Your village was small, wasn't it?"

Emma nodded.

"How were you known?"

"Emma, daughter of Ian."

"Ian? That's it?"

"Do you need more?"

Nora sighed again. She did. "You're going to need more of a designation than that. Obviously Blackstone chose two words that fit together. You want to do that?"

To her surprise, Emma's eyes filled with tears.

"Emma?"

"I am lost," she whispered. "That is what you must call me. Emma the Lost."

"It's not usual—"

"I do not care," Emma said. "You asked me to chose."

Nora nodded. "So I did." She took a deep breath. "We no longer call ourselves using articles, like 'the.' So we will simply call you Emma Lost. Is that all right?"

Emma nodded.

Then Nora grabbed the remote. "Okay. Let me explain—"

The doorbell chimed. Emma crouched, hands over her ears. Nora grabbed her and pulled her up. "That's what our door knocker sounds like."

"Oh," Emma said.

Nora helped her to the sofa then went up the stairs to the door. As she pulled it open, her mother swept in, carrying two bags that smelled of kung pao chicken, sesame beef, and something made with curry.

"I thought you'd leave me out there forever," her mother said as she headed toward the kitchen. She was wearing a summer dress that flowed around her like a scarf and accented her hair which was, at present, a bronze blonde not found in nature. "I stopped at Chen's, and you wouldn't believe the crowd. Fortunately they knew me and—"

"Mother," Nora said.

"—of course I had to wait for almond cookies, so I took fortune cookies instead—"

"Mother."

"—and they weren't going to give me steamed rice, so I had to call Mr. Chen up front. Or is that his name? I never know. Anyway—"

"Mother!" Nora said.

"Nora, dear, you don't have to be so sharp." Her mother's face peered around the cabinets. "Oh, is this your friend? I didn't see her. Hello. I'm Amanda Lowenstein, Nora's mother."

Emma had her mouth open slightly but didn't say anything. Then she blinked and said to Nora, "You do not have the same final name."

"No," Nora said. "Mother's name comes from her third husband."

"Fourth, dear," Amanda said.

"This is Emma Lost, Mother," Nora said.

"Lust? What kind of name is that? Lust?"

"Lost. As in found."

"Oh," Amanda said. "It's still a strange name." She disappeared back into the kitchen. Emma grabbed Nora's hand.

"You are not leaving me with her?"

"Only for a few hours."

"I would like to come with you."

"That would be harder."

"For you perhaps," Emma said.

"Actually, believe it or not, it'll be harder for you.

She's overbearing, but she has no magic. Remember that. And if you can't stand being around her anymore, excuse yourself and go to the room where you changed clothes. That's your room. She won't go in there."

"Do you promise?"

"Yes," Nora said. She squeezed Emma's hand and then went into the kitchen. Amanda had taken all the stoneware serving bowls out of the cupboard and was scraping the contents of the cardboard cartons to them.

"Mother!" Nora said, starting to pull one away and then realizing she was too late. "You're supposed to eat them out of the cardboard."

"Your lax kitchen habits are but one reason Max left you," Amanda said.

"Max didn't leave me," Nora said, putting her hands on her hips and surveying the disaster her kitchen had become in a matter of moments. "I left him."

"Even so," Amanda said, putting the rice in the last bowl and then shoving that bowl into the microwave, "he would have fought for you if you gave him a proper home."

"You didn't give Dad a proper home."

"And see where it got us?"

The rice spun in the microwave. Squidgy sauntered into the room, tail high, sniffing as if the food were for her. Nora, resigned, took out plates.

"Mom, I'm not going to stay long. But I should warn you that Emma is a bit unusual."

"Everyone from your generation is unusual, darling," her mother said, somehow forgetting that she was part of a generation that painted itself colors and danced naked in the mud.

"She has amnesia, and it's a weird form of amnesia."

Amanda took the rice out of the microwave, fluffed it with a fork, and then frowned at Nora. "Weird?"

Nora nodded. "She can't remember much about anything. She doesn't even know simple things, like what a television is."

Amanda frowned. "I've read about amnesia, dear, and that's not how it works."

"Not usually," Nora said, "but her doctors say this is a strange case."

"Then why aren't they monitoring her?"

Good question. Nora hated lying to her mother. "It's too complicated to explain."

"And how do you know her name?"

"Just her first name, Mother," Nora said, letting the exasperation creep into her voice. "She chose 'Lost' herself."

"I think 'Doe' would have been better. More common."

"Emma's not a common woman."

"I am getting that sense."

Nora took one of the bowls and moved it to the table. In the living room, Emma was seated on the couch, petting Darnell. Nora was beginning to wonder if the fickle cat liked Emma better.

"Please do not take her out of the apartment and don't under any circumstances let anyone in."

"Not even her doctors?"

"Especially not her doctors." Nora grabbed another bowl and carried it in. "If someone takes her—"

"Takes her? As in kidnaps her?"

"—call the police first and me second."

"It sounds like I need hazard pay," Amanda said,

bringing the plates to the table. "Emma, dear, do you prefer silverware or chopsticks?"

Emma looked up and glanced first at Nora as if she needed help with the answer.

"You know," Nora said, "I don't think it'll make any difference. I think they'll be equally confusing."

"Oh, dear," Amanda said, sinking into her chair. "This is worse than I thought."

"Now you're beginning to understand," Nora said.

Emma wandered toward the table, Darnell following her like a dog. She sniffed the bowls, the movement delicate. "This is food?"

"Chinese food," Nora's mother said.

"Chinese—?"

Amanda frowned. "Well, Cantonese, I think. Or is it Szechwan? Nora, help me out."

Nora suppressed a smile, sat down, and spooned rice on her plate. "Actually, Mother, you started it. You can get out of it. I'm just going to eat."

———

"Bah!" Ealhswith said as she flung a slice of pepperoni and sausage pizza across her living room. The slice stuck to her white wall and then slid, slowly, onto the white carpet, leaving a tomato stain that looked like blood.

She stood, wiped off her hands, and debated whether or not to make the short trip to New York. A good slice of pizza would be worth it, given the mood she was in. In fact, she could go for a long day of shopping and eating and theater in the City, a day to take her mind off everything.

Everything, including Emma, Blackstone, that

irritating little lawyer woman Nora, and the fact that
Oregon—Portland, Oregon, in particular—had the worst
pizza on the planet.

It had been Ealhswith's mistake. She had forgotten
how bad Oregon pizza really was. She'd called for a
delivery en route, hoping for a bit of comfort food while
she decompressed from this horrid, horrid day. Being
ordered out of a lawyer's house. How low was that? Not
to mention the fact that Emma was actually awake. Now
Ealhswith had to maneuver her back into her tidy little
coma and somehow blame Blackstone for it after she got
that annoying attorney out of the way.

The Fates would hate it if Ealhswith did something
permanent to that little meddler. But Ealhswith might
do something else, something that wasn't permanent but
which was annoying.

She just had to figure out what it was.

Ealhswith clapped her hands together, and the pizza
vanished, along with the bloody stain against the wall.
Her living room was white on white, as clean as she
could get it, and she loved it that way. Her home was
always ready for visitors, not that she had any and, if she
ever did have any, they would be impressed at how perfect her decor was. Except, of course, for her bedroom.
She would never let anyone in there.

Ealhswith's stomach growled. A trip to New York
was an indulgence at the moment. She would have to
make do with something else. She certainly couldn't
try for another abysmal pizza. Maybe some Thai
food. Portland did, at least, have good Asian cuisine.
Ealhswith wouldn't have been able to live here if all of
the food were abysmal.

She set down her remote and scratched a grease smear off her white couch. Barbara Stanwyck in *Double Indemnity* would never have allowed herself to get uninvited. Nor would Bette Davis in any film she was in. Not even Kathleen Turner, in that terrible remake of *Body Heat*, would have allowed herself to be manipulated by a person less powerful than she was.

Following the rules was for milquetoasts like Sarah Michelle Gellar and that flat-voiced redhead who played the exceedingly dull Dana Scully on the *X-Files*. Television and movies had it all wrong, of course. Powerful women weren't soft-spoken or the defenders of all that was holy. Mortal entertainment made certain that all the truly powerful women died at the end of their films, usually through a mistake that no powerful woman would ever make.

It had been years since Ealhswith watched the end of a movie—especially one with a proper villainess. She found series television just as difficult to finish. Still, Ealhswith turned to her rather substantial DVD collection in moments like these, moments when she felt as if she had lost control—however temporarily— of her life.

She watched key scenes—like the one where Sharon Stone turned a routine police interview into a seduction in *Basic Instinct* or the moment when Anjelica Huston put wimpy little Drew Barrymore in her place in that saccharine—and mistold—film, *Ever After*. Ealhswith got her inspiration from scenes like that, and from novels, and plays—Shakespeare wrote some great female parts and could be forgiven for the little weaklings he called his heroines. Lady Macbeth surely could put them all to shame, and as did Kate, wonderful Kate, whom, it was clear, would forever make Petruchio's life a living hell.

Ealhswith shook herself out of the thought. As inspiring as she found all of those stories, none of them helped her figure out how to get Emma back. The lawyer had, for the time being, effectively barred Ealhswith from Emma's life by quoting rules and legalities, and cultural norms, like any good wimpy heroine should.

Rules, legalities, and cultural norms. Ealhswith crossed her arms. Rules, legalities, and norms. All the things she absolutely hated. But as she had learned over the years, things she could use to her advantage.

So young Miss Barr wanted to use mortal legal arguments to fight a magic battle, did she? Ealhswith smiled. Why not? It could be done.

Not if she followed all the rules. But most of them. And what were rules for if not to be broken? Especially if a person didn't get caught.

Ealhswith laughed her cruel villainess's laugh, the one she had been practicing since she saw her first film noir in the late 1940s. A cold, calculating laugh.

She was an expert at bending the rules, an expert at not getting caught. After all, if she could trick the Fates, she could trick a simple little mortal court. It would be a pleasure to beat that pesky attorney at her own game to get Emma back—and to rip out Blackstone's heart in the process.

Chapter 6

AFTER A LUNCH CONVERSATION IN WHICH NORA'S mother tried to explain China ("it is the largest country on Earth—" "How do you know this?" "Because—oh, I don't know"), its location in relationship to theirs ("It's in the Far East." "And we are where?" "In America." "Which is where?"), and its regions and cuisines ("Now Hunan is the hot one, right, Nora?" "I don't know, Mother." "And that is China?" "No, it's Chinese." "Then why do you not call it Chinese?"), Nora fled the loft, only to have to return a moment later for her car keys and purse. When she walked back in, her mother was explaining how rice was grown ("in paddies" "which are?") and Nora just shook her head, took the purse and keys, and left again before she could get sucked back into the conversation.

As she took the stairs down, she wished, she really did, that Emma had opted for at least part of the magic spell which gave her the history of the world. With all these simple questions and the amount of things she had to learn, this was going to get real tiring, real fast.

Halfway to the office, Nora realized she was still wearing her filthy sweatshirt and jeans. She thought for a moment about driving home then decided against it. The last thing she wanted to explain was why she needed different clothes for work.

Instead she stopped at the Saks downtown and bought herself a new suit. It was made of linen, and she wore a light pink blouse with it and even indulged in a pair of Italian leather shoes. She deserved it, and somehow she managed to make the entire purchase in only a matter of minutes.

She left the store wearing the suit, carrying her grimy clothes in the Saks bag. From there, the drive to her office was short. She was still in the same building she had been in ten years before, but she had taken over one of the penthouse suites. Her law firm was no longer just hers; she had junior partners and baby lawyers and law clerks, so many people bustling about that if she wasn't careful, she would call one by the wrong name. As she pulled into the familiar parking garage, she found herself thinking what a difference ten years made.

Ruthie had stayed with her, using part of the money from the first bizarre episode with Blackstone for night classes in business management and in legal secretary training. Somewhere in that first six months, she dropped the deadbeat boyfriend, who then found some other poor schmo to support him. Ruthie started dating a series of self-made men, all of whom owned their own businesses, and all of whom eventually wanted to hire her away from Nora. Ruthie had declined offers of jobs and offers of marriage, for which Nora was profoundly grateful. She never would have thought, after their rocky start, that Ruthie would become indispensable. And right now, Nora wanted to see Ruthie, to help her get this strange case under way.

Ruthie had her own office inside the three-room suite that was Nora's private space. Nora had to pass reception, where the latest college intern sat, overwhelmed by the ringing phones and the growing mass of paper, and where the regular receptionist kept everything in order. The receptionist had been with Nora for eight years. She was a solid, unimaginative woman whose friendliness was her greatest asset. She waved at Nora, who nodded back, and then she answered a few phones herself, clearly knowing where her paycheck came from.

Nora walked behind the big oak reception area, grabbed a thick wad of paper which were messages that had accumulated since the last time Ruthie grabbed them, and then headed through the waiting area (filled with nice plants and current magazines) into the heart of the law office. Through double glass doors, clerks and legal secretaries bustled past the open files and library shelves. Inside one of the meeting rooms, one of the junior partners was holding a conference with several older men in conservative black suits. In another meeting room, two baby lawyers were seated side by side, law books open before them, files scattered across the table.

The offices were full and more than one attorney was hurrying out the back, briefcase stuffed, and looking harried. All those attorneys, all those billable hours. She was the only senior partner, and it was her firm. Even though the junior partners got a percentage of the firm's revenue, no one got as much as she did. She knew this was one of the reasons Max was playing hardball in the divorce; no matter how much he made defending the guilty, his income would never match hers. She could retire now, leave the management in the hands of the ablest junior partner, and make a good living for the rest of her life. She chose not to do that. Every morning—except this morning—she was here, heading the staff meeting, keeping track of cases and clients, and making certain everything ran smoothly. That she hadn't been here this morning felt odd, as if the entire world were out of sync. Which, in some ways, it was.

The law clerks greeted her with nervous head-bobs. The two main secretaries all looked surprised to see her walking in so late. If Nora took a day off, she took the full day. But she rarely did. While she worked fewer paying cases, she still spent most of her time here. She managed difficult clients, and she did a lot of pro bono work, representing clients—mostly domestic abuse cases that revolved around children or child custody—who couldn't pay. Some of those cases broke her heart. Others redeemed her notion of the way that human beings cared for each other even in times of crisis.

And that, more than anything, was probably why she had taken on Emma. She had seen in the middle of all that turmoil, the potential for one young woman to get hurt. In many ways, Emma was already hurt; by all the lost time, all the lost years. She needed a chance to get her feet beneath her before she made her own choices, which was exactly what most of those women Nora had represented needed before they could figure out how to take care of themselves and their children.

"Boy, will Ruthie be glad to see you," said Steven, one of the junior partners, as he passed, laptop under his arm. "She's been breathing fire all morning."

"It's afternoon," Nora said.

"It's gotten worse," he said with a grin.

"Thanks for the warning."

Nora squared her shoulders and walked through the

narrow corridor that led to her office suite. She opened the door, thinking how much this little setup resembled the one she had started with several floors below, and barely registered the client sitting in the corner. Instead she looked at Ruthie.

Breathing fire was probably a bad analogy. Turning the room frigid with her chilly attitude was better. Ruthie had cleaned up in ten years. Her power suit was more expensive than the one Nora was wearing, and her jewelry was tasteful gold chains with matching diamond studs. Her long hair had been tamed and pulled back, and she'd stopped wearing contacts, deciding long ago that glasses gave her more authority.

Ruthie pulled those glasses down her nose and looked at Nora like a one-room school teacher disciplining the class clown. "If you were going to take a morning off, you should have warned me. The entire office is behind because of you. It took the staff fifteen minutes to decide which junior partner should lead the meeting; I had to type up minutes special for you—"

Nora knew that part wasn't true. One of the other secretaries had done it. Ruthie had learned to delegate tasks like that years ago.

"—I canceled four appointments, let Mrs. Seldayne cry on my silk blouse, and thanked the good Lord that your court appearance for that sweet three-year-old and his wretched mother was yesterday and not today. You have more messages than I care to count, there is some kind of financial crisis in accounting that needs your fullest attention *now* or so I'm told, and this so-called gentleman refuses to leave my office and wait where all the other clients do."

That last part made Nora pay attention. No one ever got the better of Ruthie. Not the new and improved Ruthie. Nora turned.

Blackstone was sitting in one of the uncomfortable office chairs Ruthie had bought for the express purpose of making certain that no one sat in her office very long. At first glance, Blackstone seemed comfortable—his long legs were extended, his slender hands clasped over his flat belly, much as they had been in Nora's office years ago—but at second glance, it became clear that he was holding the position through sheer willpower. Another battle of wills, this one with Ruthie. The man was the most stubborn person Nora had ever met.

"I don't have time for you today, Mr. Blackstone," Nora said. "We had our discussion earlier."

He stood, shaking one leg slightly, as if it had fallen asleep. "All I need is five minutes, Nora. Please—"

She thumbed through her messages, even though he was probably the only person on the planet she could never ignore. Still, she managed to focus on the messages. At least half were marked "urgent." "And I don't recall ever giving you permission to use my first name, Mr. Blackstone."

"I'm sorry," he said and sounded so contrite that she actually looked at him. That was a mistake. Her gaze got caught on his silver eyes with their long lashes. It took a moment before she could break the look.

"I am very busy, Mr. Blackstone."

"Where's Emma?" he asked.

"In my care, as I promised she would be," Nora said. "That's all you need to know."

Ruthie sat up. She'd seen variations of this drama

played out in this office countless times. To her, this must have seemed like a domestic abuse situation. Nora gave her a small "wait" signal with her left hand.

"You can't continue to take care of her yourself. You know this is foolishness," he said.

"I know nothing of the sort, Mr. Blackstone. Now, if you'll let me by—"

"Nora—Miss Barr—Mrs. Farnsworth—"

"It's always been Barr," Nora said.

"Please. I—" He extended his hands and then dropped them, as if he knew that pleading with her would do no good. He shook his head and started for the door.

As he passed her, Nora got the distinct sense that he truly was upset, that this was not an act he was putting on for her benefit. For the first time since she had met him, Blackstone needed help.

"All right, Mr. Blackstone," she said. "You have fifteen minutes. No more. Ruthie will let us know when your time is up."

She nodded to Ruthie, who looked surprised. No one had ever convinced Nora to change her plans before.

She took the other pile of messages off Ruthie's desk and opened the oak door that separated Ruthie's office from hers. Both offices had connecting doors to a conference room that wasn't used as much as Nora had thought it would be.

As she always did when she stepped inside her office, she paused to look at the bridges crossing the Columbia River and the buildings and mountains beyond. No city was prettier than Portland, and she didn't tire of looking at it. The beautiful day continued, and for once, the sunshine didn't bring with it the haze that had been growing with each summer. Everything was fresh and clear, as if the air were chilly instead of hot.

Blackstone stopped behind her. She could feel his warmth against her back, smell that scent she had noticed on him years ago, a scent of leather and something exotic. She stepped away from him, mostly to be out of range of that intoxicating smell, and headed toward her desk, the same oak desk she had always had, the one her father had given her before he died. It almost looked small in this large room, but it was the one thing that reminded her of who she was, where she had come from, and what she was doing here. It was that desk that made her realize a woman could spend her entire life chasing money and die with cash in her hands and nothing else. She decided she didn't want to die that way, and so she began her pro bono work, quietly and with great fervor. It became the centerpiece of her life as her marriage to Max had fallen apart.

"Close the door, Mr. Blackstone," she said as she put the messages on her desk. She tapped the intercom and asked Ruthie to hold her calls. Then she turned her attention to him.

He still had his hand on the door, as if he weren't certain whether or not he should come into the room. His hair was messed, his shirt was rumpled, and he had an expression on his face that was something Nora had never seen before. It looked as if he were trying to keep his normal aura of bemused calm but was too upset to do so. The mask kept slipping, revealing a younger, softer man, a man she could like. A lot.

She kept her voice cool as she said, "Have a seat, Mr. Blackstone."

He came closer but did not sit down. "It wasn't supposed to be like this."

"What wasn't?"

"Her waking. I thought—" he stopped himself, shook his head, as if the sentence wasn't worth finishing.

"That she'd run into your arms?" Nora asked. "She did."

"I know," he said. "But I thought she'd take the spell and come with me. I didn't expect her to be so angry."

"She said you didn't know each other long."

He put his hands on the back of the chair, almost as though he needed its support. "It seemed like a long time then. When you're young, you know."

"She's still young," Nora said.

He nodded, once, the movement curt. "It's like I don't know what to do now that she's awake."

"The fight with Ealhswith had become everything, hadn't it?"

"No." He pulled the chair back then walked around it and sat down. His posture was rigid, not the pretend relaxation he had had outside. The mask was completely gone from his face. This man was open to her, his eyes wide, his mouth mobile. He looked lost. As lost as Emma.

He raised his hands, cupped them, and kept them apart, as if forming an imaginary box with his fingers. "It's as if she wasn't a person anymore."

Nora waited. This was important, although she wasn't sure why.

"And yet I knew she was. I always had this idea that she and I would walk off into the sunset."

"Once you got rid of Ealhswith."

"Once we had our own life."

Nora threaded her fingers together. "But you've had a life. For a long time. Without Emma."

"I know," he said. "I'm beginning to realize it."

"So is she," Nora said.

"My God," he said, bowing his head and sliding his hands into his hair, messing it further. "What we did to her, I didn't realize—" He raised his head. His hair was standing out in tufts. He looked like a little boy, a little boy who had just discovered that the world didn't work the way he wanted it to. "You have to let me see her. I need to make this right."

"What would you do?" Nora asked. "Send her back to her own time?"

He shook his head.

"Give her a thousand years of false memories?"

He closed his eyes.

"Put her back to sleep?"

"No," he said, standing. "No."

"What can you do?" Nora asked again.

"Make her forget," he said. "That's the best I can do."

"What would she forget?"

"Everything," he whispered.

"Everything?" Nora asked.

He shrugged. "Or everything since she awoke. She could remember her childhood, her past."

"Then she'd still be confused by this world," Nora said. "All you would do was make certain she had forgotten her anger at you. You're better off having her forget her name, her background, her world."

He shoved his hands into the back pockets of his jeans and bowed his head. "That's not a solution either, is it?"

"Not if what she tells me is true," Nora said. "If she will come into her own magic someday. And then, of course, there's Ealhswith to deal with."

"Yes," he said.

"I don't think magic can solve this," Nora said.

He frowned, as if he had never encountered anything like that before. "Still," he said, "she needs help, and I don't think you can give it."

"You can't," Nora said. "She's afraid of you."

"Afraid?" He turned, startled. All the power she had felt from him, all the charming warmth that had been so much a part of him, was gone. This was Blackstone, the man behind the games. She longed to reach out to him, but she didn't dare.

"Yes," Nora said gently. "Think of what you've done to her, you and Ealhswith."

He sank back into the chair.

"You took everything from her. Her past, her future. Everything she was familiar with, and you've replaced it with nothing. You're not even someone she recognizes."

"But she ran to me," he said.

"She says you look older. Angrier. She says you're someone else." Nora rubbed her thumbs together, then stopped when she realized she was making her own nervousness visible. "You are, you know. Ten years changes a person. I can't think what a thousand would do."

He rubbed his hands along his thighs, then grabbed his knees and leaned forward like a supplicant who wasn't sure if he should humble himself too much. "She was supposed to be my soul mate. She is my destiny. That's what they said."

"They?" Nora asked.

He shook his head, then bent it forward so that she couldn't see his face at all. A few stray strands of silver along his crown caught the light. Emma was right. He didn't look like a boy. He looked like a man full grown.

He took a deep breath, slapped his thigh, and then stood. "I take it she's Sancho's responsibility now?" The mask was back. His face was smooth, as if nothing could touch it, or him. As if he didn't have a heart at all.

"Actually, no," Nora said. "He was responsible for the microbus. It's still in its garage. I did my part."

"She can't be on her own." Blackstone came forward and leaned on the desk. The scent of him swirled around her, leather and exotic and enticing.

"She isn't," Nora said, holding her ground, even though his face was just inches from hers. "She's already taking action."

"Action?"

"She hired me to act as her representative."

"You can't."

Nora raised an eyebrow. "Why not?"

"Because—you work for Sancho."

"I don't see why warehousing a microbus conflicts with becoming the attorney for a woman who needs to establish herself in a strange new world."

"You claimed, in your apartment, that you were protecting Emma on the behest of Sancho. Now you're saying you represent her. That's a conflict."

"That's called thinking on your feet. I had to do something to convince you and Ealhswith that I had some authority."

"Speaking of Ealhswith, how are you going to protect Emma from her?"

"I'm not sure yet, but I'll come up with something."

"Let me see Emma. Let me talk to her. This is just foolishness."

"No," Nora said.

He leaned back, as if her word had been a physical blow. "No?"

"When we first met, ten years ago, I told you that you had no rights to this girl, remember?"

"She was in a coma then. She—"

"You still don't, Blackstone." It was hard for Nora to keep her voice level. He was still too close to her. And she wanted to give in to him, to keep him around. But she didn't dare, not if she was going to protect Emma. "She makes her own choices, and she is not ready to see you."

"I can simply appear in your apartment."

"Do that," Nora said, "and I'll have the police after you so fast, your head will spin."

"So I really am uninvited."

It was her turn to lean back. Obviously "uninvited" was an important concept to him. He had used that word with Ealhswith when she had been in the loft, and she had left almost immediately. "Yes," Nora said. "You are uninvited."

He sighed, slapped his hands on the desk, and stood up. "You are making this impossible."

"I am doing what I think best."

"Treating me as you would treat one of your divorce cases, the domestic cases, where the husband is persona non grata?"

"You are not a husband, you are not married to Emma, and you are exhibiting behavior that I could easily convince the police is stalking. I don't like it, and neither does Emma."

He headed toward the door, then stopped. "I don't suppose I could hire you?"

"For what?"

"I don't know," he said. "To help me with Emma perhaps?"

"No," Nora said.

"Why not?"

"Because that," she said, "is a conflict of interest."

He let out a hissing breath. "You are a difficult woman."

"You don't know the half of it."

He ran his hand through his hair, smoothing it this time, as if he were trying to tame its mess. He didn't look at her for a moment, and she wondered if he were trying to figure out another way around her, a way to charm her, seduce her, to make her think the way he wanted her to think.

"It's hard for me to let go," he said, his back to Nora. "I've been protecting her for a thousand years."

"For a thousand years," Nora said, "she couldn't move. She can now."

"I know." He shook his head slightly. "I know."

He was silent for a moment. Nora had learned long ago to wait, to let the other person break a silence. That way, she discovered so much more.

He turned so that she could see one side of his face. She couldn't quite read it, not at that unusual angle. "I never meant to harm her," he said.

"You should tell her that."

"You won't let me."

She smiled. "Touché."

"She'll need help. I know it. Please, tell her she can come to me. I won't—do anything to upset her. I promise."

At least he didn't say he loved her. Nora didn't know why that mattered, but it did. It felt as if they were getting closer to the truth somehow, with that little sentence removed from the conversation.

"I'll tell her," Nora said.

He nodded, looked away. "And I want you to call me too, if you have trouble with Ealhswith, the Fates, or the magic. Sometimes…" He didn't finish the thought.

"Sometimes?"

"These things snowball," he said. He grabbed the doorknob and turned. This time, she could see him, and he looked just like the man she had met—minus the snake. She would have to ask him about that sometime.

"Snowball?" she asked.

"I hope you don't find out." His smile was slight, and it didn't go to his eyes. "I guess Sancho was right about you."

"In what way?"

"He said you could handle whatever came up." Blackstone shrugged. "Perhaps he foresaw this."

"It wasn't hard to see."

"For you, maybe," Blackstone said. "It blindsided me." He let himself out the door, closing it softly behind him. She stared at it for a moment, then stood.

She was shaking. She hadn't realized it until she was alone. She was shaking from the morning's events and the conversation with Blackstone. Hell, just being alone with the man made her nervous. She had to use all of her mental powers to concentrate. She had never found a man so attractive. Not even Max.

Especially not Max.

She grimaced and went to her minibar, where she kept mostly colas, some yogurt and fruit in case she didn't get lunch, and some ice cream for emergencies. She opened the door, stared inside the refrigerator, and decided she was only going to eat because she was nervous.

And upset.

And terrified.

Maybe that little man Sancho thought she could handle anything, but she didn't. She had talked a good game about defending herself and Emma against Ealhswith and helping Emma make the transition, but she wasn't sure she could do it.

And she knew she couldn't do it alone.

She grabbed a can of Diet Coke, opened it, and put it on a coaster on her desk. Then she dictated her file notes for Ruthie. Before Nora gave them to Ruthie, she would have to swear her to confidentiality, maybe even have Ruthie review her agreement with the firm. This one shouldn't get out, not to the secretaries, not to anyone. They would all think Nora was crazy.

A knock on her door startled her. "Come," she said.

Randolph, another of the junior partners, came inside. He was slender and small, trim in an efficient way. His suits were always meticulous, his hair styled neater than any woman's in the office, and his hands manicured the way that only Ruthie had been able to match.

"Sorry," he said, looking over his shoulder. "I know I should wait for the partners' meeting tomorrow, but is that your newest client?"

"What?" Nora asked, feeling as if she had entered into a conversation in the middle.

"Alex Blackstone."

"Alex?" She blinked. Of course he wouldn't use Aethelstan. Not in this day and age. But Stan seemed the logical shortening of the name. Not Alex.

"Yeah," Randolph said. "It was your office he was leaving, right?"

"Yes," Nora said, gathering herself so that she didn't say anything she shouldn't. "But he's not a client. He's connected to a case that I can't talk about."

"Damn," Randolph said. "That's one big fish."

"You know him?"

"You don't?"

The feeling of being in someone else's conversation continued. "Should I?"

"Don't you read the papers?"

"Yes, I read the papers."

"Then you should know."

"What?"

"Who Alex Blackstone is."

"Maybe I just don't read the papers as closely as you," she snapped.

"Obviously not," Randolph said.

She waited. So did he. That was when she realized this was one of those petty lawyer games, and she didn't have time to play. "So," she said. "Who is he?"

"The hottest restaurateur in Portland. Kind of our answer to Wolfgang Puck. Only he blends cuisines from all over the world into his own. And he does theme nights. You know, War of the Roses Night, a Moveable Feast night—"

"Moveable Feast?"

"You know, Paris in the twenties."

"No, I didn't know," she said, annoyed. "So he's famous locally."

"On the verge of becoming famous nationally, I think. And his restaurant has been open less than a year."

"What's it called?"

"What?"

"The restaurant," she snapped, not wanting to play anymore games.

"Quixotic."

"Figures," she muttered.

"What?" Randolph asked.

"'Quixotic' is an adjective," she said. "I thought restaurant names were supposed to be nouns."

He looked at her as if she had gone crazy.

"Never mind," she said. "Look, I've got a lot on my plate, so unless you came here to do more than gossip—"

"I just wanted to find out if we had gotten his legal business. It's become quite a coup among the firms in town. A lot of them are chasing him—"

"We're not."

"Well, since he's been here, do you mind if I—?"

"Yes."

Randolph frowned. "That's not like you. What kind of case is he connected with?"

"A messy one," Nora said. Then she frowned. "Say, do you know any good general history professors, or maybe English professors with a specialty in medieval lit? I'd even settle for a comp lit prof or a specialist in arcane languages."

"Is this for the case?"

"Randolph," she said. "Just answer the question."

"I can have my clerk dig some up. He's fresh out of the U of O."

"I'd prefer someone from Portland."

"Whatever," Randolph said. "If I find this out for you, can I help on the case?"

She put her micro voice recorder down. "What is your interest in Blackstone?"

"He's going to be worth a lot of money, Nora. Especially once he goes national. This is the age of the famous chef. They license a thousand things, from special recipes to franchises to television shows. Think of the income to the firm."

"You think of it," Nora said. "I've got to get through this first."

"Mind if I call him?"

"Yes," she said. "It would be a conflict of interest."

"Don't tell me," Randolph said. "He beats his wife."

"He doesn't have a wife," she said. "I don't know why everyone assumes he does."

"What everyone?" Randolph said. "I was guessing."

Nora frowned at him. She was distracted and tired and not up for a conversation like this. "Do me a favor and don't talk about this."

"You still want the names of the professors?"

"Please," she said.

"All right, but someday you'll have to tell me what this is all about."

"I will," she said, "when it's all over."

If it ever ends, she thought, and felt a surge of fear. The magnitude of what she had gotten into had finally hit her. She only hoped she was strong enough to hold her own until Emma got on her feet.

If Emma ever got on her feet.

Nora closed her eyes. Sometimes it didn't pay to have

legal training. It always taught you to see the worst.
And the worst in this case was not something she really
wanted to consider.

Only she didn't know how to stop herself.

When she opened her eyes, Randolph was still
there, staring at her. "Something's really wrong, isn't
it?" he asked.

She nodded.

"I won't hassle you about it any more," he said. "But
if you need help, you come to me, all right?"

"Yeah," she said, knowing she wouldn't. She wasn't
sure she could get help from anyone. At least, not anyone normal.

And that was the biggest problem of all.

———————

For the second time that day, Blackstone stood outside
a building with Nora inside and stared at his car. It was
becoming, to him at least, a symbol of everything that
was wrong with the computer age. Why did a status
symbol have to be so very small?

He had parked in a parking space near a newly planted
maple tree. The street was lined with a dozen of these
newly planted trees, apparently some city planner's attempt at beautification. Downtown Portland was beautiful enough; it didn't need trees that would someday tower
over the road or block the view from the lower windows.

He felt particularly protective of those lower windows. For the past ten years, he had gazed at them and
thought of Nora toiling away in her ratty office. He
hadn't realized, until today, that she had graduated to an
entire floor at the building's top.

The Porsche was baking in the heat. For some reason, he hadn't wanted to go into the parking garage. The garage almost felt as if it were too filled with memories, too much a part of his past.

His past with Nora, not Emma.

His fists were clenched again. What was wrong with him? He should have charmed Nora, forced her to un-uninvite him, and gone to see Emma. But charming Nora would be difficult, if not impossible, and even if it were possible, he didn't want to.

He wanted her to like him for his own sake. And for the first time in the last millennium, maybe the first time in his life, he wasn't confident of being liked. Nora seemed to see down inside him, and he was getting the sense that she didn't approve of what she saw.

Why should she? In her opinion, he had imprisoned for a thousand years a woman he claimed to love, then he had treated that woman insensitively when she had awakened from her coma, and he hadn't once told her that he loved her.

Somehow he hadn't been able to say the words. At least, not with Nora in the room. Even if she hadn't been in the room, he wasn't sure how convincing he would be. He wasn't sure how he felt about Emma—besides guilty and slightly ashamed. He could blame this whole thing on Ealhswith and his own inexperience, but somehow that seemed wrong.

It was time he took responsibility himself.

Responsibility meant that he be the one to work with Emma, he be the one to train her in the ways of this brave new world, he be the one to show her how wonderful the twenty-first century could be.

Somehow he had to get Nora to trust him. He shook his head slightly. That wouldn't work. Not after all she had seen.

He leaned on his hot tiny car and crossed his arms, staring up at the building where she had once had an office the size of a closet. She had come so far since he last saw her. She didn't look like a kid just out of high school anymore. She looked like exactly what she was—a powerful woman full grown. She had been an attorney for ten years, and she saw things clearly. She would know when someone was trying to manipulate her, even someone as good as he was.

In fact, she would be expecting that.

He shook his head. If only they could work together. But she wasn't ready to do that either. And he didn't have time—actually Emma didn't have time—for Nora to gain his trust.

So he would have to play things her way. He would have to see if he could bend the rules of her world, her legal world, so that he could spend time with Emma.

And for that, he needed his faithful sidekick, the man Nora only knew as Sancho Panza. Blackstone knew Sancho's real name, of course, but those who had come into their magic never used real names—not casually, anyway. It was too dangerous.

Sancho was in the South of France, or so he said. Sometimes he just disappeared for weeks at a time, coming back looking sadder than he had when he left. Blackstone always had the sense that Sancho, for all his bravado, was lonely, but he could never confirm it. The one thing Blackstone knew was that he was Sancho's best—and only—friend.

It was time to cash in on that friendship. Blackstone couldn't get to Emma, but Sancho could. If they argued this right, Sancho would leave Nora's with Emma at his side—and then Blackstone would be able to talk to her, to help her, to make her see reason.

And somehow, in the middle of all that, he would find a way to convince her to forgive him.

Chapter 7

WHEN NORA GOT HOME, SHE FOUND HER MOTHER and Emma in the living room, deep in conversation. Emma looked calmer. Darnell was on her lap. Nora felt a twinge of jealousy—even the cats thought Emma was the be-all and end-all of women—and then put it aside. Nora stood for a moment, taking in the scene before her.

Apparently, Emma had gotten used to Nora's mother. And a few other things. Emma was holding the television remote as if it were the Holy Grail and occasionally, she would point it at the TV. She kept turning to the Home Shopping Network. After a moment, Nora's mother would change the channel to CNN, and after a while, Emma would change it back.

It was going to be a long night.

As Nora came inside, carrying her Saks bag and her briefcase, her mother waved gaily. "I have dinner in the refrigerator," Amanda said. "Emma helped."

Emma smiled at her, as if she had completed the greatest accomplishment of her life. "I like the stove," she said. "It is so easy. Even if food is strange here."

Amanda patted Emma on the shoulder and stood up. She walked to Nora, took her bag, and said, "Let me help you put your new clothes away."

"They're old clothes," Nora said. "I'm wearing the new ones."

"So you are." Amanda brushed imaginary lint off her shoulder. "They'll need to be dry-cleaned."

"Mother."

Amanda shrugged. "Come along."

And Nora let Amanda lead her into her own bedroom at the top of the stairs.

"Good," Amanda said. "Now—"

"It's not that private here," Nora whispered.

Amanda took her arm and led her into the upstairs bathroom, pulling the door closed. Nora had remodeled the room with the rest of the loft, making the bathroom her own private sanctuary. There was a separate area for the toilet, double sinks because the designer had insisted, a fancy shower with its own stall, and The Tub. The Tub was on a raised platform with windows that opened to the city. The shades were down now, and the room was dark. Nora flipped on a light. Amanda blinked as if unaccustomed to such brightness.

"The problem is worse than you know," Amanda said, keeping her voice low.

"I doubt that," Nora said.

"Emma believes she is a witch."

"I know," Nora said.

"A witch without powers."

"I know that too," Nora said, wishing that she had been able to convince Emma to lie.

"A witch without powers from the Middle Ages."

"The Dark Ages, Mother," Nora said.

"I thought there was no difference."

"There is quite a difference," Nora said. "The Middle Ages were modern compared to the Dark Ages."

"Oh, dear," Amanda said. Then she slapped Nora's arm. "You knew this."

"Yes."

"And you didn't tell me."

"Yes."

"Why not?"

"Because I thought it might bother you."

"It does bother me. Does her psychiatrist know?"

Nora didn't know how to answer that. So she tried the indirect approach. "Everyone knows who needs to know."

Amanda's mouth formed a thin line. "Emma says you're protecting her."

"Yes," Nora said.

"She says her mother and her boyfriend are after her."

"More or less."

"You're not equipped to handle that. Why isn't she in one of those shelters?"

"Believing she's a witch from the Dark Ages?"

"So they'll put her in an institution. And frankly, Nora, I'm beginning to think that, no matter how sweet she is, she belongs in one."

"If I do that, Mother, then she'll eventually be remanded into the custody of her mother. Or her boyfriend if he can convince them he's her husband. And I've met the man. He can convince you that the Moon is made of cheese."

"I'm not convinced it's not," Amanda said archly. "I think that whole landing thing was a public relations hoax."

"Mother."

Amanda shrugged. "That Nixon. He'd do anything to win any competition."

Nora knew better than to get Amanda started on her

own weird brand of politics. "Mother, please. We were talking about Emma."

"Yes, and I do see your point. But really, you are no match for a determined woman and a strong man."

Nora smiled. "I'm match enough," she said, hoping she exuded confidence she didn't feel.

"Well," Amanda said, "you'll obviously need help caring for this girl. I'll be back in the morning. I'll be your assistant until you can find this girl the help she needs." Amanda leaned closer. "I think we made progress today. She's really quite convincing about this Dark Ages thing. She asked more questions! I had no idea I knew so much about so little!" Amanda frowned. "She won't forget all of this by tomorrow, will she?"

"No," Nora said.

"Have you ever thought there is a real possibility that she is who she says she is?"

Nora peered at Amanda. Her no-nonsense mother, who wasn't even willing to believe in manned space flight, let alone magic. "What do you think?"

Amanda blinked, then leaned back. "If this is mental illness, then the girl should win an Academy Award."

"They don't give awards for illness, Mother. Only acting."

"That's what I mean."

"What's what you mean?"

"Crazy people aren't this consistent."

"And consistency makes her sane?"

"Well, she does believe what she's saying."

"And that makes her sane?"

"You know what I mean."

"Actually, Mother, I don't." Nora put her hand on her mother's back as she opened the door. "But I'm willing to go with it, whatever you mean, as long as you don't tell anyone about Emma."

"You know me," Amanda said, placing her index finger over her mouth. "Mum's the word."

"Good," Nora said. "Staying for dinner?"

"No, dear. I'm quite exhausted by all this *thinking*. I don't know how you do it, day in and day out."

Nora suppressed a grin. "I get paid to."

"I hope so," Amanda said. "Emma claims not to know what money is."

"That's not a surprise either," Nora said.

"You seem quite calm about this."

"Actually," Nora said, "I'm too overwhelmed to be upset."

"That seems sensible, my dear," Amanda said. "No use wasting energy on things we can't change."

Then Amanda pulled open the door and let herself out of the bathroom. She made her way through the bedroom, calling out some nonsense to Emma. Nora remained there for a moment, holding on to the tile countertop for support. She would make it through this day, she promised herself. She had to. There were only a few hours left. And if she was lucky, she would wake up tomorrow and realize that this was a long, extended, extremely detailed version of her reoccurring nightmare.

No such luck, of course. That was her first thought as she struggled out of sleep, hearing the doorbell chime below. She glanced at her digital clock. It read 1:30 a.m.

She had been in bed a little under two hours. It had taken her forever to convince Emma to go to sleep. She had the feeling Emma was angling for sharing a room, so that she could hear the comfort of Nora's breathing. But Nora had to draw the line somewhere. Besides, sharing a room in this loft also meant sharing a bed, and Nora wasn't about to do that, no matter how responsible she felt toward Emma.

The doorbell chimed again. Nora threw back the covers, imagining Emma cowering in her own room, worrying about the strange sound. Nora slipped on a robe but couldn't find any slippers. She hurried down the spiral staircase, the metal cold against her bare feet, and looked through the peephole at her guest.

She saw no one.

Great, she thought. A phantom caller. Just what she needed. Life had gotten strange today, and it seemed it was going to continue being strange. Her heart was pounding. Did opening a door make someone invited? Was this a trick that Ealhswith was playing on her? Or, God forbid, Blackstone?

Then, through the peephole, she saw a tiny hand rise out of the darkness and strain to reach the door chime. Even though she was expecting it, the sound made her jump.

She pulled the door open a smidge, leaving the chain on, and looked down. Sancho Panza, or whatever his name was, stood before her, his hand just going down to his side.

"It's about time," he said.

"It's the middle of the night."

"I'd be having breakfast in France," he said.

"You're not in France."

"More's the pity."

He was wearing a natty ice-cream suit and a bowler that made him look like something out of Renoir. She stared at him. He would also be at home in a Fred Astaire movie, one of the early shipboard romances—was that *Top Hat*?—with Ginger Rogers, or on stage with the Broadway musical *Ragtime*, even though she doubted he would have fit all that well into E.L. Doctorow's book. He was too short. Not that he was tall enough for the stage, either. And he would have made Fred Astaire look like a giant—

"Are you going to let me in, or do I get to stand in this wretched hallway until dawn?"

She blinked. Boy, she was tired if she let herself go on mental tangents like that. "I don't receive clients in my home. Office hours are nine to five."

She started to close the door, but he stuck his foot in it. "You weren't at your office at nine this morning, were you?"

"Yesterday morning," she said. "It's tomorrow already."

"*Were you?*"

"If you don't know, you're the only one in your social set who doesn't."

He grinned. He had been toying with her, testing her. She hated that. She pushed his polished spat with her bare foot, trying to get it out of her door. "I'm going back to bed," she said.

"Not yet." He reached into his pocket and pulled out a pile of paper that didn't look as if it had fit into the space. She recognized one piece. It was a birth certificate, with Emma's name on it.

Her new name.

"I told you," Nora said. "I don't deal in illegal documents."

"Neither do I," Sancho said. Then his grin widened. "Do you really want to have this meeting in your office?"

She sighed and pushed on the door. "If you want me to let you in, you need to move your damn foot."

He did. She toyed for a moment with shutting him out entirely but decided she still wouldn't get any sleep. He would continually ring the door chime or knock or do something to keep her awake.

She unchained the door and opened it. Sancho's hand was hovering near the chime. "Thought you forgot me," he said.

"Wish I could," she muttered. "Come on in."

He did. She closed and locked the door behind him. Then she surveyed the living room, wondering why the sound hadn't awakened Emma. Maybe it had. Maybe she really was cringing in her room.

"Excuse me a moment," Nora said as she flicked on a light. "I'll be right back."

She went down the hallway to Emma's room, knocked, and then pushed the door open. Emma was asleep, her hands beneath her perfect oval face, her long hair sprawled around her. She looked like a princess, a fairy-tale princess, like the ones in the cartoons Nora had seen as a child, or the detailed illustrations that had lined her favorite children's books.

Darnell was sprawled in Emma's hair. He looked up at Nora, his yellow eyes catching the light. His expression was not pleasant.

"I'm the one who feeds you," Nora whispered.

It didn't seem to make a difference to him at all.

She sighed and went in closer to see if Emma was faking, but her breathing was soft and even. Nora whispered her name, and Emma did not respond. Good. The girl probably was exhausted, even though she had slept for a thousand years. Her brain probably ached from all the things she had seen, heard, and learned that day.

Nora tiptoed out of the room and pulled the door closed. Then she went back to the living room. The little man had turned on more lights. He was standing beside the unshuttered window in the kitchen, staring at the city.

"Nice view," he said.

She didn't answer. Instead she went back up the stairs to her bedroom and changed into a pair of jeans and a T-shirt. She had felt at a disadvantage, talking to a man in a suit in her living room, even if that man were Sancho Panza.

When she went back down, he was on the sofa, the identification papers spread like cards on the coffee table. He was perusing them as if they were a tarot deck.

"We can't use them," she said.

He looked up at her. "Why not?"

"Because you couldn't have gotten them legally."

"And you can?" He perched on the edge of the couch like a little boy, his feet not touching the floor. His bowler was on her favorite chair. Before sitting down, she removed the hat and put it on an end table.

"Of course you have no answer for that. Why would you? Why would anyone?" He smiled. "You haven't encountered anything like this before."

"And you have?"

"Just once," he said. "But the thousand years spanned a less complicated time."

Her entire body stiffened. "How old are you, exactly?"

"Exactly?" He ran a hand through his short hair. "I'm not sure exactly. Calendars have changed a lot since I was born. If you use the Julian system, then I'm one age; the ancient Egyptian, another; and the current system, I am a third age. Add to that the fact that no one recorded the moment of my birth and you have quite a mess."

She sighed. "Do you always give such rambling answers to such easy questions?"

"Do you always ask such difficult questions expecting easy answers?"

She decided once more that she didn't like him. She leaned forward, examining the identification. It looked complete. Everything was here, from a birth certificate to a passport to that special ID card that was given to people who didn't qualify for a driver's license. All of them listed Emma's age as twenty and her last name as Lost, even though Nora had told no one that was what she had chosen.

"How did you know Emma's last name?" she asked.

"It was in the air." He glanced at her sideways. "Did you wake her?"

"Emma? No."

"Well, you have to. I'm here to take her away."

"And how do you figure to do that?"

"You're done. The job I hired you for is over. You can keep whatever remains in your escrow account as payment for a service satisfactorily rendered."

Nora's hands felt clammy. "My office will issue you a refund in the morning."

"No—"

"I don't need any more money."

He smiled. "True enough." He started picking up the ID. "So, would you get her for me?"

"No," Nora said.

"No?" He reacted in much the same way Blackstone had. Did no one say no to these people?

"No."

"Why not?"

"Because Emma's my client now."

"She can't be. She has no identity, no money, and— it's some sort of conflict, isn't it?"

"No," Nora said.

"But you were to guard her for me. And then when I came for her, you were done."

Nora shook her head. She was waking up and spoiling for a fight. She hadn't realized it, but she had been spoiling for a real fight all day. "You asked me to guard a microbus and its contents. You said nothing about a woman."

"She was in the microbus. You know that. You helped her get out this morning."

"For all I know, she crawled in this morning, and I helped her escape," Nora said.

Sancho narrowed his eyes. For some reason, that look on him scared her a lot more than it had when Ealhswith had made the same expression. "I asked you to guard Emma."

"I can show you my notes from the time," Nora said. "I keep detailed notes. But I also have an excellent memory. And I believe what you said to me was that you wanted me to store the microbus. You gave me a little worksheet to show how you came up with the figures for my payment, and on top was the phrase 'Microbus Storage.' I told you I would not inspect the contents of that bus, and I would not relinquish the keys to anyone but you."

"Then why did you?"

"Why did I what?"

"Inspect the contents of the bus."

"I didn't."

"You have Emma."

"I opened the back because I had been having horrible nightmares. There I found an envelope with my name on it. I followed the instructions in the envelope."

"Seems like you broke your word."

"I did not."

He shrugged. "She was in my bus."

"As of this morning," Nora said. "But no human could be in there for ten years."

"Who says she's human?"

"Who says she's not?"

They glared at each other. "You're going to be difficult about this, aren't you?" he asked, and she could swear that she thought he was suppressing a grin.

"No," she said. "I'm just sick of the way that Emma's been treated."

"Really?"

"Really. Your friend Blackstone thinks that she will just run into his arms after he's robbed her of centuries."

"Don't judge him too harshly."

"Why not?"

"Because you don't know the whole story."

"Do you?"

He shook his head. "I think it's still playing out."

"Would it make a difference if I did know the whole story?"

"Probably not," Sancho said. He shoved the ID at her. "You'll need this."

"I can't use illegal ID."

"You won't. Emma will." Then he frowned. "She is all right, isn't she?"

"No," Nora said. "She's scared and traumatized and thoroughly confused by this world. And she won't accept Blackstone's help to get her through the hurdles."

"I thought you wouldn't let her accept Blackstone's help."

"Magically. He said he can give her a memory of the last thousand years."

"Stupid infant," Sancho said. "That's not what she needs."

"Oh?" Nora asked. "What does she need?"

"A good teacher. And frankly, my dear, you're not it."

"Why not?"

"What were the Europeans doing to the pagans in 1575?"

"Burning them, I assume."

"Assume." He frowned. "And the Chinese?"

"What about them?"

"What were they doing to people with magical abilities in 1575?"

"Our 1575?"

"Your 1575."

She shrugged. She didn't know enough about Chinese culture to know if they had a particular attitude toward magic or not.

"What about the Jews?"

"What about them?"

"When, if ever, did they accept the wisdom of the Kabbala?"

"The Kabbala?"

"What about Africans?"

"What about them?"

"How did they feel about magic?"

"When? In 1575?"

"Sure, for the sake of argument."

"I don't know," she said.

"Clearly," he said. "You know so little that you didn't even ask me which tribe."

"I didn't ask you that about Europe, either."

"I assumed you knew."

"Don't assume," she said.

"Exactly."

"I don't know anyone who would know all that," she said.

"Except me, Blackstone, and Ealhswith."

"I'm not having any of you get near Emma."

"I can."

"No," she said. "You can't. I met you as Blackstone's friend. Right now, he's a danger to her."

"Says you."

"Says Emma."

"As if she knows. He's protected her for a thousand years."

"So you say."

"Can't you believe the evidence of your own eyes?"

"What I've seen makes me wonder if he stole her from Ealhswith, who, granted, wasn't taking good care of her either. I have to go with that."

"You have to go with your heart."

That stopped her. "What does that mean?"

He grinned. "You know."

"Just because Blackstone is good-looking and charming doesn't mean I'll accept whatever he does."

"I didn't say that."

"You were implying it."

"No, I wasn't." He chuckled. "But I like your misunderstanding."

In spite of herself, she blushed. "You need to get out of here."

"No, I don't," he said. "You invited me in."

"Now I'm uninviting you. Get out."

"You still have something that's mine."

"If you're referring to Emma, you're about a hundred years out of date. People can't be property anymore."

"Actually, I was referring to my microbus. I want it back."

"Fine," she said. "Come to my office tomorrow. We'll liquidate the escrow account, and I'll give you your keys."

"Give them to me now."

"No," she said. "We're going to be official about this."

He grinned. "You like to say no."

"Not really."

"Yes, really. And you're good at it. This is so wonderful."

"I don't see why it's wonderful," she said.

"You will," he said. "Believe me. You will."

Ultimately Nora chickened out and left the identification for Amanda to explain to Emma. Nora had trouble enough with the shower. The idea of bathing every day was apparently a novel one to someone from the Dark Ages. Which was why, Nora supposed, as she grabbed a bowl of cereal before heading to the office, they were called the Dark Ages. It was probably a bastardization of their real name: the Dirt Ages.

At least Emma hadn't screamed when she went into the shower, but she had cringed for a very long time. It took Nora a while to figure out that Emma was also afraid of the hot water, after her experience the day before. Nora turned the water temperature from frigid to lukewarm, and Emma was happy. At least she was happy until Nora showed her the soap.

Emma came out of the bathroom looking fresh and rosy and even more beautiful than before. She made Nora's favorite sundress look much better than Nora did. Darnell followed Emma wherever she went; he hadn't even shown up for breakfast that morning, the little traitor. Which made Squidgy happy. She had all the food to herself.

For a ten-year-old cat, Darnell sure was loose with his affections. Particularly when, in the past, he wouldn't give anyone except Nora the time of day.

Nora left the moment Amanda arrived, not willing to answer any more questions abut how cereal was made; where the cows were; how the refrigerator worked, and why she wore shoes that elevated her several inches off the ground. As Nora walked out the door, she promised Amanda some help in the next day or so, and she gave her permission to take Emma to a small park nearby. Fortunately Portland was a city of parks—it had, Nora once heard, more parks per capita than any other city in the nation. What it meant for her was that she didn't have to go far to find greenery.

Nora did make her mother promise to take her cell phone along and not to let Emma out of her sight.

The office, after the chaos of her house, was a welcome respite. It didn't matter that the staff had a million questions for her or that her message pile had duplicated. It didn't matter that Max's attorney wanted yet another list of the assets that Nora had taken from their joint home, unwilling to believe, she supposed, the first one. This one she would have to sign and notarize. The next step would probably be to get a deposition or a court order to search her loft. At some point, she would have to have her own attorney call Max and remind him that Nora was not a prosecutor, trying to hide her tactics to get Max put away on federal charges.

She breezed through the partner's meeting, skipping over her business with Emma and the reason she had met with Blackstone. That was one of the nice things about owning her own law firm; she didn't have to answer to anyone. They all had to answer to her.

Her mood was almost buoyant when she went to her own office. The mood collapsed immediately when she saw both Sancho and Blackstone waiting in Ruthie's uncomfortable chairs.

Ruthie looked at Nora with a pained expression on her face. "I asked them to wait in reception," she said. "Somehow they talked me into letting them remain here."

That was twice in two days Blackstone had made Ruthie do something out of character. Nora would have to forbid him from using even tiny magic spells on her secretary.

"Into my office," she snapped. "Now."

Sancho jumped off the chair and saluted. He wasn't wearing his suit anymore. Instead, he had on a polo shirt and a pair of khakis. Blackstone looked positively underdressed next to him, wearing what Nora was beginning to see as his signature T-shirt and jeans.

She opened her office door, and even the sight of the city, spread out before her, did not please her. She could see haze forming over the river, indicating that the day would be both hot and gray. Just what her mood needed.

She set her briefcase down but did not go to her chair. Instead, she turned, leaned on her desk, and waited until the men came into her office.

It took Blackstone a moment; he was giving Ruthie a small rose—where he got it, Nora had no idea. He hadn't been holding it a moment before. Ruthie looked pleased and embarrassed at her own pleasure, all at the same time.

When Blackstone entered and closed the door, Nora said, "Stop toying with my secretary."

He grinned at her, that full-watt kick-you-in-the-stomach grin that got her every time. "Jealous?"

"No," she said a little too fast. "I just don't like Ruthie being played with."

"Protective."

"At times."

"You two understand each other better than you know," Sancho said, and hoisted himself into the nearest chair.

"I know why you're here," she said to Sancho. "Why did you bring him?"

"I thought you missed him."

"I kicked him out of my office yesterday."

"So he said," Sancho said.

Nora sighed. She reached into her top desk drawer and removed the microbus keys, along with the key to the lock. Then she wrote down the name of the storage place and the garage number. She pressed the intercom and told Ruthie to figure out the amount left in the escrow, minus this month's fees, and to close the account, giving the remaining money back to Sancho in the form of a check.

"I believe that's all our business, isn't it?" she asked coolly.

"Not really," he said. "I would like the opportunity to speak to Emma."

"I'll ask her about it."

Sancho nodded as if he had expected as much. Then he turned to Blackstone. Blackstone glared at him. Sancho glared back.

"Is this for my benefit, or can you two stare at each other elsewhere?" Nora asked.

"I think Blackstone would like to ask you a question," Sancho said.

"Then he should ask it. I have a long day ahead," Nora said.

Sancho got down off the chair. "I'm going to check on the check," he said.

"Why does this feel like a setup?" Nora asked as Sancho left.

"Because it is," Blackstone said. He remained in the back of the room. He hadn't come close at all this time, and she got the sense that he was nervous. "Look, you and I started off on the wrong foot."

"Not really," she said, her grip tightening on the desk.

"I mean, I would like to talk to you a little, get to know you better."

"So you can grill me about Emma?"

"No, actually," he said, sounding confused, as if he couldn't understand why she would think such a thing.

"Then why didn't it come up before now? You met me ten years ago. That may not be a lot of time to you, but best-case scenario, that's one tenth of my life."

He smiled. "You were interested in Max."

She frowned. "How did you know?"

"The three wishes."

"What?"

"I granted you three wishes. Success. Financial independence, and Max."

Her mouth opened, then shut, then opened again. She didn't say anything for the longest time, and when she finally could get her vocal chords functioning again, she said, "If you granted me three wishes, and Max was one of them, I should be living happily ever after by now."

Blackstone shook a finger at her. "That wasn't one of the wishes."

"I never *asked* you for anything."

"You didn't have to," he said. "You were radiating desire."

That wasn't for Max, you idiot, she almost blurted. But she caught herself in time. "You can read minds?" she asked, a second too late.

"No," he said. "But people's wishes are usually clear enough, if you observe them."

"And you observed that the greatest desires in my life were success, wealth, and Max?"

"Not wealth, exactly," he said. "Enough money to get by."

"Well, I have that." She went around her desk to her chair and sat down hard. "And so what you're saying is that all of this was your doing. None of it was mine."

He rolled his eyes, then sat in the chair Sancho had vacated. "Why can't women take gifts?"

"Don't lump me into a category with other women."

"Why not?"

"Because—" she stopped herself. Then her eyes narrowed. "You've done this before."

"Many times."

"To women."

"Of course."

"You're a bigger idiot than I thought."

He frowned at her. "That's a hell of a way to say thank you."

"For telling me I haven't done anything in ten years."

"Jesus, Nora," he snapped. "You did. I made sure you had enough money to get by when Sancho gave you the escrow and when Max gave you that finder's fee. You did the rest."

"Success?" she asked.

"At the time, success to you was keeping the doors of your office open."

He was right, but she didn't want him to see it. The fight she had been spoiling for had finally arrived.

"And Max?"

"You were never going to ask him out, and he was so damn shy that I figured I'd give you both a nudge."

"And see where it got us? Thousands of dollars in legal fees."

"You can afford it."

She glared at him.

He shrugged one shoulder. The gesture was winning, but she wasn't in the mood to be won. "Didn't you have some good years?" he asked.

They did. Those first years were fun. When they were still young attorneys, when they really didn't have money or a decent place to live. The time that Darnell (damn that cat) had jumped on the counter and taken six bites out of the beef roast they were going to serve Max's boss—six separate bites, from different parts of the roast—and Max and Nora had spent a giggly, frightened few moments figuring out how to carve the damn thing (the roast, not the cat) so that they could serve it without embarrassment. The trip to the coast that they couldn't afford. The long Sunday afternoons watching old movies and eating ice cream, the afternoons that always ended in bed.

Blackstone was watching her too closely.

"What?" she asked. "A year or two is the duration of wishes these days?"

He grinned. "You did have some good times."

"I'd have been stupid to marry Max if I didn't. And I'm not stupid." She pushed her chair away from her desk. As she did so, her gaze caught the stack of waiting messages. Even though she wanted to keep fighting with this man—she wanted to do anything to keep ...in in her office, fight or not—she needed to get to work. She had a lot to do, and not all of it concerned Emma.

"So let me get this straight," she said. "Ten years ago, you granted me three wishes, and now you're using that fact like a trump card so that you can spend time with me."

He shrugged again, only this time it was the other shoulder, and this gesture was more affecting than the first one.

"And you want to spend time with me because you find me charming and witty and utterly involving."

"I do want to get to know you better."

She nodded. "And keep tabs on Emma even though you won't visit her."

"Unfair, Nora."

"No, it's not." She pulled her chair closer to the desk and went into tough attorney mode. "Frankly, *Mr*. Blackstone, I'm very disappointed in you. I thought you were smooth and convincing. I thought you could charm the pants off a snake." Then she paused. "Although, come to think of it, I never did see pants on your snake. What happened to it, anyway?"

"It died," he said flatly.

"Sorry. Heartbreaking."

"Yes, actually."

She wasn't going for the sympathy. She couldn't muster any for a snake anyway. "You have been obvious and lame and insulting this morning. If you wanted something from me, you should have asked for it—"

"I did," he said. "Yesterday I asked for time with Emma."

"See?" Nora said. "I knew this was about Emma."

"And this morning I've asked for time with you. I am asking for what I want."

"In a way that guarantees that you won't get it."

"You would prefer me to charm you like I've been charming the efficient Ruthie? Hmm? When I came in here, you berated me for doing that very thing."

"Ruthie was unsuspecting."

He leaned closer to her. Leather again. Why did she find the scent of leather so sexy? Maybe she didn't. Maybe it was that faint scent beneath it, that touch of him.

"People who are being charmed aren't supposed to know it," he said. "That's part of the charm."

When she didn't respond, he leaned closer. If she raised her fingers, she could touch the skin on his face. She wondered if it would be as smooth as the skin on his hand had been, if it would be as warm, if it would feel as familiar as her own.

"I could manipulate you, Nora, if that's what you want. Silly me," he said, "I thought you were the kind of woman who liked to think for herself, who appreciated a man for what he is."

"What are you, Mr. Blackstone?" She kept her voice cool, which ultimately amazed her, considering how jumpy her insides were. "A man who seduces women? A man who lies to women? A man who considers women possessions?"

"Not fair."

"Not fair? What are you then?"

"A man who thought he had found someone he could talk to," he said. "A man who is profoundly disappointed."

Then he blinked, as if he couldn't believe what he had just said, and leaned back. He shook his head once and stood.

"Mr. Blackstone?"

He turned. "You know, I've never met anyone who pisses me off like you do."

"Except Ealhswith."

"Not even Ealhswith. I just hate her. You—I come in

here, thinking I can have a rational discussion, and I end up yelling like a berserker."

"A what?"

"A soldier, you know, one who has—the word berserk, ah, you know—they were prevalent after the Hundred Years War—oh, hell." He spread his arms out. "I am babbling. I haven't babbled in centuries. Damn, woman, what are you doing to me?"

"Saying no," she said sweetly. "Apparently you people aren't used to it."

He stared at her for a moment, and as he did, an entire symphony of emotions played in his eyes. With each mood they seemed to change color, from silver to gray to blue to black to brown and back to silver again. Nora watched the changes, mesmerized.

"You did say no, didn't you?" he said, almost to himself. "And I'm not listening. I haven't listened at all, which is also not like me. I'm usually quite a good listener. When it doesn't matter."

He shoved his hands in his pockets and bowed his head. She could no longer see those marvelous eyes, and she wanted to.

"You've said no," he continued, "and Emma has said go away, and Sancho told me years ago to change my attitude toward the coffin and Ealhswith, and I haven't listened to a one of you."

He raised his head. His eyes were so pale, she almost couldn't see them. "Well, I'm listening now." He took a deep breath. "I'm going. It's been a real pleasure knowing you, Miss—Mrs.—Ms. Barr. I promise I will never charm your secretary again."

He stared at her for a moment, and when she said

nothing, he bowed. The movement was sweet and elegant, his right arm sweeping out as if he were removing his hat with a flourish. She could imagine him in sixteenth century French clothing—the ruffles and feathers of *The Three Musketeers* fame—and it suited him as well as the jeans and T-shirt did now. She started to reach for him, but he rose, turned, and left her office so quickly that she was still in half a movement as her door slammed closed.

She stared at it for a moment. She had told him to leave, but she hadn't wanted him to. She wasn't ready for him to walk out of her life like that. But that was what she had asked. That was what she had demanded.

She almost ran after him, but her own pride stopped her. What if that was what he wanted? What if this were still part of the game he had played with her from the beginning? Three wishes and sleeping beauties and evil stepmothers.

And magic. Always magic.

She sat back down at her desk. She would take care of Emma first. Then she would worry about Blackstone.

The thought seemed rational, and it should have calmed her. But it didn't. As she picked up her stack of messages, she found herself worrying, wondering, doubting she would ever see him again.

Blackstone drove himself back to the restaurant, taking side streets and gunning the Porsche, daring a cop to pull him over. No cop did, and he was disappointed. He wanted to fight with someone, get arrested, and then reverse the whole thing as if nothing had happened.

But no one seemed to notice his speed. No one except an elderly woman who had been walking her black poodle. She had shaken a finger at him as he passed.

Sancho hadn't been in Ruthie's office when Blackstone left. The efficient Ruthie had blinked at him with a bit of confusion when he asked about Sancho and had said in what Blackstone knew was not Ruthie's normal voice, "He disappeared."

In front of her, probably. To freak her out. Sancho was like that. Blackstone had never entirely gotten the point of unsettling the mortals.

Except for Nora, of course.

And she appeared utterly unflappable.

He didn't know where that bit about the three wishes had come from. He had actually reminded himself, as he got up that morning, not to mention them to her. The last time he had granted a woman three wishes, she had nearly torn his eyes out. That had been about 1750, and he had vowed never to do such a thing again.

Apparently resolutions only lasted 250 years.

He pulled the car into his private space behind the restaurant and got out. Three other cars were in the lot. He unlocked the kitchen door and entered to the smell of sautéed garlic and onions mixing with the fresh scent of cilantro. Two of his chefs, dressed in their regulation whites, were hovering over a large soup kettle, discussing the fine art of spices. His sous chef was working on a roux at the far stove.

Blackstone had designed this kitchen himself. It had several stove tops, half a dozen grills, and three restaurant-size dishwashers. It also had seven small ovens and two large ovens, an emergency microwave, which he had banished to the back, and several refrigerators, including one large enough to stuff six men inside. The freezer, which stood to one side, filled a room all on its own.

Sancho was standing beside the baker, pulling apart a just-completed loaf of sourdough. Blackstone's baker, a woman who had won more contests than the rest of the staff combined, was glaring at Sancho, pastry scissors clutched in her left hand.

"You know I don't like anyone eating in the kitchen," Blackstone said, taking the loaf from Sancho.

"Well, your maître goon won't let me in the dining room," Sancho said.

"Then maybe you should take that as a hint."

"Touchy, touchy." Sancho snatched the bread back. "I take it the meeting didn't go well."

"That woman is the most stubborn, difficult—" Blackstone stopped himself. His staff was staring at him. He never lost his temper—at least, not over a woman. Occasionally over a poorly created dish. But never over a woman. "Come into my office."

He led Sancho past the wire racks filled with pots, pans, and simple white dishes to the closet-size room he used as an office. On one corner of the desk sat a computer, its screen covered with tiny fish, and a phone sat on the other corner. In between were order forms, index cards filled with his scrawled recipes, and bills. Blackstone shoved them aside and leaned against the desk.

"She won't let me see Emma," he said.

"She won't let me see her either," Sancho said. "She has a good point."

"Does she?" Blackstone asked. "It seems to me that she's just being stubborn."

Sancho grinned. "Then you're well matched."

"I was talking about Nora."

"So was I."

They glared at each other for a moment. Then Blackstone broke the glance. "I didn't expect her to be so much trouble."

"Nora or Emma?"

"Both," Blackstone said.

Sancho shook his head. "I've been trying to warn you. You've been handling this all wrong. Right from the start."

Blackstone pushed off the desk and wished there was more space in the office. He didn't want to be this close to Sancho. "I was a young magician. I didn't know the right spells."

"We've been over this," Sancho said. "I'm not talking about the first spell. I'm talking about the fight with Ealhswith."

"You think I should have left Emma with her?"

"No," Sancho said. "But you have to understand why Emma's a bit peeved."

Blackstone ran a hand through his hair. "I do understand." He sighed. "Nora got through to me on that."

Sancho's smile widened. It was as if he had a secret he didn't want to share with Blackstone. "Nora's pretty special, isn't she?"

"I'm promised to Emma."

"You keep saying that." Sancho crossed his arms. "It's almost like you're trying to convince yourself."

"The Fates said she was my soul mate."

"Did they?"

Blackstone sighed. He wished they hadn't, but they had. "Yes, that's what they said."

"Sometimes I think your memory is faulty."

"And sometimes I think you want the impossible from me." Blackstone had to work to keep his voice low. "I need your help getting Emma away from Nora."

"I don't think it'll work."

"But Ealhswith'll go after them."

"Probably," Sancho said.

"And they're undefended."

"I think if the illustrious Ms. Barr heard you say that, she'd show you just how defended she is."

Blackstone bowed his head. He had been admiring her courage just the day before. He knew she was strong. And she had gotten to him this morning. She had shown him how he hadn't listened—to anyone. He had created a part of this mess, as surely as Ealhswith had.

Maybe it was time to start listening, then.

"What do you think I should do?" he asked softly.

Sancho's eyes widened, as if he hadn't expected to be consulted for advice. "You're asking me?"

"I think you're the only other person in the room."

"Well." Sancho cleared his throat. "I think you should do what the ladies want."

"I should leave them alone?"

Sancho nodded.

"But Ealhswith—"

"Will do something, and eventually it'll be too much for Nora, and she'll come to you for help. You can be her white knight."

"I don't think she believes in white knights."

Sancho's eyes twinkled. "Not now, maybe."

Blackstone shook his head. "I don't want to manipulate her."

"Interesting," Sancho said. "Why not?"

Because he liked her too much for that. But he couldn't admit it to Sancho. Some things had to remain personal. "I don't think the Fates would approve."

"When has that stopped you?" Sancho asked.

"If I leave Emma and Nora alone, they'll be in so much danger."

"Then keep an eye on them. A discreet eye."

"And what happens if I get caught?"

Sancho shrugged. "Nora'll yell at you again."

"She doesn't like me much, does she?"

Sancho raised his eyebrows. "Oh, I think she likes you more than she wants to admit."

Blackstone sighed. "This hasn't gone the way I planned, Sancho."

Sancho stared at him for a moment, then nodded sagely. "Love never does."

Chapter 8

NORA SPENT THE NEXT TWO DAYS CATCHING UP ON work—it was amazing how far behind she got when she skipped a single day—going to court, answering calls, taking care of cases. She bent her own rules because she couldn't think of a way around them and used the identification that Sancho brought to create an identity for Emma. Her mother spent days with Emma and Nora spent evenings, and the questions were slowly getting less intense.

Nora was even beginning to tolerate her mother's presence at dinner.

Darnell, on the other hand, didn't even acknowledge Nora's existence anymore. Squidgy liked this turn of events; she was acting as if she were the only cat in the house. Darnell was acting as if Emma were the only person; Nora felt it only fair.

Emma was slowly beginning to accept some of the bits of daily life in this world: the noise, the plumbing, and the food. She didn't like the way that everything seemed to be too difficult to be made at home. She wanted to make her own soap (even though she loved the lavender-scented specialty soaps that Nora had bought to soothe herself after her divorce), her own clothes (Amanda suggested buying fabric but Emma wanted to weave her own) and her own shoes (Nora drew the line at running a tanning operation out of her own home). They found a spinning wheel at an antique store and placed it in

Emma's room, and somewhere Nora's mother managed to get unspun wool (which Nora thought looked like a pile of Squidgy's hair balls). When Emma got too over-whelmed, she went and spun. She was asking for a loom next, and Nora's mother promised to look for one on one of her evenings off.

Nora didn't know what she would have done without her mother. It was Amanda who realized that going to the nearest park, even armed with a cell phone, was a bad idea. There were too many strange people about. So Amanda decided to drive Emma to greenery, thinking it would get Emma used to the car, and reward her by letting her be in nature. Nora's mother also made sure that they didn't follow any set routine, and often she used different cars. She and Nora traded vehicles more than once, and Nora's mother had taken to going to car dealerships and test-driving new models, taking Emma and the poor salesman to some park for a picnic as part of the ruse.

In addition to all her catch-up, Nora spent the last two days interviewing professors. Most came in because they were curious—law firms rarely hired medieval his-tory professors for deep research—and most were com-pletely unsuited to what she needed. She didn't know what she was looking for exactly, but she would know it when she saw it.

The last interview on Friday proved to be the one she was waiting for. The man who walked into the room looked like he had been transplanted from a previous era. His salt-and-pepper hair (which was more pepper than salt) had been combed once, but on the way to the office it had obviously been tossed by the wind, and he hadn't noticed. His salt-and-pepper beard (which was more salt than pepper) had been trimmed, but still looked as if it were waiting to explode into an unruly thicket. He wore a woolen suit coat despite the heat, and a wrinkled cotton shirt with matching cotton pants. Unlike all the other professors, he didn't wear Birkenstocks. He wore normal sandals. His toes were long and hairy, and Nora found herself thinking of hobbits as she looked at his feet.

"Ms. Barr?" he asked, extending a hand as compact as his feet. "I'm Jeffrey Chawsir."

She had seen the name written down, of course, but it wasn't until he said it that she realized how it was pronounced—and what it sounded like.

"You've got to be kidding," she said before she stopped herself.

He shrugged. "It's spelled different."

"But you're a professor of medieval studies. Don't you think that's a bit of coincidence to be named after Geoffrey Chaucer, author of the most famous piece of fiction from that period?"

"Actually," he said, "*Canterbury Tales* postdates my period. I specialize in the twelfth century, not the fourteenth." Then he grinned. It was the grin that sold her. It was crooked and warm and made his face like that of a Disney grandfather about to dispense wisdom. "Besides, a man has to start somewhere."

"Meaning?"

"After a while, a boy gets tired of hearing 'you've got to be kidding' after he introduces himself to adults."

"I went to school with a Tom Sawyer," Nora said. "No one said 'you've got to be kidding' to him."

He shrugged. "With him, they probably thought it was

a mistake on his parents' part. After all, Tom is a common name, and so is Sawyer. But Chawsir isn't, and Jeffrey, well, men my age are usually named John or David or Michael. People think my parents did it on purpose."

"Did they?"

"Yes and no," he said. "My mother's father was named Jeffrey. They thought it would work. I'm the first person in my family to finish college, let alone high school."

"So it wasn't intentional."

"Not in the way you're thinking."

She held out her hand and indicated the chair. "Please, have a seat."

He did, and as he sat, he adjusted the line of his trousers. She hadn't seen a man do that in years. She leaned on the desk, something she often did when she was interviewing people. It didn't seem to upset him.

"I must say," he said in a professorial tone, "I've been very curious about this. This is my first time in a law firm."

"Really?" she said. That was unusual in this litigious age. "Not divorced?"

"Never married."

"And obviously never sued."

"Or accused of a crime." He grinned that crooked grin again. "A boring life."

"Only if your requirements for an interesting one force you to go to a lawyer's office."

He laughed.

She leaned back. "I can't tell you what this is for, at least not yet. So please, bear with me."

He nodded.

"I need honest answers from you. I've already

received assessments from your dean and from some students and colleagues. Now I need to find out how comfortable you are with certain things."

"All right," he said that with a measure of caution, like he was humoring a difficult child.

"Do you mind tutoring someone?"

"Not at all."

"Would you be willing to spend eight hours a day tutoring someone?"

"For the right fee. And if the job could be completed before the semester begins at the end of September."

She ignored that part. She would deal with that when it happened. She doubted Emma would be ready for anything by the end of September. That was a very short two and a half months away.

"Do you feel strong in world history from the Dark Ages to the present?"

"Strong? My specialty is the Middle Ages."

"For example," she said. "If I were to ask you to name the presidents of the United States, could you?"

"Of course. I'm a history buff."

"Could you outline the history of Japan for me?"

"Now?"

She waited.

"Do you want me to start with the myth about the Emperor and his family descending from the sun, or with the formation of the Shogunate?"

She smiled. "That's plenty. Could you name the kings of England before William the Conqueror?"

"Not if I want to be accurate. There's some debate as to whether they were kings of England or simply strong leaders of particular regions."

Her smile grew. "Can you cook over a fire?"

"This involves camping?"

"No. A hearth fire."

"I've never done it. I know the principles."

"How about the principles of magic."

"What kind?" he asked. "I'm familiar with all the European varieties. I get the Persian ones confused."

She placed her hands on the side of her desk, holding onto its carved top. "If I told you I was a witch, you would say—?"

"Are you a member of Wicca or do you follow some of the darker arts?" He spoke with no judgment at all.

"And if I told you I knew actual magic, you would say—?"

"I would love to see some sometime."

She let out a large sigh of relief, stood up, and extended her hand. "Wonderful. You're hired."

"I don't even know what the job is."

"Purposely." She reached for the intercom and buzzed Ruthie. "Here's what I can tell you. This job requires strict confidentiality. You can't tell anyone—girlfriend, boyfriend, best friend, mother, father, anyone—what you're doing or where you go to do it. You must have an open mind, and you must work eight hours a day, at least five days a week. For that you will be paid the starting salary of my associates, which is"—she picked up a piece of paper and glanced at it—"exactly double what you earn at the university for the same amount of time."

He blinked at her, looking a bit confused. "I'd like to know what the job is."

"In order for me to tell you any more—"

Ruthie opened the door, brought papers in, and set them on the desk. As she did so, she glanced at the professor as if she couldn't believe what she was seeing. And then she left, closing the door behind her.

"—you'll have to sign these confidentiality documents and not tell anyone what you have seen."

"Is this some sort of case?"

"It's a bit stranger than that," Nora said. She handed him one of the documents. He scanned it.

"Ah, hell," he said. "I guess I can sign this. What's a few hours out of my life?"

"You might be surprised," she said.

Nora had had all of her interviewees checked out by her favorite private detective firm, but even so, she wasn't one to trust easily. Instead of taking Jeffrey Chawsir to her home, she had Amanda rent a hotel room in one of Portland's more exclusive hotels, not far from Nora's office. She called her mother and asked her to bring Emma to the hotel. Nora would bring Chawsir.

He signed the preliminary confidentiality documents and then they walked to the hotel. When they entered the gold-trimmed double glass doors of the hotel and stepped into the mahogany and gold lobby, he got visibly nervous.

Nora suppressed a smile. Did he think this was an elaborate seduction?

"You can relax, Professor," she said. "I'm holding the meeting here so that you know as little as possible, should you decide to back out of this."

He nodded, a tight nervous movement that meant he

wanted to believe her but didn't really. They entered the elevator and went to the eighth floor.

As they stepped off the elevator, she could hear her mother's voice, muffled, but filled with an unmistakable exasperation. "Bidet!" Amanda was saying. "It's a bidet!"

"Oh, shit," Nora whispered. She had taken care of all the bathroom explanations, and Emma hadn't liked a one of them. Nora sprinted for the room door, which wasn't too far from the elevator, and unlocked it. The professor still stood near the elevator.

"I do not understand 'bidet.' It makes no sense, if there is this toilet already." Emma. And she was raising her voice.

"Come on," Nora said to the professor, and then pushed the hotel room door open. "We're here!"

"Thank heavens!" Nora's mother said from the bathroom. "Will you explain to this child—"

"Mother," Nora said. "Both of us are here."

"Oh," Amanda said.

"The professor would like to meet his pupil," Nora said as the professor came in the room. She closed the door behind him. They were in a suite, with a small living room complete with couch, two easy chairs, a desk, and a large television set.

The professor frowned at Nora as if he couldn't quite imagine what he had walked into.

Emma came out of the bathroom. She was wearing her own pair of jeans (she had decided she liked jeans) and a loose-weave top that Nora's mother had found at some outdoor clothing stand. She looked angry, as she often did when confronted with cleanliness rituals.

Bodily functions were not her strong suit. At that moment, Nora promised herself that it was up to Amanda to explain tampons and gynecologists to Emma. It was about time Amanda explained those items to somebody; heaven knew she hadn't explained either to Nora.

Emma said, "I still do not comprehend all these items for such simple functions. It would seem to me that one sink and one hole in the ground would be sufficient—"

"Emma," Nora said, loudly, hoping to drown out the rest of Emma's words, "this is Professor Jeffrey Chawsir. He wants to meet you. He is considering helping you with your education."

Emma peered at him. He peered back, apparently not impressed by her beauty. Nora stared at him. He was the first man who hadn't looked at Emma as if she were a supermodel come to life.

"What sort of help do you need with your education?"

"Ah, everything," Nora's mother said from the bathroom. "The girl is a blank slate."

"That is not true," Emma said. "I am very well educated for my time."

"Your time was a long time ago, sweetie," Amanda said as she came out of the bathroom. She stopped when she saw the professor. Their eyes met, and Amanda actually blushed. Nora had never seen Amanda blush, not in thirty-five years, not through four husbands, and certainly not when anyone else would have blushed. "Jeffrey."

"Amanda." He held out his hands, took hers, and brought her in for a kiss that lasted a moment too long to be formal. Emma looked at Nora and raised her eyebrows. Nora shrugged in return.

The professor stepped back. He was blushing, just like Amanda was. "I never thought I would see you again."

"Never is a long time when you get as old as we are."

"You haven't aged a day since I saw you last."

Nora's mother laughed. "You still have that wicked way with a lie."

He took her hand and led her to the couch. "I didn't realize you were in Portland."

"I have been for decades," Amanda said, making the word sound like "days." "I didn't realize you were either."

"I'm not. I'm in Eugene, teaching medieval studies."

"Medieval studies. You've always enjoyed the past."

"Still enamored with the future?"

Nora's mother sighed. "Not like I was."

"Mother?" Nora asked.

Amanda glanced at the professor. "Jeffrey and I went to school together. High school."

"And part of college," he said.

Amanda looked down. "I don't like to think of that."

Nora had no idea her mother had gone to college. She had always insisted that Nora go, saying that without it, a girl had to depend on her man.

He kept Amanda's hand clasped in his. "Your daughter wants to hire me."

"I know," Amanda said. "It's to help me."

"Actually," Nora said. "It's to—"

Amanda shot her a look that meant be quiet in every language known to man.

"—help me," Emma said.

"I'm caring for the girl," Amanda said. "And believe me, she needs some help."

Emma scowled at that. Nora did too. "Let me tell him, Mother."

"No," Amanda said. "You two leave us. We'll discuss this."

"I can't take Emma out of here, Mother," Nora said.

"That's all right," the professor said. "I'll take the job."

"You don't even know what it is," Nora said.

He smiled. "I know all I have to," he said.

~~~

So they became a strange foursome, Nora, Emma, Amanda, and the professor. They worked out a system where Emma got her daily dose of education, Nora got her work done, and the professor and Amanda rekindled their friendship, whatever it had been. When Nora arrived home at night, she heard from Emma about all the wonderful things she had learned, from the evolution of clothing (one day's lesson) to an overview of the history of the western world (one week's lesson). The professor seemed to understand that his pupil was odd, and he obviously didn't agree with Amanda's explanation of why, but he didn't quiz Emma either, and he never brought it up to Nora. He simply did the work, and in doing so, calmed Emma more than Nora or Amanda ever could. It seemed that knowledge gave Emma strength, real knowledge, knowledge she could question, not the superficial knowledge that Blackstone had promised her.

Nora respected that about Emma. Emma seemed for all her apparent youth and confusion to know herself real well. She knew how she functioned, she knew how she learned, and she knew who she was, despite her drastic change of time zones. Nora wasn't that grounded in her own world. She couldn't imagine being that grounded in someone else's.

They spent a month like this. A month in which no one mentioned magic, or Blackstone, or Sancho—who hadn't even cashed his check—or Ealhswith. Nora wouldn't let her mother relax her vigilance, and neither, strangely, would the professor. Emma had no real desire to explore much beyond the apartment, the parks, and selected portions of the city. Those seemed to be more than enough for her, which, when Nora thought about it, made perfect sense.

They had finally settled into a routine, and Nora felt as if she could put the strangeness of the past month behind her, as she had put the original meeting with Blackstone and the subsequent burning of that neighborhood behind her. Her mood improved, her workload felt good, and the divorce was progressing.

And then, everything changed.

———ww———

It began with a call from another attorney. Hank Geffon was an older man, known for his work in difficult cases. He was good. He was expensive. He was quite apologetic.

"Nora," he said. "Do you have a client named Emma Lost?"

"Yes," she said. She was in her office, in the middle of some dictation, finishing a preliminary report in a case that she hoped wouldn't go past the judge. The question made her stiffen. How had another attorney learned of Emma?

"Do you know her mother, Ally Swith?"

"Ally Swith?" Nora asked, instantly on alert. Ealhswith? These people and their fake names. "My client's mother is dead."

"Hmm," Hank said. "I think we have a problem here, Nora. I'm going to have to send over some documents, unless you want to let me know how to reach Emma Lost."

"No can do, Hank. My client guards her privacy."

"So I hear."

Nora's hands had become clammy, but she had good control of her voice. "What else do you hear?"

"That Emma Lost has been institutionalized for the past decade or more. My client says she's tried this before. She's been declared incompetent. My client says that she's Emma's legal guardian."

"And she's her mother?"

"That too."

Nora couldn't remember what Sancho had put on the birth certificate. To be completely honest, she hadn't looked. Not that it mattered. The damn documents were fake.

"You're right, Hank. We do have a problem. Who is this Ally Swith?"

"She says she's your client's mother."

"I mean who is she, Hank? What does she do? Where does she live? Where's she from?"

"Nora, I think we're getting into an area we should avoid." His tone was ever so slightly patronizing. She felt her shoulders relax an inch. He didn't know. And he hadn't thought to ask.

"I don't think it's anything to avoid," Nora said.

"Let me send over the documents, and you can look them over. Then call your client. We'll proceed from there."

He hung up. Nora stared at the phone for a long time, then swore softly under her breath. She should have known better than to trust Sancho. Hadn't Max said, all those years ago, that Sancho had worked for Ealhswith? What if he'd been working for her all along? Nora had taken the documents because it was easier, because she didn't have to do it herself.

She closed her clammy hands into fists and counted to ten. She was getting way too worked up. She wasn't keeping her usual professional calm. Why? Because she already felt guilty about those documents. Maybe they could save her. Maybe Sancho had already taken care of those things.

Not that she would want them introduced as evidence in court. That would be all she needed; turning in fake (illegal!) documentation to a judge.

But not every case went to court, and as good and expensive as Hank was, he really hated to sweat. If she made him think this case would be difficult, then she might have him, no matter what Ealhswith did.

Slowly she unclenched her fists. Her breathing was becoming regular. What was it that Max told her, early on, during her first difficult case? There wasn't anything that a good attorney couldn't overcome. It wasn't about the truth, it was about the story and whose story was the best. If it did go to court, Nora's story would be the best, plain and simple. If. Court was a big if.

"Damn," she whispered again. She should have known that Ealhswith went away too easily. She had trusted it, had thought those simple words were enough to drive the woman away. She hadn't thought it through. The woman had fought Blackstone for the custody of

Emma for a thousand years. Why did Nora think she would suffer a different fate?

And what the hell was so important about Emma anyway that Ealhswith was willing to fight that hard? It wasn't about parenthood—she wasn't Emma's mother, or even her stepmother—and it couldn't be about mentoring. You'd think that after, say, two hundred years, even the most dedicated teacher would give up.

No. There had to be something else. And she would find out what it was.

—⁓—

"That's it for the first volley? That's it?"

Ealhswith paced around Hank Geffon's huge office. It was ostentatious, with too much brass trim and mahogany furniture. A man's office, a place that projected the wrong kind of power.

What had she been thinking coming here?

"Trust me, Mrs. Swith. We must proceed slowly." Geffon's unctuous voice grated on her nerves. She turned, wondering if he would look better as a monkey or a mouse. He was fat and balding and wore a suit that was worth more than his sofa.

A snake. Some sort of reptile. Something without a voice box.

Her fingers twitched, but she held them tightly against her. She couldn't change him, not here, not in his office.

"Slowly?" she said. "All we've been doing is go slow. I came to you a month ago."

"First, we had to draw up the papers. And find your daughter's primary psychiatrist."

That had been a trick. The weasly little man from

the nearby mental institution had looked surprised as each and every word about Emma had come out of his mouth. He'd even sweated. Ealhswith had had to work on repressing a smile. It was so easy to make these creatures lie.

He looks like he had something to hide, Geffon had said.

No, she had thought. He had nothing to hide at all.

"Your conversation just seemed too polite to me," Ealhswith said. "Why didn't you let her know we have them dead to rights and that she should let me see my daughter?"

"I did." Geffon folded his hands. "Trust me, Mrs. Swith. Your daughter will be back in your custody by the end of the week."

Ealhswith whirled, facing all the LeRoy Neiman limited editions on the wall. What had she been thinking, hiring this man? He couldn't even afford originals. As if anyone would want originals of *athletes*. Ealhswith nearly spit to show her disgust.

"Who knows what my daughter has been through?" she said, attempting to keep her voice level. Her fingers were still twitching. "She could have been irreparably harmed by now."

"I showed you the detective's report," Geffon said. "Nora is a good and dedicated attorney, and she seems to have taken a personal interest in your daughter for some reason."

"She hasn't gotten her professional help, though, has she?" Ealhswith said. "Emma needs her doctors."

Geffon sighed. "Right now, Emma seems fine."

"Emma is not fine! She thinks she's a witch from

the Dark Ages. Who knows what she'll do!" Ealhswith added just enough panic in her voice to sound like a worried mother. She kept her back to Geffon so that he wouldn't see how calm she actually was.

"Mrs. Swith, if we don't take the proper legal action in the proper manner, the court could overturn your petition. I know Nora. I tried to hire her for this firm once. She's one of the best attorneys in the city, and she'll make sure every i is dotted and every t is crossed. If we don't do the same, you could lose custody of your daughter."

Ealhswith clenched her fist. Becoming a snake was too good for this worm. Maybe she'd change him into an actual worm. A night crawler, or half a dozen night crawlers. Then she'd sell him for bait.

Instead, she turned and let her anger show in her eyes. "Are you saying, Mr. Geffon, that I need a better attorney?"

His mouth opened slightly. The worm obviously wasn't used to being questioned. "No," he said. "I'm saying that I'm more than a match for Nora if you let me do my job."

Ealhswith suppressed a sigh. She had no idea the wheels of mortal justice ground so slowly. Too slowly for her. But now that she had them in gear, she wouldn't stop them.

Although she would take a new tack.

"Is your detective's report accurate?"

"Of course." Geffon bristled for a moment, and then she shared her most cunning look with him. It seemed to calm him. "Why do you ask?"

"Because, if the report is true, your fine attorney friend is leaving my daughter with a professor and a woman with no discernible occupation, who seem to spend their days taking her to various parks. Is that the proper treatment for a mentally ill girl?"

"No," Geffon said. "I've mentioned it in my report. I could get a local psychologist to comment on the inappropriateness, though. You realize I'll have to add that to your tab."

"Of course," Ealhswith said. She didn't care about the money. Let the worm spend a small fortune. It wouldn't matter in a day or so anyway. What did matter was that she take action on her own.

And she already had a plan.

A plan Ms. Nora Barr left open for her.

Ealhswith was uninvited—in Nora Barr's home. But Nora Barr didn't control the public parks.

Ealhswith rubbed her hands together. Sooner or later, even the best opponents made a mistake.

———

Lunch at Quixotic was apparently very good. That was Nora's first thought as she circled the block several times, looking for a good parking space. The tiny lot beside the restaurant was full. Quixotic wasn't too far from Powell's Bookstore, just off Burnside, on one of the side streets that had been undergoing part of the neighborhood renovation. The building was old, but the decor was new. The neon outside made the entire place very appealing to the young crowd, but the hint of wood and greenery made it comfortable for adults as well.

The line going out the door was the thing that looked daunting to Nora. She doubted the owner would have time to talk.

She hesitated. Was she really here to discuss Ealhswith, or had she decided that she had gone too long without seeing Blackstone? Was she here for a Beautiful-Man Fix or to get information?

Beautiful-Man Fix. That was what it had to be. She could have called him. It would have been smarter to call him. In fact, she would do that.

She switched her briefcase to her other hand and started back to the car. At that moment, a familiar nasal voice said beside her, "You know, he's got a table set aside for you."

She looked down. Sancho was standing at her right, near her briefcase—in fact, she had almost whacked him with it—and he was staring up at her. He was wearing a seersucker jacket and matching pants. They looked very seventies. She wondered if that was his decade of choice, or if he were merely going through all his light fashions—from all the centuries—during the hottest part of Portland's summer.

"He can't have a table set aside for me," she said. "He doesn't even know I'm coming."

"He's reserved it every day since he opened the place. I think it's reserved for you."

"Not Emma?"

"Emma, Shemma. Don't you realize she's like a cosmic McGuffin?"

"A what?"

"Don't know your Hitchcock, do you?"

Nora frowned. She had seen all of Hitchcock's movies. "I don't remember any McGuffin in Hitchcock's films."

She braced herself, expecting Sancho to pull out some other Hitchcock, some famous writer or well-known politician. Instead he snorted and said, "See what I mean?" which of course, she didn't. When she didn't respond, he said, "He's going to want to see you. I assume you're here to see him."

She swallowed. Now that she was so close, she was chickening out. "I can just as easily talk to you. It's about Ealhswith."

"I never talk about Ealhswith."

Nora felt silly looking down at him. She crouched.

Sancho slapped her arm. "Don't do that. You'll make me look five years old."

"I'm used to looking people in the eye."

"Well, I'm not. You're making me nervous."

"You're making me nervous."

"I'm older than you. Respect your elders, for God's sake, and stand up."

She did. Then she crouched again. She wanted to see his expression when she asked him the next question: "You're not still working for Ealhswith, are you?"

Color filled his face, and it didn't look like the color of someone who was embarrassed or caught red-handed. It looked like a flush of anger.

"Je-Zus," he said. "Just stand. Stand up. Stand."

She did.

He shook his head, then jumped once, as if he were a kid trying to kill a giant ant. The people in line were staring at them.

"Aethelstan told you this, didn't he? That I worked for her. I never did. I *never* did. I was an apprentice for a summer. One summer. I thought she could teach me alchemy. No one can teach anyone alchemy, but that's a whole different story, and one that goes on for about six hundred years. Her first scam, I call it, and I fell for it, until Aethelstan explained the properties of gold to me. He wasn't right either, not then. I mean we knew nothing about science, but he was closer than she was, and besides, he made more sense, and I hate it when he tells people that I used to work for her."

"Don't apprentices generally work for the people they're apprenticed to?"

"That's not the point!" he shouted.

"What is the point?"

"I quit."

"All right," she said. "I had to ask. And I do need to talk to you."

"Aethelstan'll kill me if I talk to you and don't let him talk to you."

"You're lying again aren't you?" she said. "There's no table."

"There is a table, he will be mad, and I'm not lying," he said. "I have never lied to you. Ingrate."

He said that last under his breath, but she caught it anyway. She let him lead her around the side of the building to the kitchen door.

Nora had been in dozens of restaurant kitchens over the years—she had put herself through school as a waitress—but never had she been in one like this. The kitchen was large with several steel tables scattered throughout it. There were several ovens, even more grills, large refrigerators in each area from salad prep to baking, and a freezer large enough to live in. A dozen people were working, all dressed in white and most of whom were men. The work areas were spotless. Even the dishwasher's space, usually the sloppiest

in any restaurant kitchen, was clean. If it weren't for
the heavenly smells coming off the stove tops and the
marvelous meals, served on simple white plates, that
were passing from chef to waiter, Nora would have
thought the kitchen was a movie set that had never
been used.

Sancho led her through the kitchen, around most of
the tables, and into a back area of the dining room. Here
the conversation was loud and laughter-filled, and the
Portland summer sunlight filtered through dozens of
windows. The decor was more modern than she would
have expected, with cast-iron wire sculptures on the wall
and a lot of neon.

Sancho started up a flight of very wide, very shallow
stairs, and then looked back at her. "Come on," he said.

She was gazing at the full dining room, the patrons
waiting at the maître d's post, thinking that she didn't
know Portland could support a place like this, at least
not at lunch. "I thought you said I had a table."

"You do."

"In the restaurant?"

"In the good section," he said. "Now come on."

He took the stairs quicker than she would have
thought possible, and she had to hurry to keep up with
him. The stairs wound around a column, decorated with
some artist's idea of graffiti, as well as the signatures of
famous patrons.

At the top of the stairs was a balcony that was partially glassed-in so that it could be used in the winter.
Right now, though, all the windows were open, and out
on the terrace were dozens of cast-iron tables with um-
brellas, and all of them had a stunning view of the city.

"Beautiful, isn't it?" Blackstone asked in her ear. He was behind her. She hadn't heard him come up—it was hard to amid the clatter of plates, the murmur of conversation, and the low jazz that filtered through it all—but she could smell him, that touch of leather and something exotic. He had to be very close, because she could also feel his warmth against her right shoulder, even though their bodies weren't touching.

"The restaurant?" she asked without turning around. "Or the view?"

He laughed, and the sound sent a tingle through her. "Contrary as always." Then he did put a hand on her back, and the tingle grew worse. Coming to see him had been a mistake. She had suspected it on the street, but now she knew it.

"Mr. Blackstone," she said, turning, and catching herself against him. He didn't move back, as any other person might do.

"Alex," he said.

"I thought your name was Aethelstan."

"It's not a name that trips easily off the tongue." He was looking down at her. She thought she had remembered his eyes, but she hadn't. They were the soft silver-blue of a summer sky. "Although I like the way it sounds when you say it."

She stared at him a moment too long. "I didn't come here to be charmed," she said, taking a step back from him.

"Pity," he said, moving the hand that had been on her back to her elbow. "You'd present quite a challenge."

She didn't smile. He led her to a table that had a view of the dining room below, the terrace, and the rest of the balcony. Yet it was on a landing all its own, a private place where conversations couldn't be overheard.

There was a reserved sign on the table, as well as two place settings, and a vase with a single rose. Blackstone pulled out a chair for her, and she sat down. Sancho seemed to have disappeared.

Then Blackstone sat across from her. As he did, a waiter showed up.

"Ms. Barr would like a glass of water, some of our special-brewed ice tea, and so would I," he said.

Nora opened her mouth to contradict him, then she realized that was exactly what she would have ordered—if she had known that they brewed their own tea.

"And bring us the mushroom and polenta appetizer, and two orders of the Chilean sea bass."

The waiter nodded and disappeared.

"I didn't come for lunch," Nora said.

Blackstone smiled. "That's funny. Everyone else did."

"And if I had, I would have liked to look at the menu."

"Next time," he said. "You'll like this."

The thing of it was, she probably would. "Don't tell me," she said. "I was radiating desire for the sea bass."

His smile grew. It was a soft smile, not his charming do-anything smile. This one was somehow more dangerous. It was a private smile, one that seemed like it was just for her. "If you were radiating desire," he said, "I would hope it would be for more than the sea bass."

Her heart rate increased, and she wished she had the mental power to slow it down. Damn the man for flirting with her. Damn her for wanting to flirt back.

"I didn't come here for lunch," she repeated. "I came to find out a few things."

His smile faded. "About Emma?"

"About Ealhswith."

His mouth thinned. The warmth he had shown her a moment ago was gone. "How is Emma?"

"Adapting better than I would have thought," Nora said. "She still has trouble with some of the basics—zippers are beyond her for some reason—but she seems to be doing well. I don't know how she is emotionally. She has that pretty well shut off."

He closed his eyes and turned his head slightly. "I've been thinking about what you said. What I did. It's indefensible. You know, about a hundred years into it, I had forgotten that she was even a person. I always prided myself on my compassion and my humanity, and somehow, I managed this."

Nora waited. There was nothing she could say to that.

He swallowed. "If I could go back and change things, I would. But I can't. So I honor your wishes—and Emma's—and I won't try to approach her. But if she ever needs anything—money, support, help with the magic—please call me. Please."

He hadn't begged before. He hadn't been this contrite before. Nora wanted to reach across the table and take his hand, but she couldn't. After all, this was her client that they were talking about, and he had treated her horribly, whether the treatment had been intentional or not.

"Why is Ealhswith so interested in her?" Nora asked.

He turned. "You're having trouble with Ealhswith?"

"Yes."

"I thought you made her uninvited."

"She hasn't come near us," Nora said.

The waiter returned with two clear blue plates and tiny appetizer forks. He set them down, then turned and grabbed a larger plate off a nearby tray. It had a mound of polenta in the center, with dozens of kinds of mushrooms on top, all covered in a sauce that smelled faintly of burgundy and garlic.

Then, as quickly as he appeared, he left.

"Your recipe?" Nora asked.

"Everything in here is made from my recipes," he said. "And usually at my hand or under my supervision. You have to collect something in a thousand years."

"Recipes?" Nora asked.

He shrugged. "I like food. And I learned long ago to get the recipe for something you like because there's no guarantee that anyone will remember how to make it when you return to the same region again."

She supposed not. Over that many years, of course things would change, would disappear. Restaurants barely stayed open long enough for her tastes. She couldn't imagine what would happen for his.

He picked up her plate and placed part of the appetizer on it. Then he set the plate before her and watched her. It seemed as though he were hoping for her approval. She wasn't sure why. She wasn't sure what this undercurrent was between them, how they seemed to speak on more than one level at once.

She took a small taste. The mushrooms were grilled—an unexpected surprise—and the sauce was more a demi-glace that had a richness she hadn't expected. The polenta added a texture that took the food to a level she hadn't tasted before, at least not at the restaurants she frequented.

"It's spectacular," she said.

Blackstone relaxed visibly. "That's the first compliment you've ever given me."

She smiled. "It's the first you've deserved."

A flush covered his cheeks, and she wondered if her words were too harsh. Perhaps she should go easier on this man. After all, he had respected her wishes. He hadn't come to her office again. He had made no attempt to contact Emma. And he hadn't even sent Sancho over to see if he could find out anything.

Blackstone took some food for himself. The mood was gone. "What sort of trouble is Ealhswith giving you, then, if she's not throwing fire spells at your front door?"

"Legal trouble," Nora said.

He raised his eyebrows. "Ealhswith?"

"It's my fault really. I'm the one who brought up the law that night, saying that she was bound by the laws of this land."

"How could she use that against you?"

With two bites, Nora had finished the food he had given her. Now, as she spoke, she took a second helping. "She has retained one of the best lawyers in the city, and through him she's claiming that Emma is her daughter, that Emma has been declared incompetent, and that for the last ten years she's been in a mental institution. She's also claiming that because of all of that, Emma's unable to take care of herself in any matter, including hiring a lawyer."

Blackstone pushed his plate away. "What would you normally do in this circumstance?"

"Investigate her claim, of course."

"And if, for the sake of argument, Emma had been in an institution?"

"I'd hire a psychiatrist or a series of psychiatrists to determine her mental condition." Nora scraped the last of the polenta off her plate. The appetizer had been excellent, but filling. She doubted she would have any room for the sea bass. "I couldn't do that in this case if I wanted to. Emma still asks basic questions that any three-year-old should know the answer to, like why do we keep voices in one box when we have a box that can hold voices and bodies?"

"Huh?" Blackstone asked.

"See?" Nora said. "Not even you get that one. And I wouldn't have either, if I hadn't seen where she was looking at the time. She thinks we store voices inside of radios and people inside of televisions. She hasn't grasped the concept that these are taped projections. Airwaves are really beyond her."

"Oh, dear," Blackstone said. He ran a hand through his thick hair. "Are you asking me to finally give her the information spell?"

"No," Nora said. "She still won't take the spell, although I've mentioned it from time to time."

And always in exasperation. Emma could try the patience of God.

Nora sighed. "I need information, though. I was going to get it from Sancho, but he brought me to you."

"I'm sure I can tell you what you need to know," Blackstone said.

It surprised her that he didn't push his ability to do the information spell on her. A month ago he would have insisted, and then insisted some more until she got angry. He really had had time to think about all he'd done. She wondered how he felt, losing the thing—the person—he had protected for a millennium. It must have been nearly impossible to step away. And he had.

"All right," Nora said. "I need to know how Sancho got the documents for Emma and how he made them look real."

"Counselor," Blackstone said. "You don't really want to know that."

"I do," she said.

Blackstone licked his lower lip. It was a nervous gesture that seemed that much more startling because Blackstone had so few of them. "You really don't want to know."

"Sancho said the documents are legal."

"They are," Blackstone said. "But what we consider to be legal and what you consider to be legal are two different things."

"How about what a judge would consider to be legal."

"Why?" Blackstone asked. "Is this thing with Ealhswith going to go to court?"

"I hope not," Nora said. She took a sip of her water, more as a stalling tactic than because she needed it. "I guess what I'm fishing for is this: Is what Sancho did unusual or can Ealhswith do it too?"

"Get legal documentation of something?"

Nora nodded.

"Of course she can."

Nora sighed. "Then the documents that she showed Hank Geffon were probably legit."

"Who?"

"Her attorney."

"You need legal documents for this claim?"

"Legal guardians are appointed in court. Ealhswith's documents would show that Emma is incompetent to live her own life."

Blackstone leaned back. "I suppose if I offered to provide documents that proved she was competent, you'd turn me down."

"I really don't want to go to court with fake documentation," Nora said. "Even if you and Sancho insist it'll hold up."

"You know," he said with a small smile, "you create a lot of problems because you're so damn ethical."

Nora shrugged. "I warned you about that in the beginning."

"So you did."

They sat in silence for a moment, just looking at each other. Was it her imagination or had his eyes grown darker? She longed to lean forward, to touch his face, his hands. She had never felt so drawn to a man before.

The waiter broke the mood, clearing his throat before he set down two plates of Chilean sea bass. Nora felt her cheeks flush, and Blackstone looked a bit startled himself as he glanced at his employee. The waiter smiled at Nora as if they shared a secret.

She immediately looked down at her sea bass. It rested on a white plate whose simplicity added to the beauty of the meal before her. The sauce was light and multicolored. The bass rested on a bed of rice, touched with cilantro and green onions. Fresh green beans acted as a garnish along the side.

The scent wafting toward her made her stomach rumble. And she hadn't even thought she was still hungry.

"This is more food than I've eaten in a week," she said.

Blackstone smiled at her. The waiter bowed and disappeared, probably to tell stories in the kitchen of the boss's flirtation. The thought made her blush again.

"I didn't think attorneys blushed," he said.

"Only ethical ones do," she muttered, her head down.

He put his forefinger under her chin, lifting her head up. "Do you know how beautiful you are when you blush?"

She pushed his hand away. "I told you in my office, Mr. Blackstone—"

"Alex."

"—trying to get to Emma through me won't work."

"And I told you, Nora, I'm not trying that."

"Then what are you doing?"

He looked at her for a long moment. "Maybe I'm trying to get your attention."

"You've had my attention from the moment we met."

He nodded, once, a brief movement. "Then maybe I'm trying to get your approval."

She felt her flush grow deeper. "Flirting with me won't do it."

"Why not?"

"Because, Mr. Blackstone, if I'm to believe you, you were promised to a girl you kept in a coffin for a thousand years. I would hope that you wouldn't change your mind after she became mobile again. She's only been awake for a month."

"And I haven't seen in her in all that time."

"I know," Nora said.

He looked down at his own food and sighed. "But you make a good point. It's insensitive of me. Which seems to be par for the course in anything to do with Emma."

He was silent for a moment. Nora watched him. He did seem confused by all this, but she couldn't tell if it was an act or not.

She took a bite of the sea bass and noted that the spices were vaguely Thai and quite spicy. The simplicity of eating brought her back to herself and reminded her that she had a few other questions that only Blackstone or Sancho could answer.

"What is going on with Ealhswith?" she asked. "I mean, both you and Emma have said she's not Emma's real mother. And I can understand a mentor fighting for a student for a while, but not a thousand years. What's going on?"

His gaze moved across her face, as if he were assessing her, as if he were afraid she wasn't going to believe what he had to say. "I used to think," he said slowly, "that Ealhswith was jealous of Emma. Emma was beautiful. Ealhswith was not. Emma was young. Ealhswith was not."

He picked up his water glass and took a sip from it.

"But, like you, I began to realize that those explanations were too simple. If they were true, Ealhswith would have given up on them after a hundred years or so. I expected her to, honestly. I expected that after a few years, she would stop searching for me, or for Emma. But Ealhswith always showed up, and always before the ten years was up—at least whenever I had Emma in my custody."

He smiled. It was a grim look.

"I supposed that Ealhswith felt that way about me."

Nora said nothing. She ate a bit more of the sea bass, which was delicious, and drank some of the tea.

Occasionally, she would nod to encourage him to go on.

"My own training progressed," he said. "And as it did, I learned about a spell that changed everything."

He glanced down, as if he were bracing himself for saying the next.

"My people," he said. "They age. We age. Our aging is like any normal person's until we come into our magic. And then we age one year for each century. Sometimes that accelerates, if we've done a lot of spells or if the Fates, our ruling body, decide we have committed a crime that requires losing some years. I used a lot of magic in the years between 1478 and 1700. I'm probably an equivalent of thirty-five human years old."

Which was exactly how old she pegged him to be. "What sort of magic?" she asked.

"It's a long story, and I don't want to go into it, but suffice it to say that Monty Python were more right than they were wrong. No one expects the Spanish Inquisition."

He took another bite of sea bass, and she used it as a cue to do the same.

"Often," he said, after he had finished chewing, "one of our number tries to buy those years back. It doesn't work. Time does not reverse for us. But it can be stolen."

"Stolen?" Nora asked.

He nodded. "There is a spell—and it's a forbidden one—that allows a dying mage to take the body of a mage who has not come into his or her powers and use it as if it were their own."

Nora frowned. "Live in it? Along with the other person?"

"No," Blackstone said. "Steal it. They switch bodies.

The young mage will die in the old mage's body, and the old mage will live another lifetime."

"You think this is what Ealhswith wants with Emma?"

He nodded. "Ealhswith has been punished twice since I've known her. The Fates sealed the details, like they always do, afraid that the rest of us will follow suit, I guess. As if we can't make moral choices for ourselves. But Ealhswith's lifespan is considerably shorter than it should be. And by keeping Emma on ice, she had her standby body ready."

"Why didn't your Fates stop her?"

"Because this battle has looked like a simple fight between me and Ealhswith, and since it involved one of us, and it predated all the protection laws, the Fates had to let it go on."

Nora was so full she felt as if she were going to burst. She couldn't remember the last time she'd had this much food at lunch—or enjoyed it so much. But she pushed her plate aside and picked up her water glass as a way to prevent herself from eating any more.

"But now Emma's awake," she said.

"Yes," he said. "And Ealhswith has to figure out a way to get her back into a state of suspended animation."

"Wouldn't that be a tip off to the Fates?"

"If she did it wrong, it would," he said. "But remember that warning she gave me? Not to kiss Emma? It was a setup. There'd be no way to prove I didn't send her spiraling again."

"Wait," Nora said. "I thought the kiss-and-tell spell meant that if you kissed Emma, she'd die, and you put her in that long sleep to keep her alive."

He nodded. "I was young. I didn't know how to get

around a spell like that, so I did exactly what Ealhswith knew I would do. I played right into her hands. Our entire community knows it. The Fates reprimanded me for it but couldn't undo it. Now if Emma ends up back in the same state while Ealhswith and I are fighting over her, I'll get the blame again."

"But you haven't come near Emma in a month."

"And neither has Ealhswith. Then she hits you with a legal conundrum, and you come to me. See? Involvement again."

Nora shook her head slightly. "How do you know that Ealhswith is doing this?"

"I don't," he said. "But she has never shown any feeling for Emma as a person. And there is nothing else that makes sense."

Nora swallowed. "Forgive me for asking a lawyer question," she said, "but how do I know that you're not wanting to do the same thing?"

His spectacular eyes widened. "Me? Keep Emma on ice until I'm an old man near death?"

Nora nodded.

"Because," he said, and then he stopped himself. Nora could almost hear the end of that sentence. *Because I love her*. He watched her face, as if he knew what she were thinking. "You won't believe me, will you?"

"Just tell me why not," Nora said.

"I'm not the kind of person who would do that," he said. "But even if I were, it wouldn't work. My magic is different than Emma's. I'm a man. I came into my powers at twenty-one. She'll come into hers at fifty or so. And we have different powers, different ways of using them, different ways of accessing them. If I could steal her body—and I don't think I can—but let's say for the sake of argument that I could, I certainly wouldn't be able to use her magic skills. I'd simply be a man living in a woman's body, with no abilities at all."

"Of course, I have to take your word on this."

"Actually, no," he said. "There are hundreds of magic texts, most of which are in your libraries. I can tell you which one to look at."

"After you and Sancho use your documentation skills to make it up."

He crossed his arms. "Does anything get past your skepticism?"

"Not much," she said. "That's why I'm a good lawyer."

"But it makes for lousy friendships," he said.

"Who said we were friends?"

A slight frown creased his forehead. He sighed softly and looked away. Then he ran his hands along his pants and sighed again. "You know," he said. "I'm not trying to hurt Emma. Or take her for my own. You have to be able to see that. I've done everything you've wanted."

Nora remained silent.

"You'll have to start trusting me at some point. It was my idea that got Emma awake for the first time in a thousand years. When you decided to help her, I let you. I could have just as easily charmed you, taken her from you, and made you forget."

Nora looked down. He could have. She hadn't thought of that. But he could have. And it was only luck that made him find her first after she had rescued Emma. If Ealhswith had found her first, she would have done that.

"I know you think I'm horrible," he said softly. "But I'm not. I just made a few mistakes."

The waiter came over, heard that last, and shifted nervously. He had brought a dessert tray with him.

"Two berries with cream," Blackstone said, without looking at the waiter. "And two coffees."

The waiter nodded crisply and disappeared into the kitchen.

"I can order for myself," Nora said.

"It's my restaurant," Blackstone said again. "I know what's good."

"But you don't know how full I am. I doubt I can eat anything else."

"You can at least taste it," he said. "As my guest."

A busboy swooped behind her and picked up the plate with her sea bass. She noted, out of the corner of her eye, that the staff were all watching the table.

"Don't you usually sit with the customers?"

"Sometimes," he said. "But not here."

"What's so special about here?"

"I've been saving it," he said.

"For Emma?"

He shook his head. "For you."

Her heart did a small flip-flop. "What's so special about me that you have to keep flattering me like this? I have to assume it's about Emma."

"It was about Emma," he said. "At the beginning, anyway. But I needed you to be rational. I needed you to make decisions. I couldn't make them for you, or Ealhswith would have been able to find Emma. It was one of my many mistakes in trying to hide her."

The waiter set two crystal champagne flutes in front of them, layered with berries, then homemade cream, then more berries, and more cream. He gave them each an ice tea spoon, and another waiter set down steaming cups of coffee.

Blackstone waited until they were gone before continuing. "Now, I guess I find you to be a challenge. I know how hard it is to get your approval and your respect. I guess I want to earn them both."

"Why?" she asked. "I'm just a simple mortal."

"If you were a simple mortal, you wouldn't have stood up to me let alone Ealhswith. You would have let us go on with our battles. You have not." He picked up his spoon. "I'm grateful for that."

He was saying thank you. She hadn't expected it from him. She felt the flush rise in her cheeks again. "I was just doing my job."

"You've never just done your job," he said. "And now you've taken on Emma on Emma's terms. It's got to be quite a task."

Nora took a bite of the dessert while she thought of an answer. The cream wasn't so much a cream as a vanilla mousse. It was a perfect complement to the tartness of the summer berries.

"The first day was the hardest," she said. "She wanted to know what everything was, from the remote control to the fabric on the couch. She still does."

He had nearly finished his dessert. He set it aside and picked up his coffee, cradling the cup between his long fingers. "I barely remember her." He spoke softly, and as he did, color crept into his cheeks. "I mean, I remember all the time we spent together, but it was so long ago. She has slept ever since and I—" He stopped and shook his head, then smiled ruefully at Nora. "I never thought this through."

It was hard on him too. She hadn't thought of that either. He had spent a lifetime—hundreds of lifetimes—protecting a woman that he no longer knew.

"She's supposed to be your soul mate, right?" Nora asked. "You'll have to get to know her, when she's ready."

He nodded. "I guess I have time." He took a sip from his coffee cup, and then set the cup down. He looked around the restaurant again, as if it gave him comfort. "Sometimes what you want, what you need, and what you have are so completely different."

Nora thought of Max. Once upon a time, what they wanted and needed were the same. Then at some point, their interests changed. Their personalities changed. In ten short years.

But they hadn't been soul mates. She had known that from the beginning. There had been none of that instant love, none of that instant knowledge, the books talked about. Only an attraction, a strong friendship, and then a separating.

"Do you believe in soul mates?" she asked Blackstone.

He continued staring over the balcony for a moment, then he turned to her and smiled faintly. "I'm afraid I do."

Nora felt a pang in her heart so deep that she nearly gasped. She made herself blink and smile. "When Emma's ready, I'll tell her about Ealhswith's plans. I'll tell Emma what you did. Maybe then you can see her."

That faint smile remained on his face. It was a distracted, almost sad look. "As I said, I have time. Now, I guess, Emma does too."

Nora finished a last sip of her coffee and then stood. "Thank you for lunch," she said, holding out her hand.

He rose, took her hand as if he were going to shake it, then turned it over in his own. His palms were warm and dry, their touch gentle. Slowly he bowed, just as she had once imagined him doing, and kissed her palm.

It was a strangely intimate gesture, and it sent a wave of desire through her that she tried desperately to ignore. He stood up, still holding her hand, then folded her fingers over the still tingling place where he had kissed her.

"You are an amazing woman, Nora," he said. Their eyes met and held for a moment.

She was the first to break the gaze. She looked away, removed her hand from his but kept the fingers over the kiss, protecting it. She no longer trusted her own eyes to keep her own feelings secret. How many other women had looked at him with such desire? How many hundreds in all of those years? Only to know that he was bound to a woman he barely remembered?

"Thank you," she said finally, looking up.

But he was already gone.

It took her a while to get to her car. She found, as she left the restaurant, that a lot of people watched her. They had apparently never seen the mysterious Alex Blackstone with a woman. A few members of the staff asked her trivial things, apparently to find out more about her, and she would have had them find Sancho, only she didn't know what name he was using in this place.

After she left, she leaned against a tree for a moment, willing her heart rate to slow. She wasn't sure what had happened in there, whether Blackstone had charmed her (but to what end?) or whether he'd been expressing a natural regret or whether he had meant every word he said.

It felt as if he had meant every word. But it might have felt that way anyway, if she'd been charmed.

She shook her head. He said he needed her to think for herself, and he hadn't charmed her for that reason. Did that standard still apply? She thought so. No matter what kind of documentation Ealhswith had had her attorney send over, for the time being, Nora still had Emma as a client. And Blackstone needed Nora to use her full faculties.

Didn't he?

She had never been this confused by a man. Not Max, not anyone. She sighed and pushed away from the tree. She wandered to her car, got in, and drove back to her office.

As she got off the elevator, she saw the receptionist pick up the phone. Nora stopped to pick up her messages, and as she did, Ruthie came running out of the back hallway. Her hair was askew, she was breathing hard, and she had forgotten to put on her shoes like she usually did when she got up from her desk.

Nora looked at her in alarm. "What is it?"

"I've been trying to reach you all afternoon?" Ruthie said, breathlessly. "What happened to your cell?"

"I forgot it."

"Of all days to be without a phone," Ruthie snapped. "What is it?"

"Your mother's been calling all afternoon."

"My mother? What happened?"

"Emma? Your new client? The one that's been staying with you?"

Nora didn't like how this was shaking out. "What about her?"

"She's gone."

Chapter 9

ALL THE WAY HOME, PARKING THE CAR, RUNNING UP the stairs, hurrying toward the door to the loft, Nora vacillated between anger toward Emma (What was she thinking, leaving now?) and worry (Did Ealhswith know? Did the uninvited words work now that Emma was outside of Nora's protection?) As she unlocked the door, someone opened it from the inside.

Her mother was standing there, eyes red. "Thank heavens," she said, rubbing her hands together in a gesture that could only be what some writers called "wringing." "Where have you been? Why didn't you call? Emma's been kidnapped."

Nora felt cold. She came inside and closed the door. "Kidnapped?"

Jeffrey was standing just behind Amanda. He was shaking his head. "I still contend that she wandered off. She's a bit confused, you know. I try, but there are just some things that throw her."

"Where was this?" Nora asked. "Why aren't you looking for her?"

"We did look for her," Jeffrey said. "At least I did. I was about to head back out when your mother said you were coming here. I thought you might want a voice of reason."

"I am being reasonable." Amanda turned, grabbed Nora by the shoulders, and shook her. "Can't you tell I'm being reasonable?"

Nora put her hands on her mother's and took a step back. "Of course you are," she said as soothingly as she could, mouthing "thank you" over Amanda's shoulder at Jeffrey. "Now tell me what happened."

"We were in that park, you know," Amanda said. "That little dinky one downtown."

"The one where all the teenagers hang out?" Nora asked.

"And the homeless, and most of Portland's criminal element," said Jeffrey with a touch of disapproval. Nora had never heard him be disapproving before. "I told her not to take Emma there. It wasn't the kind of park we usually took her to."

"It's pleasant there in the daytime," Amanda said. "Besides, there's a lovely Hunan restaurant nearby where I was planning to get some takeout. Jeffrey and I had discussed it, and we thought we needed to gradually introduce Emma into this century—"

"Mother," Nora said, "Just tell me what happened."

"Jeffrey went off to get lunch—"

"I thought you were going to."

"Well, Emma and I were having a lovely discussion about vendor carts—"

"They were fighting," Jeffrey said. "Emma wanted to try a hot dog, and Amanda was trying to explain how no one should eat a hot dog and that made Emma want one more and then Amanda started to explain what was in one—"

"*What happened?*" Nora asked again.

"That was when I went to get lunch," Jeffrey said.

"She went to get one herself," Amanda said. "We'd been explaining money to her, and she had a twenty dollar bill. I was trying to tell her not to, but she ran, and she got to one of those vendors, and while he was making her one of those horrible things, this woman came up—"

"Woman?" Nora asked, feeling a chill.

"Yes," Amanda said. "A tall woman wearing the most inappropriate dress. You'd think she was going to the opera. And she had black hair—"

"With a white streak?"

"Yes!" Amanda said.

"Ealhswith," Nora said. "Shit."

"You know this woman?" Jeffrey asked.

"Yes," Nora said. "Then what?"

"Then the vendor started to hand her the hot dog, and—" Amanda's voice shook. "And—"

"And?"

"She and that awful woman vanished."

"People don't vanish, Amanda," Jeffrey said. "That's what I've been trying to tell you."

"Then what happened to her?"

"I don't know," Jeffrey said. "She got distracted. She wandered off. I've been telling you to tell Nora that perhaps Emma needs professional help."

Nora swallowed hard. "What time?" she asked. "What time did this happen?"

"About noon," Amanda said.

About noon. Not long after Geffon had served her the papers. It had been a bait and switch. Get Nora preoccupied with the legal aspects and steal Emma right from under her nose. And if Nora hadn't needed her Beautiful-Man Fix, she might have stayed at the office until late, researching the case. Ealhswith had no way

of knowing that the people who were with Emma were
baby-sitting her and would call Nora.

"This is serious, isn't it?" Jeffrey asked.

"What did you think?" Amanda said. "The girl is
missing. She doesn't even know how to read."

He sighed. "I'll go back out and look for her. Nora,
call the police. Let's file a missing persons—"

"No," Nora said. "That fits right into her plan."

"What?" Amanda asked. "Emma has a plan?"

"Ealhswith's," Nora said. "If I file a missing persons,
and Emma turns back up, we look incompetent. If the
police do find her, they'll think she's incompetent."

"What are you talking about?" Jeffrey asked.

Nora shook her head. Of course they didn't know.
She hadn't told them. She had only told one person.

The only person who could help her.

She walked to the telephone, picked up the business
card, and dialed Blackstone's cell phone number. He
picked it up on the first ring.

"What?"

"It's Nora." Her voice was calm, even though her
hands were shaking. "I need your help."

"What's happened?"

"Ealhswith's taken Emma."

"Where are you?"

"At home."

"I'll be right there." He hung up before she could
say anything else. She clung to the receiver as if it were
a lifeline to him. She turned to Jeffrey and her mother,
about to explain who Blackstone was when he appeared
in front of the door.

There was no smoke, no loud bang, nothing like in

the movies. One moment the space was empty. The next moment, he was there.

Amanda screamed. Jeffrey took a step backward and nearly tumbled down the stairs.

Blackstone looked half wild. He glanced around until he saw Nora. "When did this happen?"

Nora hung up as she spoke. "As I came to see you, I guess."

"As?" he snapped. "*As?*"

"I just found out."

He turned toward Amanda, who backed into Jeffrey. Jeffrey put his arms around her as if to steady her. "And who are these people?"

"My mother, and Jeffrey Chawsir. They—"

"You are not Geoffrey Chaucer," Blackstone said. "I know him. He was self-righteous, arrogant, and one hell of a writer. Besides, he was much shorter than you."

Jeffrey, who obviously had never encountered anything like this, said with complete dignity, "I am Jeffrey Chawsir."

"A man suffering from delusions is not what we need right now," Blackstone said. "Get them to leave. We have important things to do."

"And they'll help us," Nora said. "Jeffrey Chawsir is his real name. It's just spelled different. He's the professor I hired to teach Emma history and to bring her up to speed. My mother has been taking care of her during the days. They were with her when Ealhswith took her."

"Ealhswith came here?"

"No," Nora said. "They have been taking her to various parks."

"Which one?" Blackstone asked Amanda. His silver eyes were flashing, and if Nora didn't know better, she would have said he was furious.

"I don't know the name of it," Amanda said. "It's the small one downtown with the street vendors and the homeless guys and the fountain and the steps that the kids—"

Blackstone raised an arm, swept it over them, and brought it down. Suddenly, they were in the very park Amanda was describing.

"—skateboard in," she said, finishing her sentence. She looked around, wide-eyed. "My heavens, Jeffrey. I guess people really do vanish. I think we just did."

"No," he said, his voice a bit wobbly. "I think we just appeared."

One of the kids going by, skateboard under his arm, glared at them. A vendor behind them slammed the door closed on his little stall and inside it, Nora heard him shout, "That's enough! I'm going home, going back to bed, and starting this day all over again!"

The sun was high, and the heat of the day had found its way into the park. Nora was standing downwind of the fountain, and a little spray of cool mist kept hitting her in the face.

Blackstone didn't seem at all disoriented by his change of surroundings. "Okay, writer boy," he said, taking Jeffrey by the arm. "Where did you last see her?"

"I didn't," Jeffrey said. "I was getting Chinese take-out. Amanda—"

"Where?" Blackstone said to Amanda.

"Right there," she said, pointing at the now closed vendor's stall. "I sent her off to get herself a hot dog. It was to be her first experiment with money. I was watching from over there." She pointed at a green bench that a bearded man wearing dirty Army fatigues was spread out on. "And then that woman showed up, grabbed Emma, and vanished."

Blackstone stalked up to the stall, waved a hand again, and the air rippled as if it were touched by a blast of heat. For a moment, a vague form of Emma appeared, and then Ealhswith appeared beside her, took her arm, and they both disappeared.

"If you didn't believe me," Amanda said in an aggrieved tone, "you could have just said so."

Blackstone hurried down the stone steps and stopped beside Nora. "It was a perfect abduction," he said. "Not a trace. Not even a residue, and there should have been one, with that kind of magic. Ealhswith has gotten very good over the years. Better than I thought."

"Magic?" Jeffrey stammered.

"What did you think this was?" Blackstone snapped. "Special effects?"

"It would certainly be easier to accept," Amanda mumbled.

"Do you know how to find Emma?" Nora asked.

"If I knew how to find her, I wouldn't have had all the problems I've had for the last millennium. I thought you had her in good hands."

"I did."

"You didn't tell them about Ealhswith."

"You said she'd be gone when I uninvited her."

"Nora," Amanda said. "I don't think bickering will get us anywhere."

"Right." Nora shook away the retort she had been

priming herself for, took a deep breath, and asked, "What are we going to do?"

Blackstone glanced at the vendor's cart, then the park itself, and then the street. He frowned, bit his lower lip, and said, "We have no choice. We have to throw ourselves on the mercy of the court."

"The court?" Jeffrey asked. But he was too late. Blackstone had already brought his arm up, swung it over them, and brought it down again.

Nora could hardly catch her breath. The air had gone from hot and dry to hot and humid, so moist that it felt as if she were breathing underwater. Her blouse immediately stuck to her back.

She was standing in a grotto, with trees that had branches which hung down around her. Amanda was standing near Blackstone and so was Jeffrey. A waterfall cascaded down the side of a cliff into a pool that was directly in front of her. Three women lay on rocks in that pool. They were naked, with bronzed skin and perfectly formed breasts, long legs and narrow waists. One had tattoos everywhere. Another had a chain hanging between her pierced nipples. The third wore diamond studs in her belly button. The first had green hair, the second a Mohawk, and the third was bald.

The nearest woman sat up. "Aethelstan!" she gasped. "You brought mortals!"

"They're not supposed to see us in our natural state!" one of the other women said.

"This is not exactly natural," the third said. "It is—as you said, Clotho—an experiment in modern teenage thinking. It is—"

"Remember the mortals," the first woman said.

"Ah, yes," the second and third said in unison, and as they did, the scene changed from the lovely pool to steps outside a stone building. It looked Greek to Nora. White columns rose from the portico, and the women stood on the marble surface. They wore long white robes and sandals. Their hair fell to the middle of their backs: one woman a brunette, one a redhead, and the other a blonde.

The blonde rested her hand on a spinner's wheel. The redhead peered at all of them. The brunette held a pair of shears.

Nora's mouth went dry. These were the Fates, then, of Greek myth. The blonde was Clotho, the Spinner, who spun the thread of life; the brunette was Atropos, who carried the "abhorréd shears" and cut the thread at death; and that meant the redhead was Lachesis, the Disposer of Lots, who assigned each person a destiny.

Who'd have thought that all of Mrs. Ramsey's assignments in high school on mythologies of the world would actually have a practical use? And to think that Nora once believed Mrs. Ramsey's class was time wasted.

"Oh for God's sake," Blackstone said to the Fates. "It's been nearly two thousand years since the Greeks had any importance."

"The last time you brought us a mortal," Clotho said, "it put us in that dreadful play."

"Crones, I believe it called us," said Lachesis.

"Standing over a cauldron, as if we have nothing better to do," Atropos said.

"'Boil, boil, toil and trouble,' or whatever the quote was," Clotho said. "The man really couldn't write, could he?"

"He's considered the best writer ever in the English language," Blackstone said.

Lachesis sniffed. "Obviously English literature leaves a lot to be desired."

"You didn't come here to discuss great books, did you, Aethelstan?" Atropos said.

They were all beautiful, which hadn't been apparent before. Their features were classic, their bearing proud. If Nora hadn't seen them change, she wouldn't have thought they were the same women.

Atropos was slapping the shears against the palm of her left hand.

Jeffrey was clinging to Amanda. Amanda was watching the three women as if they were misbehaving children about to get into trouble.

"No," Blackstone said. "I came here to discuss Ealhswith."

"Oh, that's a surprise," Clotho said in a tired voice. "We've already ruled on the Ealhswith matter."

"Things have changed," Blackstone said.

"Oh?" Lachesis asked. "Did that poor child finally come out of her coma?"

Jeffrey coughed.

"Tell the mortal to speak up or shut up," Atropos said.

"Writers don't fare well here, scribe," Blackstone said over his shoulder.

"That's becoming obvious," Jeffrey said.

"Thank heavens you're not a writer," Amanda said.

"I doubt mortals fare much better," Nora said as a warning.

"You are perceptive," said Clotho, smiling at Nora. "Didn't we tell you she'd be perceptive?"

She directed the question at Blackstone. He frowned. "You didn't say anything about her at all."

Lachesis sighed. "Aethelstan, you are the slowest—"

"Shush," Atropos said. "He told us he wanted to discover on his own how the world worked, remember?"

"How can I forget?" Clotho said. "The arrogance of the newly magicked male."

"That was a thousand years ago," Blackstone said. "I've learned a bit since then."

"Obviously not," Lachesis said, nodding toward Nora.

"I came here about Emma," Blackstone said. "Leave Nora out of this."

"She's very involved," Atropos said.

"In fact, she's been left out too long," said Clotho.

"She's been involved for the last ten years," Blackstone said, "which is probably ten years too many."

"Why do I feel like I fell asleep in that Chinese restaurant?" Jeffrey muttered.

"Tell the mortals to be quiet," Lachesis said.

"No," Blackstone said. "I need their testimony."

"Testimony?" Atropos said. "This is an official proceeding?"

"We thought this was about them," Clotho said.

"No," Blackstone said. "I told you. It's about Ealhswith."

"Don't get testy with us, boy," Lachesis said.

"Stop playing word games," Blackstone said. "Emma's in danger. She needs your help."

"If she needs our help," Atropos said, "and she's out of that little coma you so needlessly placed her in, she can come to us and ask for help."

"No, she can't," Blackstone said. "She hasn't come into her magic yet."

"Hmm," Clotho said. "We should look into that. She is one thousand thirty. She should have come into her magic nine hundred and eighty years ago."

"One thousand and thirty?" Jeffrey whispered a bit too loudly to Amanda.

"That's what she said," Amanda whispered back.

"The mortals are blathering," Lachesis said.

"Aethelstan, shut them up, or we will," Atropos said.

"No," he said. "You will listen to me. With Nora's help"—and he came to her side, put his arm around her, and held her close as he spoke—"Emma was finally able to break out of my spell. But she was in a suspended animation. She hasn't learned or grown for the past thousand years—"

"You, of course, spelled her," Clotho said.

"No," Blackstone said.

"I didn't think you were still incompetent, Aethelstan," Lachesis said.

A tremble ran through him. Nora squeezed his side for reassurance.

"I am not incompetent," he said. "I—"

"Emma didn't want his help," Nora said. She bowed a little, as much as she could with Blackstone's arm around her waist. "Forgive me for speaking to such an august body. I presume you're the Fates that Black—Aethelstan's always talking about. You need to know that Emma grew upset about her lost thousand years, and I interfered, giving her my protection."

"Your protection?" Atropos said. "Forgive me, my dear, but that's like a fly protecting a gazelle."

"Nonetheless," Nora said. Her heart was pounding. She couldn't believe she was doing this. If she had thought Blackstone and Ealhswith powerful, she was risking everything talking to the women who ruled them. "Emma didn't want Blackstone's—I mean, Aethelstan's—help, so I forbade him from assisting her."

"Blackstone?" Jeffrey asked, turning toward him. "*The* Blackstone."

"Actually, yes," he said. "But not the one you think. It was a messy—"

"Enough!" the three women cried together. The four intruders stood at attention. Blackstone's hand tightened around Nora's waist, and he pulled her so close that she almost lost her balance.

Clotho let go of her spinning wheel and leaned toward Nora. "You say you forbid Aethelstan from assisting Emma, and he listened to you?"

"He wasn't happy about it," Nora said. "So I uninvited him. In my world, he has no rights to Emma."

"In ours," Lachesis said, "he has an obligation to help her."

"He did," Nora said. "He gave her immunity from diseases, and a spell that enabled her to speak English, and another one that protected her muscles so that they wouldn't atrophy, and a few others that I've forgotten, but she drew the line at the memory spell, the one that would give her a cursory knowledge of the last thousand years."

"That makes no sense," Lachesis said. "If she took all his other help, why stop there?"

"Because she didn't know the whole story when she took the initial help. In fact, I was the one reading the spells off a piece of paper. Blackstone—um, Aethelstan—hadn't even shown up yet because he didn't know where I had hidden her. Then we met with him, and Emma learned what had happened and, well, she got mad."

"Of course she got mad." Atropos waggled a finger at Blackstone. "We warned you about that."

"Too late," he said. "You wouldn't tell me how to undo the spell I'd cast."

"We did tell you," Clotho said. "We told you to leave the girl untouched for ten years. Seems like you finally had a chance to do that."

"By hiding her from Ealhswith," he said. "But Ealhswith has her now."

"So find her," Lachesis said. "Leave us out of it."

"I can't," he said. "This is very serious."

"Yes, it is," Atropos said. "You've let an unequipped girl with no knowledge of her world run around loose in a modern mortal city. That threatens all of us."

"No," Nora said. "I did."

Blackstone frowned at her, as if to keep her quiet, but she ignored him.

"I was the one who was supposed to be helping her. My mother"—Nora nodded toward her mother, who surprisingly took a small bow—"baby-sat her and did a good job, I think, even this morning, despite what happened. And Mr. Chawsir—"

"Oh, no," Clotho moaned. "Another one of those English writers."

"We'll have to call the meeting short," Lachesis said.

"I hate to be portrayed as a crone," Atropos said.

"I'm not that Chaucer!" Jeffrey said, then shook his head as if he couldn't believe the insanity he had walked into.

"I can vouch for that," Blackstone said. "The writer has been dead for centuries. This man is a mere professor."

"No one is a mere professor," Amanda said, rising to her full height. "Mr. Blackstone, or whoever you are, you owe a great debt to Jeffrey. He's the one who taught Emma things that no one else could, and she was happy to learn them. It gave her a sense of confidence to learn on her own."

"That's not what we're discussing," Blackstone said. His back was rigid with stress.

"Yes," Clotho said. "What are we discussing?"

"Emma!" Blackstone snapped. "We need to get her away from Ealhswith."

"So say you," Lachesis said, "and frankly, Aethelstan, you haven't been very trustworthy on this subject."

He let go of Nora and took a step forward. She moved with him. He glared at her, but she didn't care. She was going to stay beside him. He needed a lot of help. These women were impossible.

"You've taken years from Ealhswith," he said. One of the women opened her mouth, but Blackstone held up his hand. "And rightly so. But she isn't willing to go gently into that good night."

"What?" Atropos whispered.

"He's quoting another English writer," Clotho whispered back.

"Actually," Jeffrey said, "he's quoting a Welsh writer."

"As if there's a difference," Atropos said.

"Don't say that to the Welsh," Jeffrey said.

The three women glared at him. Blackstone ignored the exchange. "Ealhswith doesn't like getting older," Blackstone said, "and she's not willing to die when her time comes. Her plan is to make a switch. She'll put Emma in her own body and take Emma's body as her own. Emma will die in her place."

"Ealhswith cannot do that," Lachesis said to Blackstone. "We outlawed that spell five hundred years ago."

"Her plan predates that," Blackstone said.

"It doesn't matter. She still can't conduct the spell," Atropos said.

"Of course she can," Blackstone said. "The question is whether or not you'll catch her."

"You made this claim once before," Clotho said. "It isn't credible. Not with the squabble the two of you have been conducting over Emma."

"I was going to let Emma go after the first hundred years," Blackstone said. "Then I discovered what Ealhswith was going to do—"

"It seems to me you just assumed it," Lachesis said. "You could offer no proof."

"—and since you wouldn't do anything, I had to. I had to keep Emma away from her."

"You weren't very successful at that," Atropos said.

"It would have been easier if I had had your help," Blackstone said.

"You really should let this go, Aethelstan," Clotho said.

"I can't!" he said. "Ealhswith has Emma, and now there's nothing to prevent her from carrying through with her plan."

"Except that Ealhswith isn't dying," Lachesis said. "She still has thousands of years ahead of her."

"She's going to put Emma back in suspended

animation. She thinks Emma is the perfect switch candidate, so she'll make sure that she will have Emma."

"Do you have proof of this?" Atropos asked, pocketing her shears and crossing her arms. Her long flowing sleeves caught on her fingers, and she had to shake them loose.

"Emma came out of her coma," Blackstone said. "I've left her alone for the last month. Ealhswith and I were not squabbling over her."

"I can vouch for that," Nora said. "Emma's been with me, my mother, or Jeffrey the entire time."

"But Ealhswith still kidnapped Emma," Blackstone said. "Why?"

"Perhaps," Clotho said, "Emma went willingly."

"I doubt that," Nora said. "Emma is afraid of Ealhswith."

"This is all supposition," Lachesis said. "We do not operate on supposition. We don't even know if Ealhswith is the one who took her."

"Yes, we do," Amanda said. "I saw it all. If Ealhswith's the one with a streak of white through her hair and a fearsome demeanor, and the worst taste in clothing—"

"Blathering!" Atropos said.

"That is not blathering," Blackstone said. "That's testimony."

"Oh," Clotho said. "If you had told us that the mortals were going to testify to pertinent events, we could have saved ourselves a lot of trouble."

She waved a slender hand, and suddenly a scene appeared before them, thin and indistinct, like a movie projection made on a piece of glass. Nora recognized the scene. It was the same one that had played when Blackstone had swung his hand like that.

It was from Amanda's point of view, in the park. Up the concrete stairs was the hot dog vendor. Steam rose around his cart, and he looked too hot by half. Emma was standing before him, wearing another of Nora's favorite sundresses. She clutched a twenty in her right hand. The hot dog vendor was talking to her, but this projection came without sound. Emma nodded, and then Ealhswith appeared beside her. Emma took a step back, but the vendor didn't notice. He was making a dog. Emma exchanged words with Ealhswith, and then, as the vendor looked up and started to hand Emma her dog, she and Ealhswith vanished.

Then Clotho ran her hand over Jeffrey, and suddenly the projection changed. They were inside a Chinese restaurant, decorated in pink, with ironwork done in Chinese characters on the wall. A woman was taking his order—

Clotho waved her hand, and the scene disappeared.

"That wasn't relevant," Lachesis said.

"I don't see why we have to go with these scruffy mortals' versions of events anyway," Atropos said. "Why can't we speak to the one with the hot dogs? He would have a better perspective. He would have been able to hear—"

"Do you want me to get him?" Blackstone said.

"Of course not," said Clotho. "There are too many mortals here as it is."

"We cannot tell from that memory if Emma went with Ealhswith by force," Lachesis said.

"Of course she did," Nora said. Why couldn't they understand? Were these women being deliberately obtuse? Was this what Blackstone had faced from the beginning? "She hated Ealhswith."

"So you say, child," said Atropos. "But according to your earlier testimony, she wanted nothing to do with Aethelstan either. For all we know, she could have decided that she was better off with Ealhswith."

"Ealhswith was her mentor, after all," said Clotho. "Perhaps she is simply going to complete Emma's magical training. The girl will need it."

"I doubt that," Nora said.

"Really?" Lachesis asked, the question a sincere one. How come they were giving Nora so much respect and were so rude to Amanda and Jeffrey?

"I have proof that Ealhswith doesn't want Emma to be her own person. Written proof," Nora said.

"Really?" all three woman asked at once.

"The papers," Blackstone breathed. He made it sound as if she had just saved his life.

Nora nodded. "They're on my desk."

"I'll get them." He vanished.

Jeffrey turned to Nora. He looked owlish and not a bit frightened. "You could have told me."

"What? That I'd been hired by a wizard?" Nora said. "That you were teaching history to a witch?"

"That everything Emma was telling me was true," he said.

"Emma spoke of our business to a mortal?" Atropos asked.

"He seems to be a savvy mortal," Clotho said.

Then Blackstone reappeared. He looked a bit windblown, and his left cheek was bright red as if it had been bruised. He held the papers in his right hand.

"I'm not sure I like the way people pop in and out," Jeffrey muttered.

Blackstone handed the papers to Nora. She perused them once, made sure they were the correct documents, and then reached them out to the Fates. The papers disappeared from her hands, and three copies appeared in the hands of the Fates.

"Instant photocopying," Amanda said. "How convenient."

"Those are," Nora said, taking a step toward the Fates and ignoring Amanda, "committal papers. They claim that Emma is incompetent to handle her own affairs and must be placed into the custody of Ealhswith, who can then make all of Emma's decisions for her."

"What is this 'schizophrenic affective disorder'?" Atropos asked.

"The disease Ealhswith claims Emma has."

"'This disease often causes its victim to believe others are acting against her best interests, which is a belief in conflict with reality.'" Clotho was reading aloud. "'Often this belief is caused by delusional thoughts generated by "voices" heard by the victim advising her of facts not based in reality.' Is this another one of those English writer tricks?"

"No," Blackstone said. "It's a legal trick. Mortals have a legal system that binds them just like ours binds us. Ealhswith has decided to play in that world to get custody of Emma."

"'Delusional thoughts,'" Lachesis read. "Is this true? Has Emma lost her mind during her long sleep?"

"Of course not," Nora said. "But Ealhswith is claiming this so that she'll be able to do anything she wants to Emma."

"Such a thing is possible within your legal system?" Atropos asked.

"Within limits," Nora said. "She can't murder her for example."

"But isn't that what you're claiming she wants to do?" Clotho asked.

Nora sighed. Nitpicky legalistic minds. She hated that. "Not in the same way. I mean, Ealhswith can't take a knife to Emma's throat. No mortal would be able to tell that the two of them switched bodies."

"Good point," said Lachesis.

"Nor would they be able to recognize a magically induced coma, which is where I think Ealhswith is going to take Emma, if she hasn't already," Blackstone said. "Last time I was an unwitting accomplice. This time, I will not be."

"What do you want us to do?" Atropos asked.

"The best case is that I want you to find Emma and bring her back to Nora's house, unharmed," Blackstone said.

"That's action before the fact," Clotho said. "We can only punish a crime or provide a window into another world. You know that, Aethelstan."

He smiled faintly. Nora wanted to put her arm around him again, to give him support. "I had to try," he said.

"So I repeat," Lachesis said. "What do you want us to do?"

"At least tell me where she is so that I can go get her," Blackstone said.

Clotho was frowning, and Lachesis looked thoughtful. But Atropos was shaking her head.

"I've done everything required of us," Blackstone

said. "I've never broken our laws. I've worked for the betterment of those around me. I've even followed the prophecies as I've understood them. I haven't done a thing wrong."

"Except that first spell," Atropos said.

"Not even that was wrong," Blackstone said. "I was trying to save Emma's life."

"You could have brought her to us," Clotho said. "We would have saved her."

"I didn't find out about you until after the spells," Blackstone said.

"Ignorance is no excuse," Lachesis said.

"It is when it makes a certain action impossible," Blackstone said. "I did everything I could then."

"And stole a thousand years from a girl's life," said Atropos.

"Not intentionally," Blackstone said. "And it wouldn't have been that long if you had but listened to me nine hundred years ago."

"You cannot blame us for your error," Clotho said.

"I'm not," Blackstone said. "I'm taking full responsibility for my actions. But in doing so, in confronting you now, I'm taking more precious time from Emma. If Ealhswith spells her again, she's trapped."

"For all you know, she may already be trapped," Lachesis said.

"Yes," Blackstone said. "But I'll try to prevent it until I know for certain."

"Why do you do this for Emma?" Atropos asked.

"Because of the prophecy," Blackstone said.

"The prophecy—?" Clotho turned to her companions.

"You know," Nora said, unable to stand the way they

were grilling Blackstone, and him without proper repre-
sentation. She wasn't sure she liked their customs at all.
"The one that says she's his true love?"

The three women laughed. Lachesis lifted her arms
above her head. "We must confer," she said, and all
three of them vanished.

Jeffrey staggered a few feet forward until he reached
the marble steps. Then he sat down. "Someone want to
tell me what's going on?"

Amanda sat beside him. "What an exhausting afternoon. I've seen it all and I still don't believe it."

Blackstone ran a hand through his hair and turned away
from them. He walked down the grass toward a fountain.
The water spouted from an overturned urn in the hands of
a boy wearing a small skirt around his waist. Around the
fountain were more marble benches, in a circular pattern
that looked deliberate. Everything was very formal here,
molded. Nora hadn't noticed its artificiality before now.

She glanced at her mother and Jeffrey, then at
Blackstone.

"Do you think we will find Emma?" Amanda asked.

"I don't know," Jeffrey said.

"Oh, Jeffrey. This is very confusing to me." She
rested her head on Jeffrey's shoulder. He put his arm
around her.

It looked like a perfect moment, and one Nora didn't
want to interrupt. She turned her back on them and
walked to Blackstone.

He was throwing coins into the fountain. She watched
as a single penny spun in the air, then splashed into the
water. It came to rest against other coins, most of which
she didn't recognize.

"I'm sorry about losing Emma," she said.

"It's my fault," he said. "I should have been protecting her. I know how tricky Ealhswith can be."

"I asked you not to."

He shook his head. "That doesn't cut it, Nora. I know what Ealhswith's capable of, and you don't. Or maybe you didn't. I suspect you do now."

"How long do we wait for the Fates?"

"Until they make their decision," he said. "They're our best hope."

The red mark hadn't left his cheek. As Nora looked at it, she realized it was in the shape of a hand. She reached up and touched his skin lightly. "What happened to you?"

"Ruthie," he said and smiled crookedly. "She was putting papers on your desk when I appeared. I guess I ended up too close."

Nora grinned. Ruthie hated it when she thought men were taking liberties. "I thought you could charm her."

"I promised you I wouldn't."

She laid her own hand over the red mark. It was hot to the touch. "She really walloped you."

He shrugged. "I caught her by surprise."

"I'm sorry."

"You don't have to keep apologizing," he said. "None of this is your fault."

"Yes, it is," Nora said. "If I hadn't played legal games—"

"Who knows where we'd be right now. Emma could have run off on that first night and been vulnerable to half a dozen things I don't want to contemplate." He put his hand over Nora's, then lowered them both. He ran his forefinger over her knuckles, his touch soft. "You should never apologize for doing what you think is right."

"That's what you were doing to the Fates. Apologizing for saving Emma's life."

"I harmed Emma in doing so," he said. "I violated one of our first tenets. Do not act until you know the consequences."

"If you had waited, wouldn't Emma have died?"

He shook his head. "Not if I'm right. Not if Ealhswith wanted her body."

"But you couldn't have known that then."

"No," he said. "And that was the Fates' argument early on. They felt that if Ealhswith wanted Emma's body, she wouldn't have done such a risky spell. But over the years, I've learned that Ealhswith does most things in a risky manner. And she does them after making an educated guess about the way others will react. She predicted I'd do that spell, and she predicted the results. In both areas, she was correct."

Nora turned her hand in Blackstone's and laced her fingers through his. "I always thought the wicked stepmother was a patriarchal myth, designed to emasculate powerful women."

Blackstone laughed softly. "Judging my culture by the standards of yours, are you?"

She shrugged. "I thought these things were all fairy tales."

"Fairy tales always have a basis in truth."

"So I'm learning."

His fingers tightened around hers. "If the wicked stepmother was a myth designed to emasculate powerful women," he said, "how do you explain the Fates?"

"I thought they were Greek."

"That's different?"

"Greece always had a large roster of powerful women. Athena, Hera, even Aphrodite. All of them strong, all of them lusty, all of them smart."

"All of them friends of mine," Blackstone said. "And they have other qualities as well. Usually good qualities, but not always. Just like mortals."

"How can you people incorporate all the myths and legends? Or claim to?"

"We come into our powers," he said, "at different times. I was twenty-one over a thousand years ago. A friend of mine turned twenty-one about two centuries before that and formed the basis for the legends of Arthur. Myth happens because we don't learn how to hide our powers, or we're still so tied to the mortal world that we use our powers in indiscreet ways. Arthur, for example, used all of his powers to create Camelot, ignoring the prophecies, yet making a place of such greatness that you know about it today. For that, he became an old man in a normal mortal span and was sent, at the end, to Avalon where the Fates decided that he would be allowed some of his powers back as long as he never visited Camelot again."

"So this is Avalon?" Nora asked.

Blackstone shrugged. "If you want it to be. Or maybe it's Olympus. Or Atlantis. Or perhaps the Catholics are right, and this is Purgatory."

"Meaning you won't tell me," she said.

"Meaning I don't really know," he said. He looked at the fountain. "Each time I come, it's different. This is the first time the Fates have looked like their Greek counterparts."

"They didn't when we first arrived."

He grinned at her. "No, they didn't."

"Are they really Clotho, Lachesis, and Atropos?"

His eyebrows raised. "Where did you learn the name of the Fates?"

This time it was her turn to shrug. "I had mythologies of the world in school. But before that, I used to read Greek mythology books when I was a kid. I read them like I read fairy tales."

"Those awful Grimm Brothers?"

"And Hans Christian Andersen."

"The twerp."

"You knew him?"

Blackstone nodded. "The Match Girl—a friend of his. He could have helped her, but no."

"I thought he's a Danish hero."

"That's because they never met him. Pompous, pretentious—"

"Aethelstan?" The voice came from behind them. The three Fates were standing on the manicured lawn, their sandals peeking out from beneath their robes. Nora was close enough to see, on the top of the blonde's right foot, a tattoo of a spiderweb. Clotho noticed where Nora was looking and slid the foot back under her robe. "We've decided."

Blackstone's grip on Nora's hand tightened.

"We weighed many factors in this," Lachesis said.

"The prophecy," Atropos said.

"The misdone spells," Clotho said.

"Ealhswith's history," Lachesis said.

"And yours," said Atropos.

"We have decided that we can tell you this," Clotho said.

"Emma is not yet in a coma, although we suspect you are right in Ealhswith's intent," Lachesis said.

"And Ealhswith is where you would least expect her," said Atropos.

"At home?" Blackstone blurted.

Clotho smiled and patted Blackstone on the cheek. "Our boy is growing up," she said to the others.

"Careful, Aethelstan," said Lachesis. "In a few centuries, you might even be as smart as us."

They all laughed as they vanished, their laughter echoing long after they were gone.

Nora couldn't help herself; she shuddered. "I don't know if I missed that. Did they confirm your guess?"

He nodded. Then he sighed. "I'll take you home. Then I'll go."

"No," Nora said. "Emma needs a champion. She's still not certain of you."

"She needs all of us," Amanda said from the steps. She stood, brushed off her legs, then held out a hand to Jeffrey. He let her pull him up.

"I don't think you all understand what Ealhswith could do," Blackstone said.

"She can't kill mortals," Nora said. "You taught me that much. That was outlawed years ago."

"Kill—?" Amanda said.

"And if she turns us into toads, she has to turn us back."

"Toads!?!" Jeffrey said.

"And, if I remember correctly, she also has to wipe our memories of the event, which defeats the purpose, or so she once said."

"My God, Counselor," Blackstone said in

appreciation. "Remind me to never cross you when it comes to your memory."

"Duly noted, Mr. Blackstone," Nora said with a smile. Then she let the smile fade. "Can we get Emma now?"

Blackstone bowed slightly. "Your wish is my command."

———

She had used too much magic today. Ealhswith stretched out on her unmade bed and popped a piece of dark chocolate into her mouth. She was tired, amazingly so, but more satisfied than she had been in weeks.

Maybe she would take a long bath. A long bath in scented water, with black candles burning on the side, and Black Sabbath on the stereo. It sounded like a wonderful, relaxing way to spend the afternoon.

She had a lot to do. She had to finish the new glass case by hand—she simply couldn't order one to size, and right at the moment, she needed to reserve her magical abilities. Sometime in the next week, Blackstone would find her, and Ealhswith needed all of her strength for that battle.

He would lose, of course. He didn't realize what was so very plain to everyone around him. He no longer cared for Emma. He was being distracted by that annoying little attorney. And that would dull his edge.

This time, he would lose Emma. Ealhswith would win. She would have Emma's body for the next thousand years or so, and when the end came, as it inevitably would, she would move herself from her own rather magnificent body to Emma's less-than-perfect one.

The Fates had already ruled that the disagreement between Blackstone and Ealhswith was personal business. In the next thousand years or so, Ealhswith would look him up, then conveniently let him "find" the glass coffin, with Emma's body inside.

Emma's body and Ealhswith's soul. Blackstone, fool that he was, would think he was looking on his soul mate, and he would revive her.

He would never guess that it was Ealhswith who would be spending eternity at his side.

She smiled and ate another piece of chocolate. "I so love it when a plan comes together," she said and got up to draw her bath.

Chapter 10

THEY REAPPEARED IN THAT SAME BEAVERTON neighborhood that Blackstone and Ealhswith had burned ten years before. In fact, Nora soon realized, they appeared on the front lawn of the house that had remained untouched in that blaze, the place where Blackstone had been arrested, the place where Sancho had parked the VW microbus in the street.

The house looked so different now. It had received a new coat of paint not too long ago, a robin's egg blue that was both vivid and an incredible eyesore. The lawn was green and lush, and flowers filled a spectacular bed before the picture window. The garage door was open, and a dark blue Saab was parked inside.

Nora turned and glanced at the neighbor's house across the street. A curtain flickered. Apparently the same nosy radio guy still lived there—or else he'd sold the place to some other nosy person.

"You can't tell me a witch lives here," Amanda whispered. "I would think she'd go for one of the older neighborhoods, perhaps on the east side. Not a newer development like this and certainly not in the *suburbs*." She said that last as if it were hell itself, which, Nora had to admit, for her mother it was.

"Shush, Amanda," Jeffrey whispered. "I live in the suburbs."

"Nonsense," Amanda whispered. "Eugene's too small to have suburbs."

Blackstone ignored the entire exchange. He took a step toward the house, then peered into the garage. He still had a firm grip on Nora's hand, and she wasn't really willing to let go either. She felt a strength in their clasped fingers, a strength she was afraid she'd lose if he let go.

"I can't believe she's here," he said. "Why would she do this?"

"Because," Jeffrey said, "she knew you wouldn't think of it."

"How many times had she done this before?" Blackstone asked.

"I don't think it pays to look back," Amanda said. "It certainly doesn't for me."

"I think Mother's actually right for once," Nora said. "I don't think, in this instance, it pays to do any sort of recrimination. We need to get Emma out of here and quickly."

"Should we fan out?" Jeffrey asked.

"Yes," Blackstone said. "I think the quicker we find Emma, the better off we'll be."

"Always hoping for something you can't have, aren't you, Aethelstan?" The voice came from the roof. Ealhswith sat near the chimney, her long robe trailing down the shingles like a wedding dress train.

"You have no right to Emma," Blackstone said.

Ealhswith smiled. "If you're going to pursue that argument, then neither do you."

"I've left her alone. I let her make her own choices."

"Over the protests of your pretty lawyer there." Ealhswith finger waved at Nora. "You realize you're early."

"Early?" Blackstone asked.

"I didn't expect you for at least a week."

His eyes narrowed. "I assumed time is of the essence."

Ealhswith shrugged and looked at Nora. "Did my attorney send my notes?"

"Yes," Nora said, drawing herself up to her full height. "They're in the hands of the Fates now."

"The Fates? Aethelstan, you'll never get them to help you." Ealhswith leaned forward slightly.

"I told them what you're planning," he said. "So they told me where you were."

"Planning?" Ealhswith raised her eyebrows. "What am I 'planning'?"

"To use Emma's body as your own," Nora said.

Ealhswith laughed. "My dear, do you know how difficult that is to prove? You have to wait until the deed is done. Are you going to wait?"

"No," Blackstone said. "Where is she?"

"Emma?" Ealhswith shrugged. "She's here somewhere. What are you going to do? Fight me for her?"

"If I have to."

"How chivalrous of you, Aethelstan. Still haven't gotten her out of your system?"

"She's my soul mate."

"Hmm, yes, well." Ealhswith stood. Then she held out a hand, and lightning flared from her fingertips. Blackstone moved in front of Nora, and the lightning hit him, illuminating his frame, showing his skeleton through his clothes. He clenched his teeth but didn't make a sound.

Nora reached toward him, then took her hands away, unwilling to burn them. "Let him go!" she shouted. "Let him go."

Ealhswith closed her fingers into a fist, and the

lightning stopped. Blackstone stumbled toward Nora, his clothes smoking. She put her arms around him to hold him up. He was warm and smelled of ozone, but nothing was burning.

"Tell him how I've always hated that word 'soul mates.' He's used it too many times in the last thousand years." Ealhswith walked to the edge of the roof. She gripped the edges of her robe.

"Let me go, Nora," Blackstone said under his breath, "or you're going to get it too. I'll take care of Ealhswith. You find Emma."

"But she'll hurt you."

"Nothing she hasn't done before," he whispered. Then he pushed away from Nora. "You don't like the word 'soul mate' because you don't have one, Ealhswith."

She screeched and extended her hands. Lightning flared again, but this time Blackstone blocked it with his palms. "Nora!" he whispered.

Nora didn't have to be told twice. She ran toward the garage, grabbing her mother along the way and beckoning Jeffrey. From above, it had to look as if they were going to hide.

They scurried into the darkness, behind the Saab. The concrete floor was amazingly clean, and unlike most garages, this one did not smell of ancient gas fumes or have any cobwebs.

"We have to find Emma," Nora said. "She's somewhere around here."

"Amanda, you go in the house through the garage," Jeffrey said. "Nora, you help your mother. I'll take the yard."

"No," Nora said. "The yard's not safe."

"I know," Jeffrey said. "But that old witch on the roof has her eye on you. I doubt she's even noticed me. I might be able to pass for a neighbor."

The air smelled of ozone. Nora could no longer see Blackstone, but a fire had started in the front yard. This was how they had burned the neighborhood the last time.

"No," Nora said. "Change of plans. Mother, go warn the neighbors to leave their houses. Blackstone and Ealhswith are going to start large fires. That's what happened last time."

"And I thought he was such a nice man," Amanda said and started toward the garage door.

"Amanda," Jeffrey hissed. "Go next door first."

Amanda nodded, and then, keeping low, she headed toward the next house on the block. A ball of fire landed in the street, ignited against some old oil, and continued to burn.

"I thought you said they had to put everything right," Jeffrey said.

"They do," Nora said. "I just don't want anyone to get hurt, even if it'll be repaired and they won't remember it."

Jeffrey leaned over and kissed her cheek. "You're as sweet as your mother."

"I'm not sure that's a compliment for a lawyer," Nora said. She headed off behind the Saab toward the door that connected the garage to the house. Outside, Blackstone came back into her range of vision. He flicked his front two fingers as if he were removing lint, and a fireball the size of Nora's head zoomed across the yard. She couldn't see if it hit its target.

Ealhswith was shouting, but Nora couldn't make out the words. Blackstone laughed in response. It was not a pretty sound.

Jeffrey pushed the air with his right hand, as if he could push her inside. Nora nodded, then took the two concrete steps and tried the gold doorknob. It turned. She stepped inside a well-lit kitchen. There were no dishes anywhere, and the appliances had clearly never been used. It looked like a model home's showroom kitchen, and still smelled new, even though Nora knew this home had been standing at least ten years.

She crossed into the living room. The carpet was white and looked as if it had never been stepped on. White leather couches and teak chairs covered the living room floor. A big screen TV dominated the room and DVDs spilled off it. *The Frighteners, American Werewolf in London, The Haunting*. Others had handwritten labels, mostly from television shows: *Bewitched, Sabrina the Teenage Witch*, and of course, *The X-Files*.

Was Ealhswith a movie buff? Was she watching because she was lonely or was she trying to pick up tips?

Nora didn't have time to find out. She walked through the living room and up the stairs that led to the second level. As she did, she hit a smell so powerful that it was like another wall. Mold and mud and stagnant water. Nora almost sneezed.

Something whooshed outside. Nora turned. The floor to ceiling windows near the front door entry showed a fire burning the pine tree in the lot on the other side of the street. It looked like the tree just exploded into flame.

Nora ran up the stairs. "Emma!" she called. "Emma!"

No one answered. She peeked into the master bedroom and wished she hadn't. More white, an unmade bed covered with a canopy and satin sheets. An opened box of chocolates was tangled in the white duvet. Another big screen television and a state-of-the-art entertainment system, with more DVDs scattered about, these mostly film noir classics like *Laura* and *A Touch of Evil*. Big stories about bad women. Nora had a hunch she knew who Ealhswith was rooting for.

The master bathroom had perfume vials and potion bottles, several of which smoked. It was the source of the smell. The tub was full of steaming water, with a skim of oil on the top. Unlit black candles were scattered along the rim. Nora backed out of that room and went back into the hallway. One room was empty except for a half assembled glass coffin. It surprised her that Ealhswith had been putting the thing together by hand. But the fact that it was half finished was a good sign. Emma wasn't in her coma yet.

"Emma!" Nora yelled again. She thought she heard something outside of the voices shouting outside. She yanked open the last door and stumbled into a menagerie.

Dogs in cages, trying to bark but unable to, their muzzles opening but nothing coming out. Cats in smaller cages, pawing at the locks. Fish in floor-to-ceiling tanks, all staring at Nora. A gerbil that had been running in its little wheel until Nora opened the door. Turtles and frogs and chameleons all in their little boxes. And a snake that looked somehow quite familiar.

Blackstone's snake? That horrible Ealhswith had taken it from him and let him think it was dead?

The house rattled, and more booms echoed outside. Nora's heart was pounding. The dogs continued their silent barking. The cats kept jiggling the cage doors. Nora parted a curtain. The neighborhood was burning. The house across the street was engulfed in flames and, as she watched, the flames traveled from one roof to the other. She looked down on the lawn. She saw someone running, but she couldn't tell if that was Blackstone.

In the distance, sirens wailed.

She let the curtain drop. Steeling herself, she grabbed the snake, and it slithered up her sleeve, like it used to do with Blackstone. Its scaly skin wasn't as sharp as she thought it would be. It was rather oily instead. Even so, she shuddered.

One of the frogs started jumping in its little aquarium. Leaping up against the mesh top, then landing on the pile of rocks, then leaping up against the mesh top, then landing. Nora frowned at it. The gerbil was peering against its glass cage, watching her.

The frog started leaping harder and harder, bashing its little head against the mesh.

With a simple flick of my finger, I could turn you into a toad.

Ealhswith had said that to her in Nora's apartment.

Aren't you being a bit clichéd? Blackstone had asked.

Nora's breath caught in her throat. The room was beginning to smell like smoke, but that wasn't what was bothering her. What bothered her was the idea she had just had, the idea that these weren't trapped animals. These were trapped people.

The frog was denting the wire mesh.

Nora leaned toward it. "Emma?"

The frog landed on its rock and nodded. Nora had never seen a frog nod. Only it wasn't a frog. It was too bumpy and small to be a frog.

It was a toad.

Nora turned to the other animals. "Are any of you Emma?"

The dogs stopped yapping and sat in their cages, their mouths hanging open and their tongues sticking out. The cats ignored her, continuing to try to grasp the locks. The fish were still staring at her, all lined up in front like computerized fish or photographs of fish. And the gerbil had its tiny paws against the glass.

"None of them are, but you are?" Nora said, turning to the toad.

It nodded again.

"My God," she said, pulling aside the mesh and grabbing the toad. It felt soft and rubbery beneath her fingers.

The snake slid out of her sleeve, hissing and snapping. The toad squirmed even more.

Nora shook that arm and let the snake drop. Then she put the toad in her shirt pocket, bent over, and grabbed the snake beside its little eyes. She raised it to her face.

"If you ever want to see Blackstone again," she said, "you'll do as I say. Leave that toad alone."

The toad was watching out of her pocket. Nora let the snake climb up her sleeve again. Then she crept through the hall, down the stairs, and into the garage.

The snake had wrapped itself around her upper bicep. The toad kept its head out of her pocket but didn't move much beyond that. It was trembling. Nora touched it lightly with her finger.

"Hang on," she whispered. "This could get rough."

The toad nodded again.

Nora walked around the Saab. Big waves of inky black smoke were roiling down the street. The house next door was gone, and so was the house beyond that. The houses across the street were cindered remains. Ash was falling from the air. She couldn't see her mother or Jeffrey.

She stepped on the slight incline that separated the garage from the driveway. Blackstone was in the center of the lawn, lobbing fireballs at the roof. Apparently Ealhswith hadn't gotten down.

The sound of the sirens had grown.

Nora waved. Blackstone looked toward her, then instantly looked away. He lobbed another fireball, then another, and another. They flew toward the roof, but obviously didn't land because the house wasn't burning. Something exploded behind the house. Ealhswith was as good at diverting his spells as he was at diverting hers.

After lobbing the last he ran toward Nora. He reached her, put his arms around her waist, and helped her into the garage.

"I think this is Emma," she said, pointing at the toad. Blackstone squinted.

"By God," he said. "It is. Get her out of here, Nora."

"Where do I take her?" Nora asked.

Blackstone looked over his shoulder at the ruined neighborhood and winced. "Good question."

"Are you hiding, Aethelstan?" Ealhswith's voice floated down from the roof.

"Just stay put," he said, and as he started to leave, the snake shot out of Nora's sleeve and made a dive for Blackstone's arm. Nora had to catch it with her right hand.

"Malcolm?" Blackstone asked. The snake wrapped itself around his arm and peered into his face. "Malcolm?" He sounded thrilled.

"You have a snake named Malcolm?" Nora said.

Blackstone nodded. "He's my familiar. And I haven't needed him more than I need him right now."

"Aethelstan, are you afraid of me?" Ealhswith sounded as if she were pleased.

"Not on your life, Ealhswith," he shouted. Then he patted Emma on the head. "You don't know how much easier you've just made this," he said, and ran back to the front yard.

Nora stepped out farther. The smoke was hurting her lungs. The air had gotten so hot that she could barely breathe.

"This time you won't find a glass coffin in my garage," Ealhswith said.

"I know," Blackstone said. He whirled, going faster and faster until he was just a blur.

A fire truck pulled up on the street, and the men on the truck stared at Blackstone. Nora did too. The toad was still trembling in her pocket.

Then black lines shot out of the whirling dervish that was Blackstone. They went toward the roof, and above her, Nora heard a thud.

"You can't do this! You can't!" Ealhswith shouted. "If you hurt me, you'll hurt Emma!"

The toad cringed in Nora's pocket.

A black-wrapped Ealhswith fell off the roof like a charred bowling ball. It hit the eave above the front door, bounced, and landed in the lawn.

Blackstone stopped whirling and stood over her.

"I can do anything I want," he said. "Because I know where Emma is, and I know how to save her this time."

He nudged the black-wrapped ball with his foot. It whimpered.

"Can't cast a spell now, can you?" he asked. "It's rather scary when you can't move your arms."

Nora stayed in the garage. She didn't trust this. Not yet.

"I think a thousand-year sleep might be a good punishment. Or maybe I should kill you so that you can't inflict yourself on anyone else." He peered at Ealhswith through the black wrapping. Nora couldn't see anything except small bits of flesh.

Then he shook his head. "But that would make me as bad as you. Your future belongs to the Fates. They'll figure out what to do with you."

He waved an arm over Ealhswith, and the entire black ball disappeared.

Several more fire trucks pulled up, and the fireman started spraying water on the other houses. Blackstone walked toward the garage.

"If you could do that all along," Nora said, "why did you let this go on?"

"I couldn't do that all along," he said. "It takes centuries of training to do that one spell, and sometimes the mage you attack doesn't survive it. I didn't dare risk it, not while Emma was in her coma."

"But she's a toad now," Nora said. "And Ealhswith did that. There are a dozen more animals upstairs."

Blackstone nodded. "As I said, I've learned a little during this last millennium."

The toad poked its head out of Nora's pocket and

watched everything with its large eyes. Blackstone's snake peeked out of his collar and hissed.

"Pleasant familiar," Nora said.

More and more fire trucks were showing up. The sky was black, the sun gone. Smoke covered everything. The ashfall covered Nora, the car, the yard. Particles floated in the air.

"But first," Blackstone said, his smile for Nora, "we take care of the neighborhood."

"Kind of you," she said.

"I remember your complaints the last time. Besides," he said, "if I don't, we'll be inundated with more and more people."

"Not to mention the loss of air." Nora coughed, and it wasn't for effect. Her throat was raw.

Blackstone turned. He seemed to be bracing himself, drawing strength, as if he had just finished a marathon and was then told he had to run for five more miles. He spread out his arms, mumbled something in that archaic Danish, and everything disappeared.

Whiteness, opaqueness.

Nora felt dizzy.

Then the buildings were back as they were. The fire was gone. The smoke was gone. The air was clean and fresh. The flowers still bloomed, and the pine tree across the street stood tall and proud. There were no fire trucks on the street, only a handful of cars that had been parked there.

The curtains moved in the radio personality's house, and Nora thought she saw a face in the window.

"Thanks," she said.

"My pleasure," Blackstone said, bowing again. It touched her every time he did that. He seemed elegant and courtly and somehow right. On any other man that action would seem like an affectation. "Now let's take care of Emma. Please take her out of your pocket and place her on the driveway."

"You're sure this is Emma?"

"Aren't you?" he asked.

Nora bit her lower lip. How to say that the toad looked like a toad to her? Actually, it looked like a frog to her, or had from a distance.

"Don't worry," he said. "It's Emma. I recognize her eyes."

Nora looked. The bulging eyes looked like frog eyes. She took the toad out of her pocket and placed it on the driveway. Then she stepped back. The toad just sat there, watching Blackstone.

He stepped toward the road. Then he raised his arms, muttered more in Danish, then repeated parts of the spell in English. It sounded vaguely like Shakespearean dialogue from Macbeth. No wonder the bard had gotten the witches scene from the Fates.

Blackstone ended it with a shouted, "Reverse Ealhswith's spells!" and then he clapped his hands. There was a loud boom, and Nora was knocked backward onto the ground.

She landed beside the Saab, but there was no concrete beneath her. She had scraped her elbows and hands on grass. Frowning she looked up. Dozens of naked people littered what was now a vacant lot, along with furniture that had tumbled haphazardly into place. The couch and chairs were in the same spots they had been in that living room, but the bed had fallen on its side. Both big screen TVs were there as well as all the DVDs.

The glass coffin had shattered.

The naked people were sitting beside each other, holding their heads. They all looked toward Blackstone, and he cursed slightly.

Nora looked at him too. Behind him, Emma sat on the grass. She was also naked. And perfect. Nora had never known another woman to look so perfect.

Emma was staring at her own hands, then at the space where the house had been.

"Good heavens, that child needs a coat!"

The voice belonged to Amanda. Nora turned. Her mother was behind her, and Jeffrey was beside her, much in the same positions they had been in before they decided to scout the neighborhood.

"Give her your shirt, Jeffrey," Amanda said.

Jeffrey started to unbutton his shirt. Blackstone took a step toward all the naked people and swore again.

Then he held his arms up and said, "To the Fates!" and clapped his hands together again.

The naked people—except for Emma—disappeared.

"What're you doing?" Nora asked.

"Sending evidence," he said.

"They were people, not evidence."

"Too many for me to deal with." He turned toward her. "It would have been a mess."

"You could have spelled them like you planned to spell Emma."

"It's not that simple," he said. "Didn't you recognize Jimmy Hoffa in there? And the crew of the *Marie Celeste*? Obviously Ealhswith has been doing this for a long time. And keeping them as some sort of vendetta."

Jeffrey got up and wrapped his shirt around Emma. That seemed to break her spell. She patted his hands and stood slowly, her gaze still on Blackstone.

"Aethelstan," she said. "I misjudged you."

He shot Nora a quick glance, so quick that she wondered if she imagined that he was rolling his eyes. Then he turned toward Emma. "No," he said. "I owe you an apology."

"No, you do not," she said. "I owe you an apology. You saved my life."

Then she ran into his arms, Jeffrey's shirt flapping around her. They spun slightly, and Blackstone looked at Nora over Emma's shoulder.

"You saved me," Emma said again. Then she grabbed his head, brought it down, and kissed him.

Nora held her breath. Blackstone looked alarmed. But Emma giggled. "See!" she said. "Even that spell has been reversed."

"I guess so," he said, and for some reason he didn't sound happy.

Emma backed out of his grasp and wrapped the shirt around herself. She smiled at Nora. "Thank you," she said. "You were great. As were you, Amanda. And you, Jeffrey. I owe you so much. I shall get you a new shirt."

He nodded, as if he were in shock. Nora was trembling. Things were moving too fast for her.

Emma grabbed Blackstone's hand. "Let us leave," she said.

He glanced at Nora. "Do you have objections, Counselor?"

"Not if my client doesn't," she said, amazed that her voice could sound so calm.

Blackstone frowned slightly and looked at Emma.

"Object?" Emma said. "No. I finally understand what has happened. I am ready to face the future. It is time to get to know Aethelstan. This Aethelstan. He says we are soul mates, you know." She smiled at all of them, and it was like a blessing from the gods. "I will make sure Aethelstan pays you for your services."

"Women don't rely on men for money anymore, my dear," Amanda said, a bit primly.

But she was speaking to the air. Emma and Blackstone were gone.

Chapter 11

TWO WEEKS LATER, NORA STILL HADN'T CLOSED THE file. She didn't know how.

Should she put in her notes that she had witnessed a gigantic magic battle? That she had seen dozens of animals change into dozens of naked people, one of whom might have been Jimmy Hoffa, and then watched as the entire group vanished? Should she mention that her client had disappeared—literally into thin air?

Every time she thought about recording any of her thoughts about the Emma Lost case, she realized how hopeless it was. How hopeless it all was.

And it was over. That's what she kept telling herself. Somehow she managed to get through the days, meeting new clients, doing new cases, going to court, talking to Ruthie. The nights were the hard part. Her apartment seemed empty, and it didn't help that Darnell had started going into Emma's room and howling until all hours, as if that would bring her back.

He was probably insulted that Emma's spinning wheel had disappeared the day after Emma had. If Blackstone was willing to come and get Emma's prized possessions, the least he could do was take the cat whose heart Emma had stolen.

But Emma clearly wasn't thinking of anyone but Emma. She hadn't been since the entire group rescued her from Ealhswith.

To be fair, Nora hadn't really been thinking of anyone but Nora either. After the first day's shock had worn off, she had bought herself two large cartons of chocolate chip cookie dough ice cream and eaten them both while she watched sappy movies. She hadn't acted like this when she separated from Max; she couldn't believe she was acting like this over a man who had done little more than smile at her.

He had probably charmed her. Blackstone, not Max. Despite his promise. He had probably raised those long, beautiful arms of his, recited something in Danish, and made her melt every time she saw him.

That had to be it. She wouldn't have fallen in love with him on her own.

Even though, in her heart, she knew she had.

And she didn't know how to talk about this. Ruthie was pretending that Blackstone didn't exist. Nora's mother was having difficulties of her own. She finally had to accept the existence of magic, after all that evidence.

"I should have trusted your father," she said to Nora. "But I thought he was foolish."

At least Amanda had Jeffrey. Nora had no one.

One night, in a moment of weakness, she had called Max. He, at least, had been sympathetic. She told him everything, and for once, he didn't pretend that she was talking about mobsters. He told her to treat herself, to be kind to herself, and he even promised to back off on the nasty parts of the divorce.

He had kept that promise. His response had been the only good thing to come from this entire mess.

Mostly she thought about Blackstone, and most of

these thoughts went through her mind in the middle of the night, long after she had exhausted herself at work— and lately, at the health club, figuring if she couldn't sleep naturally, and sleeping pills left her groggy, she would try good old-fashioned exercise. But that simply made her muscles sore and made her bed seem even more uncomfortable than it already did.

Squidgy didn't like her tossing and turning either. The cat had taken to sitting on her headboard, waiting until Nora had finally dropped off, and then jumping on the bed, waking her up. She was beginning to think sleep would be as elusive as Blackstone was.

Although she knew how to reach him. All she had to do was go to his restaurant, but she didn't really have a reason to. Their business was completed. The wicked stepmother had been vanquished. He was now living happily ever after with Emma.

As much as she wished them both well, Nora really didn't want to see what eternal happiness looked like. Especially when she had a hunch it would pass her by.

It was 3:00 a.m. on a Thursday night, two weeks after Blackstone had defeated Ealhswith, that Nora's doorbell rang. She knew because she looked. She also knew because it had been the first time that she had fallen asleep at anything like her normal time in weeks. So of course someone had to ruin it.

As she got up, she slid her feet into her slippers and grabbed her robe. The doorbell rang again as she hurried down the stairs. When she reached the door, she peered through the peephole. And saw nothing.

"Dammit, Sancho," she said. "Can't you show up during business hours?"

"These are business hours," he said from the other side of the door. "In England."

"I'm not in England. Come back tomorrow."

"This is tomorrow."

"You know what I mean."

Outside the door, she heard the unmistakable sound of a chuckle. "That's why you're so perfect, you know."

"Flattery won't get me to let you in."

"Come on, Nora," Sancho said. "Aren't you in the least bit curious why I'm here?"

He got her there. Through her exhaustion and her frustration, she had to admit curiosity. Maybe Blackstone had sent him.

Maybe pigs flew.

Maybe if someone cast the right spell on them, anyway.

She pulled the door open. Sancho came inside. He was wearing a velvet smoking jacket and a pair of matching trousers. "Aren't you hot?"

"It's cold in Australia," he said. "It's their winter."

"You're not in Australia. This is Oregon, or have you forgotten?"

"I haven't forgotten a thing." He pushed the door closed and walked toward the couch as if he were the one who lived here. Darnell, who had been sleeping in Emma's room, came out and stared at Sancho.

"Is that Emma's cat?"

"No," Nora said. "It's my cat. But it seems to have adopted Emma."

"Mind losing it?"

"To Emma? Why should I mind? The damn cat screeches for her all night anyway."

"Good," he said and plunked down on the couch.

"You didn't come here to ask me about a cat."

"No, I didn't." He ran a hand over his brow. "You weren't kidding. It is hot here. I thought the Northwest cools off at night."

"It does. It was one hundred today."

"Zowie." He stood and removed the smoking jacket, revealing a tuxedo shirt beneath. For some reason all that velvet looked good on him.

"If you didn't come for Darnell, then why are you here?"

"To see if you'll go to Blackstone."

It felt like a punch in the stomach. No one had spoken his name around her since the day after he disappeared. She'd had to clarify things for her mother and Jeffrey, who looked skeptical when she described Emma as the love of Blackstone's life, and then Nora had gone into a self-imposed silence.

"If he wants to see me, he knows where I am," she said, perching on her armchair. Sancho was hot, but she was too cold. Her robe was thin and she had the windows open. It had cooled down to at least fifty-five degrees, and a breeze was blowing that chilly air inside.

Sancho rolled his eyes. "He won't come to you."

"Then why should I go to him?"

"You still haven't figured it out?"

"No," Nora said.

"You're his soul mate."

"Right," she said. "And you are the king of England."

"No," he said. "I was the king's assistant."

"If one considers Arthur a full king of England, and not king of a smaller kingdom called Camelot."

Sancho's eyebrows went up. "Blackstone told you that?"

"Parts of it."

"And here I am now, acting like a matchmaker." He shook his head. "How the mighty hath fallen."

Nora rubbed her cold hands together. "Blackstone and I are as different as two people can be."

"Oh?" Sancho asked. "You seem similar to me. You're both strong personalities who act in the face of anything that comes your way. You're dynamic and interesting and basically unflappable."

"And I'm a mortal, and he's not. I'm thirty-five and he passed that mark 986 years ago. He's met everyone from King Arthur to Jimmy Hoffa and the most famous person I know is my soon-to-be ex-husband. He's—"

"For a lawyer, you make terrible points," Sancho said. "And you're as bad at putting two and two together as Blackstone is."

"What does that mean?"

"When you went to see the Fates, did they talk to you?"

"Of course."

"But what did they say about your mother and her lover?"

"Her lover—?"

"Oh, stop. You're not twelve. You knew that your mother's been sleeping with this Chawsir fellow. You just haven't wanted to acknowledge it." Sancho leaned forward. "I think it's true love, by the way."

"Since when did you become a romantic?"

"Look up your Geoffrey of Monmouth. I've always been a romantic." He leaned back. "What did the Fates say about your mother and her lover?"

"They said they were blathering."

He nodded. "And you have cats. Your mother doesn't."

"What's your point?" Nora snapped.

"You'll find out after menopause."

"Oh, shit," Nora said. "You're not implying I'm one of you."

He grinned. "You do catch on then, after someone clubs you over the head with it."

She put a hand over her eyes. She wasn't sure she was willing to let the implications of what he had just said sink in. "Why is this relevant?"

"Because," he said, "You and Blackstone aren't as different as you think."

"But he's off living happily ever after with Emma."

"Really?" Sancho said. "With little Emma?"

Nora's heart rose for just a moment. "He's not?"

"Come see for yourself," he said and waved an arm. She caught it halfway up.

"I'm not going to see him dressed like this," she said.

"So you're coming with me?"

She sighed. What could it hurt? "Will this be a Dickensian visit? You know, like the Ghosts of Christmas Present?"

He grinned. "How did you know that was me?"

"I didn't really," she said.

"Those English writers," he said, as if she hadn't spoken. "They always had to find a way to process their experiences."

She stood. She'd had enough. "If you were the Ghost of Christmas Present, how come Dickens portrayed him as tall?"

Sancho shrugged. "Revenge? A bad memory? Political correctness?"

"In 1843?"

He stood too. "All right," he said. "I'll be honest with

you, if it'll make you stop haranguing me and get you out of that ratty robe."

"It's a nice robe."

"It's not as nice as your normal clothes," he said pointedly.

She crossed her arms.

"I'm Andvari." He said that as if she should know the name.

"That's a relief," she said. "I was beginning to think you were Rumplestiltskin."

"No," he said with a bit of irritation. "My name is Andvari. That's the name I was born with. Andvari."

"So?"

"Don't they teach Norse myths in school anymore?"

"I don't know about anymore," she said, "but twenty years ago, they taught mostly Greek and Roman myths."

"Blatant discrimination," he said. "The Norse say that I was forced to give up my horde of gold and the magic ring that created it to Loki as payment to Otter's father for Otter, whom Loki had slain. I got a bit pissed, so I put a curse on the ring. There's more that has to do with dragons and gold piles, but that's the essence of it all."

"Is it true?"

"Is what true?"

"The myth?"

He shrugged. "I was bad-tempered when I was young."

She shook her head. "I don't know what I should believe anymore."

"I haven't lied to you," Sancho said. "Not once. Come with me to see Blackstone. Then you can make up your mind about him."

"One more thing before I go," she said. "Did he charm me?"

"The way you've been treating him? If he did, then all that would mean was that he was very bad at charming. And he isn't. But you've been countering his wishes from the beginning. No one does that, usually. He's smitten, lady, and has been for the past ten years. Why do you think he opened his restaurant in Portland?"

"So he could keep an eye on me while he guarded Emma's coffin."

"Baaaaaad idea, which is what I told him at the time," Sancho said. "He should have been in Hawaii or Iceland or somewhere else remote so that he wouldn't lead Ealhswith to you or Emma, but he didn't listen. He wanted to be close to you."

"You are so full of it," Nora said.

"I may be," Sancho said. "But I'm not lying. And I'm tired of standing around." He snapped a finger. Suddenly she was warmer. She looked down. She was wearing a black jacket with tasteful beaded embroidery running along the side, a pair of matching black pants, and black pumps.

"These aren't my clothes," she said.

"Consider them a gift," he said and waved his arm. Before she could catch it, he swung it all the way around. One minute she was in her apartment, and the next she was in Quixotic's kitchen.

She had to duck as a china plate whizzed by her and smashed against the wall. Blackstone was standing slightly to her side. He had his arms crossed and a bemused expression on his face.

Emma had grabbed another plate and was about to throw it. Sancho took Nora's arm and moved her behind one of the stainless steel tables.

"Can they see us?" Nora whispered.

"Of course we can see you," Blackstone said. He still hadn't looked in their direction.

"Do not speak for me!" Emma said as she lobbed another plate at him. He stepped to one side as the plate flew past and shattered against the wall. There was a large pile of broken china behind him.

"Are you going to keep throwing until you hit me?" he asked.

"Perhaps I will continue even after that!" she said and threw another plate. It sounded like a gunshot as it exploded against the wall.

"Then you'll owe me the cost of the china," he said.

"I owe you nothing!" she yelled.

"What's going on?" Nora asked.

"I think it's Ealhswith's influence," Blackstone said.

"It is not!" Emma shouted, picking up another plate. "It is you! You who treats me as if I am a common—wench!"

She threw the plate on that last word, and Blackstone stepped in the other direction. The plate slammed against the wall but did not shatter. It landed on top of the china shards and rolled off them, spinning as it hit the floor. It continued to spin for a moment, and then it shattered, as if in regret.

"I am treating you like a modern woman," Blackstone said.

"He has commanded me to slave in his kitchen!" she said, reaching for another plate.

"I'm trying to teach you a skill so you can pay your own way," he said.

"I am not to pay my own way. Well-bred women do not work!"

"In this century they do," Blackstone said. "Tell her, Nora."

Nora suppressed a grin. She'd had arguments like this with Emma, although never one that came to blows. "Oh, no," Nora said. "You're on your own."

"Merlin!" Emma shouted.

Sancho raised his head just slightly above the table. "Yes, milady?" he said with so little sarcasm that only Nora seemed to catch it.

"Take me out of here!"

"Never to return?" he asked, a bit too gleefully.

"Never to return," she said, stamping her foot. "I will not be anyone's wench, whether it is ordained or not!"

"I'm not sure it was ordained," Sancho said. Blackstone turned to him.

"You know the prophecy," he said.

"Of course I do," Sancho said. "I'm just not the one who misinterpreted it."

Nora frowned at him. Blackstone tilted his head, as if he were remembering something.

Sancho lifted his head higher above the table. "Milady, if you take your hands off the plates, I'll get you out of here."

Emma had already picked up another plate. She weighed it in her small hands before setting it down again. "Take me away *now*!" she said.

"Your wish is my command, milady," Sancho said, walking toward her, his hands raised as if he were the bad guy in a spaghetti western. "I only hope Amanda doesn't get as pissed as Nora does when she's awakened in the middle of the night."

He waved a palm over Emma, and together they disappeared.

Blackstone sank against the steel table beside him. He ran a hand through his hair, then looked at the destroyed dishes. "Lord, what a mess. What'll I tell my staff?"

"The truth?" Nora said as she stood. Her knees cracked. She had been in that position a long time.

"How much of it?"

She shrugged. "Practice on me."

He looked at her. His entire expression softened. "I missed you," he said.

She wasn't going to give in that easily. "You had Emma."

"Emma." He glanced at the spot where she had been. "Emma hasn't acknowledged how angry she is about losing a thousand years. Emma still blames me for that."

"Surely soul mates can overcome that," Nora said.

He sighed. "If Emma and I were soul mates, why was I thinking of you the entire time I was with her?"

Nora's heart started to pound. "The grass-is-always-greener syndrome?"

He shook his head. "I waited for Emma for a thousand years."

"But you didn't remember her."

"No," he said. "And I had no idea her temper was this bad." He walked to the side of the kitchen and grabbed a broom.

"Why not use magic on that?"

"And waste it?" he asked. "It all takes a slight toll. I'd

rather use magic on important things." He picked up a dustpan and crouched, starting to sweep.

Nora crouched beside him. "It's easier if you pick up the big pieces first."

She demonstrated, delicately lifting the main section of that last plate and cupping it in her hand. Then she picked up other pieces that were just as big.

Blackstone set down the broom and followed her lead. He leaned close to her, and she inhaled, letting the scents of leather and his own exoticness overwhelm her.

"What's the prophecy?" she asked.

"The one Sancho says I misinterpreted?"

"You can call him Andvari. It's okay."

Blackstone whistled. "Such control he gave you. His real name. Do you know what kind of magic there is in someone's real name?"

"Like Aethelstan?"

He grinned. "I always wondered why I told you my real name that day and not the Alex that I've been using for centuries."

"What's the prophecy?" she asked again.

"We all get one," he said, dumping his handful of broken glass in a nearby garbage can. "Mine was—" and then he spoke Greek.

At least, it sounded like Greek.

"How about in English?" Nora asked as she dumped her shards into the garbage can. Then she turned. Blackstone had his eyes closed.

"Are you all right?" she asked.

He shook his head. "I'm blinder than a dead wombat," he said.

"That's the prophecy?"

"No, but it may as well be," he said.

"So what was it?" she asked. "In English."

He cleared his throat and sat on the floor. "At the end of the first millennium AD—not that it said AD since we have a different timekeeping method than mortals, but that's what it meant—"

Nora sat beside him. He took her hand.

"—you will meet the woman who will show you your destiny."

"That doesn't say anything about soul mates," Nora said.

He shook his head. "You don't understand," he said. "All of our prophecies are about love."

"All of them?"

He nodded.

"Was your Greek bad, then?"

"No," he said. "I was twenty-one. I guess I was thinking with the wrong part of my anatomy. And Ealhswith took advantage of that."

Nora squeezed his hand. It felt so good to be beside him. She had missed him too. "So what destiny did Emma lead you to?"

He raised his eyes to hers. "You."

Nora smiled. "Surely there've been other women—"

"Not like you think," he said. "No one I've ever really loved. I've been concentrating on Emma."

"But how can you be sure that your destiny is me?"

"Simple." He put his other hand on her cheek and rubbed her lips with his thumb. "You're the only woman I've ever met because of Emma. And from the moment I saw you, I wanted to be beside you."

"You're beside me now," Nora whispered.

"I'm going to stay here," he said. "Forever."

And then he kissed her, a long, slow, lingering kiss that warmed her all over. She leaned into it, slipping her free hand into his hair. It was as thick as she had thought it would be. He tasted better than she could have hoped, and when their lips finally separated, she felt slightly disoriented, surprised. She had never felt like that before, not after a simple kiss.

"Forever's a long time in your world," she said against his mouth.

"Our world," he said.

"You haven't asked me if I want forever," she said.

He threw his head back and laughed. "A modern woman, with her own life. Here I was, trying to remake Emma into you." He seemed to catch himself and put a finger beneath Nora's chin. "Do you want forever?"

She shook her head, and that stricken look she was coming to recognize flitted through his eyes. He barely caught it, tried to mask it, his features becoming smooth.

Then she grinned at him. "I doubt forever will be long enough."

He laughed again, wrapped his arms around her, and eased her onto the floor.

"Be careful of the glass," she said, before she realized that they were in her bed, with Squidgy staring down at them in baffled surprise from the headboard. Darnell howled downstairs.

"One more thing," Nora said as Blackstone's fingers found the pearl buttons on the jacket Sancho had given her. "Will you send Darnell to Emma? He's miserable without her."

"I'm glad one of us is," Blackstone said. He waved a

hand, and Darnell vanished midhowl. Then Blackstone wrapped his body around Nora's and proceeded to show her what forever would be like.

Forever would be spectacular.

Until that night, she hadn't believed happily ever after would ever be possible.

She had been wrong.

About the Author

Before turning to romance writing, award-winning author Kristine Kathryn Rusch edited the *Magazine of Fantasy & Science Fiction* and ran Pulphouse Publishing (which won her a World Fantasy Award). As Kristine Grayson she has published six novels so far and has won the *RT Book Reviews* Reviewer's Choice Award for Best Paranormal Romance and, under her real name, Kristine Kathryn Rusch, the prestigious Hugo award. She lives in Oregon with her own Prince Charming, writer Dean Wesley Smith (who is not old enough to be one of the original three, but he is handsome enough) as well as the obligatory writers' cats. www.kriswrites.com.

Watch for the third in
Kristine Grayson's Charming series:

THOROUGHLY
Kissed

Coming June 2012
From Sourcebooks Casablanca

Hex Appeal

BY LINDA WISDOM

"Kudos to Linda Wisdom for a series that's pure magic!"

—Vicki Lewis Thompson,
New York Times bestselling author of *Wild & Hexy*

JAZZ AND NICK'S DREAM ROMANCE HAS TURNED INTO A NIGHTMARE...

FEISTY WITCH JASMINE TREMAINE AND DROP-DEAD GORGEOUS vampire cop Nikolai Gregorivich have a hot thing going, but it's tough to keep it together when nightmare visions turn their passion into bickering.

With a little help from their friends, Nick and Jazz are in a race against time to uncover whoever it is that's poisoning their dreams, and their relationship...

978-1-4022-1400-4 • $6.99 U.S. / £3.99 UK

Wicked by Any Other Name

BY LINDA WISDOM

"Do not miss this wickedly entertaining treat."

—Annette Blair,
Sex and the Psychic Witch

STASI ROMANOV USES A LITTLE WITCH MAGIC IN HER LINGERIE shop, running a brisk side business in love charms. A disgruntled customer threatening to sue over a failed spell brings wizard attorney Trevor Barnes to town—and witches and wizards make a volatile combination. The sparks fly, almost everyone's getting singed, and the whole town seems on the verge of a witch hunt.

Can the feisty witch and the gorgeous wizard overcome their objections and settle out of court—and in the bedroom?

978-1-4022-1773-9 • $6.99 U.S. / £3.99 UK

Hex in High Heels

BY LINDA WISDOM

Can a Witch and a Were find happiness?

Feisty witch Blair Fitzpatrick has had a crush on hunky carpenter Jake Harrison forever—he's one hot shape-shifter. But Jake's nasty mother and brother are after him to return to his pack, and Blair is trying hard not to unleash the ultimate revenge spell. When Jake's enemies try to force him away from her, Blair is pushed over the edge. No one messes with her boyfriend-to-be, even if he does shed on the furniture!

Praise for Linda Wisdom's Hex series:

"Fan-fave Wisdom… continues to delight."
  —*Romantic Times*

"Highly entertaining, sexy, and imaginative."
  —*Star Crossed Romance*

"It's a five star, feel-good ride!" —*Crave More Romance*

"Something fresh and new."
  —*Paranormal Romance Review*

978-1-4022-1819-4 • $6.99 U.S. / £3.99 UK

50 Ways to Hex Your Lover

BY LINDA WISDOM

✦
✦
"**A magical page-turner...had me
bewitched from the start!**" ✦

✦

—Yasmine Galenorn,
USA Today bestselling author of *Witchling*

**JAZZ CAN'T DECIDE WHETHER TO SCORCH HIM WITH A
FIREBALL OR JUMP INTO BED WITH HIM**

Jasmine Tremaine is a witch who can't stay out of trouble.
Nikolai Gregorivich is a vampire cop on the trail of a
serial killer. Their sizzling love affair has been on-again,
off-again for about 300 years—mostly off, lately.

But now Nick needs Jazz's help to steer clear of a maniacal
killer with supernatural powers, while they try to finally
figure out their own hearts.

978-1-4022-1085-3 • $6.99 U.S. / £3.99 UK

DEMONS
ARE A
GIRL'S BEST FRIEND

BY LINDA WISDOM

A BEWITCHING WOMAN ON A MISSION...

Feisty witch Maggie enjoys her work as a paranormal law enforcement officer—that is, until she's assigned to protect a teenager with major attitude and plenty of Mayan enemies. Maggie's never going to survive this assignment without the help of a half-fire demon who makes her smolder...

Praise for Linda Wisdom

"Hot talent Wisdom does a truly wonderful job mixing passion, danger, and outrageous antics into a tasty blend that's sure to satisfy."
—RT Book Reviews

"Entertaining and sexy... Ms. Wisdom's stories have something for everyone." —Night Owl Romance

"Wickedly captivating... wildly entertaining... full of magical zest and unrivaled witty prose."
—Suite 101

978-1-4022-5439-0 • $7.99 U.S./£4.99 UK